PRAISE FOR THE SANDMAN SLIM SERIES

"Kadrey provides biting humor, an over-the-top antihero and a rich stew of metaphoric language in this testosterone- and adrenaline-charged noir thriller. . . . Darkly atmospheric settings, such as a posh gentleman's club where angels are tortured in an attempt to bring about Armageddon, bring this violent fantasy into sharp, compelling focus."

—*Publishers Weekly* on *Sandman Slim*

"Endlessly inventive and high-octane. . . . Kadrey's an excellent writer who's able to juggle all of it without dropping a single pin."

—*Locus* on *Kill the Dead*

"I've encountered a lot of fictional characters with bad attitudes and vengeance on their minds, but after finishing up *Aloha from Hell*, the third book in the Sandman Slim series, I've officially moved Stark into a category of his own. . . . I hope Kadrey keeps putting out Sandman Slim books for the next twenty years. They're that much fun to read."

—*Wired* on *Aloha from Hell*

"A hell of a good time."

—*io9* on *Devil Said Bang*

"A deft mixture of urban fantasy and light comedy, the fifth Sandman Slim novel is sure to appeal to the author's growing fan base, not to mention readers of such writers as Jim Butcher, P. N. Elrod, and F. Paul Wilson."

—*Booklist* on *Kill City Blues*

"[Kadrey's] use of arcane lore is more in-depth and profoundly informed than any in urban fantasy. There could be a whole encyclopedia about the magic, monsters, and cosmic geography of Sandman Slim. Like one of his clearest influences, the horror master H. P. Lovecraft, Kadrey rips the skin off the real world, revealing the supernatural nerve endings and metaphysical meat underneath. And his prose couldn't be more visceral if it were carved into flesh."

—*Entertainment Weekly* on *The Getaway God*

"Six years after stumbling into Sandman Slim's seedy, seamy world, I'm still hungry to go back every time. To get lost in it. I have yet to be disappointed. But if this is escapism, it's the most masochistic kind I can imagine."

—*NPR* on *Killing Pretty*

"The book takes Stark to hell and worse, risks the lives of everyone he loves, and features some of the most epic battles ever written by Richard Kadrey, a master of the form. [But] it's this internal struggle that kept me reading right through to the last page."

—Cory Doctorow on *The Perdition Score*

"Kadrey's Sandman Slim series just keeps getting better, and this ninth installment packs some of the darkest twists and blackest humor yet. . . . With plenty of gruesomely fascinating characters, visceral descriptions and a final shocking showdown, this is a sensational installment to a fiendishly good series."

—*RT Book Reviews* on *The Kill Society*

"Packed with humor, *Hollywood Dead* is effortlessly entertaining, rewarding, demon-filled fiction that manages to hide a few more serious messages amongst all the fun."

—*Los Angeles Times* on *Hollywood Dead*

"The prose simmers with Kadrey's characteristic blend of cynicism and absurdist humor, but the nuanced character development and exciting relationship-building make this feel like a brave new direction for the series. This addictive urban fantasy works in its own right—and sets things up for what promises to be one hell of a finale."

—*Publishers Weekly* (starred review) on *Ballistic Kiss*

KING
BULLET

ALSO BY RICHARD KADREY

KING BULLET

A SANDMAN SLIM NOVEL

RICHARD KADREY

HARPER Voyager
An Imprint of HarperCollinsPublishers

KING BULLET. Copyright © 2021 by Richard Kadrey. All rights reserved. Printed in the United States of America. No part of this book may be used or reproduced in any manner whatsoever without written permission except in the case of brief quotations embodied in critical articles and reviews. For information, address Harper-Collins Publishers, 195 Broadway, New York, NY 10007.

HarperCollins books may be purchased for educational, business, or sales promotional use. For information, please email the Special Markets Department at SPsales@harpercollins.com.

Harper Voyager and design are trademarks of HarperCollins Publishers LLC.

FIRST EDITION

Designed by Paula Russell Szafranski

Library of Congress Cataloging-in-Publication Data has been applied for.

ISBN 978-0-06-295157-1

21 22 23 24 25　LSC　10 9 8 7 6 5 4 3 2 1

To Cass.
Last time around's for you.

The past is never dead. It's not even the past.

WILLIAM FAULKNER

When the end of the world comes, I want to be in Kentucky. They're always twenty years behind everything.

MARK TWAIN (ALLEGEDLY)

ACKNOWLEDGMENTS

Thanks to my agent, Ginger Clark, and everyone at Curtis Brown. Big thanks to my editor, David Pomerico, and the whole team at Harper Voyager. Special thanks goes to David Southwell for insights into the wonders of Hookland. Also, Cassandra Khaw, Michelle Belanger, and everyone who made me feel at home in Austin.

I also want to thank the readers who went on this weird journey with me. I never thought Stark and I would make it this far, and we wouldn't have without you. I'm grateful to each and every one of you.

Thanks,
RK

I COME TO alone and confused, so I grab my gun. It's a Colt Peacemaker. Heavy in my hand. The weight is familiar and the smell of gun oil is comforting. I cock it and scope out the area.

But there's nothing to see. Just an old bedroom in a run-down apartment with the L.A. sun creeping in from cracks at the bottom of the shades where I nailed them to the windowsill.

I put the Colt back in its holster by the bed. Nothing to see here, folks. Just some nutcase who can't remember the simple truth of it all.

I'm home.

I've been waking up here for weeks now and every damn morning it's still a shock. It's not because of the dreams. I don't have dreams half the time or, if I do, I can't remember them. No, mornings are confusing because I'm still getting used to being in the old apartment I shared with Alice twelve—or was it thirteen?—years ago. I could probably pin down the exact date, but I don't want to. Too many memories down that road. Still, I'm back where everything began. The last place I lived before Mason sent me to Hell and I became Sandman Slim.

I want to say that there's something profound about it. That it was inevitable and some invisible hand led me back here. But the universe doesn't work that way. There's no savior nudging us toward salvation like a bunch of brainless lamb chops. Mr. Muninn has enough on his hands stitching Heaven and Hell back together again. And Lucifer—back when there was a Lucifer—was too busy preening in the mirror to care.

No, we're on our own and that's fine by me. I can drink and eat a Yule log cake for dinner and stay up late watching monster movies. I'm home and free.

So why does everything feel so fucking—*off*?

As I head to the bathroom to brush my teeth, I hear Fuck Hollywood in the kitchen making coffee. She's been sleeping on my couch for the last week or so, ever since she dumped her shitty skate rat boyfriend, Buzzard. At first, I thought it would be weird having someone around in the old apartment, but it's been kind of nice. She's like the loudmouth little sister I never had. And we have the same taste in movies, so she can stay as long as she wants.

She's reading a magazine when I come into the living room.

"We're out of coffee, but I saved the last cup for you," she says without looking up. She's wearing a T-shirt at least three sizes too big for her. I get my coffee and stand over her.

"Is that my T-shirt?"

"Nope."

"It looks like one I got at a Cramps show probably before you were born."

"You're so old. Maybe you should sit down."

"Don't change the subject. That's my T-shirt, isn't it?"

She drops the magazine on her lap and looks up at me.

"Let's just say that if someone *were* to borrow someone's T-shirt around here," she says, "they would certainly return said T-shirt to the rightful owner washed and folded and with a pretty ribbon on top because the other person was being such a little princess about everything."

"I'm not being a little princess."

"Whatever you say, Snow White."

Like I said, my bratty little sister.

I sit down with my coffee and turn on the TV. Ringo Lam's *City on Fire* is on and I watch while Fuck Hollywood reads. After a few minutes, she puts down her magazine.

"Stark."

I hit pause on the movie and say, "Is the sound bugging you? I can mute it and just go with the subtitles."

"Yeah, it is bothering me a little, but that's not what I wanted to say."

"Okay. So, what's on your mind?"

"I've been here, like, eight or nine days now."

"That's cool. It's fun having you around."

"That's nice to hear. But what I wanted to say is . . ." She trails off.

"Are you okay? Has your ex been bugging you? I can have a word with him."

"That's not it," she says. She pauses for a minute and says, "I've been here for a long time now and I've never stayed the night with a guy who didn't try to fuck me. But you didn't pull that."

She comes over and hugs me.

"Thank you."

I pat her on the arm.

"You're family now. We're going to take care of you."

"It's nice knowing not all guys suck."

I can't think of what to say right away. I knew Fuck Hollywood had been through some rough times, but the way she said "But you didn't" kind of breaks my heart. I mumble the first thing I can think of.

"You're safe here."

"That means a lot to me."

I gulp down the rest of my coffee and get up.

"I'm going to pick us up more coffee before heading to Bamboo House. You want anything?"

She grins at me.

"Are you running away? You really don't take compliments well, do you?"

"I don't know what you're talking about. I'll be back soon."

She points to the coffee table.

"Don't forget your mask."

A surgical mask. I'm so sick of masks.

The epidemic started maybe three months ago. At first it looked like just another bad summer cold. Then the hospitals filled up. Then people started dying. And they kept dying so fast the city couldn't bury them right. It had to dig out mass graves in the Angeles National Forest to hold the dead. L.A. itself—all four thousand square miles of concrete and palm trees—feels like a cheap balloon ready to pop.

I don't know how civilians get anything done these days.

The subway shut down months ago. A few of the bus routes still run, but with almost half of the drivers dead, they don't exactly keep a regular schedule. The streets are empty enough parts of the day that gutsy types can get around on bikes and skateboards. A nice idea, except then you're plowing face-first through a goddamn biblical plague of flies from all the garbage. No one has had a pickup in weeks. If trash was snow, Hollywood would be in a blizzard. You can practically ski down the side of the overflowing dumpster next to Maximum Overdrive. I keep waiting for all the shit to turn sentient and start demanding protection money.

I grab my jacket off the back of a chair.

"Why do I need a mask? I'm immune to everything."

Fuck Hollywood leans forward.

"It's your civic duty to set an example."

"You're going to have to come up with something better than that."

Before I can respond, she takes a mask from the coffee table and slips the loops over my ears. Then quickly grabs her phone and takes a photo.

I touch my face.

"What did you just put on me?"

"Nothing."

I take the mask off and look. On the front is a blond girl with a helmet and a sword.

"What the hell is this?"

"That's She-Ra, aka Princess Adora, aka He-Man's twin sister."

"Why can't I just wear He-Man?"

"He-Man is a dork. We don't have He-Man."

"I look ridiculous. There has to be something else."

She grabs the other masks, throws them under the sofa cushions, and sits on them.

"There aren't any other masks."

I look at her.

"What are you going to do with that photo?"

"Nothing."

"If that shows up online, you're dead. So is everyone who sees it."

She's still laughing at me as I head out to get coffee.

In the hall, I adjust the mask so it fits better. I think about throwing the damn thing away, but it's probably better if I wear it. I'll be just another drone in the crowd.

And let's face it, no one wants to see my face.

Her goofy mask aside, it's nice that Fuck Hollywood is staying at my place. She's just a kid, and I'd worry about her otherwise. Of course, I worry about everybody these days, especially Candy and Janet. With Vidocq gone, they're pretty much the two most important people to me.

I light up a Malediction only to remember Princess Adora. Another reason I don't like these things. I pinch out the cigarette and try to push the worry and nonsense out of my head for a few minutes and concentrate on what kind of food to pick up while I'm out. Burgers or burritos? No more pizza. I swear, that's all Fuck Hollywood lives on. How someone that little can put away that much cheese and pepperoni and still have a functional digestive system baffles me. Maybe she's Sub Rosa, but only on the inside. A hoodoo stomach that can stretch forever as she stuffs pounds of burned crust down her gullet.

It makes me laugh a little, trying to picture how magic innards might work, when I spot some asshole tagging the wall by the elevator. The door to one of the nearby apartments is kicked open and someone's tossed furniture and clothes all over the hall. I'm not big on coincidences and I have a sneaky feeling that Michelangelo was helping himself to some baubles before he decided to slop paint in the hall.

Quiet as a baby bunny, I come up behind him and slam his head into the wall. Not hard enough to knock him out, but hard enough to rattle his molars. He drops his brush and the paint can he was working with. Now that I'm close, though, something is strange about the scene. The paint smells wrong. I lean over the can and give it a sniff. It's blood. And there's too much of it to have all come from him.

With my boot, I roll art boy over onto his back. Like me, he's wearing a mask, but his is a complicated painter's rig with a wide filter in the front. He decorated the mask with nostrils and pointy pink ears so he looks like a paint—or blood—spattered pig. I grab him by the overalls and haul him to his feet. He's still woozy when I get him up, so I take off his mask and slap him a couple of times to get his attention.

"Hey, Porky. You do not come into my home and start shitting the place up without my permission, which you definitely don't have. Explain to me why I shouldn't drag your dumb ass to the window and drop you like one more bag of trash?"

He's awake now and smiling like a baboon. It's quite a sight. He has double sets of silver fang implants in his upper and lower jaw. His face looks like it was scarred with acid, but in careful patterns. Spirals on his cheeks and chin.

His ears have been burned to points and someone etched "PIGGY" across his forehead. The tip of his nose is gone, completing the look.

I have a bad feeling I know who and what he is.

After I slap him a couple more times I say, "What's your name?"

That makes him laugh—deep, hysterical guffaws. Porky is on something and high as the Goodyear Blimp.

He blinks at me, blood from a cut on his forehead pooling in the circular scars on his cheeks. He whispers, "Shoggot."

Fuck.

This is just what I need right now. Shoggots are a Sub Rosa gang. By far the craziest. They live by a myth that they're like me—Nephilims. Only in their shriveled little brains, they're the offspring of one of Lucifer's fallen angels and a mortal woman. They ugly themselves up to resemble what they imagine Hellions look like. They got the ugly part right, at least. But the more I look at him, the more I feel like there's something else wrong here besides Porky's paint. No. This doesn't add up.

I say, "You're not a Shoggot. Shoggots are Sub Rosa. You're a civilian. Just some ordinary asshole living by a tall tale that isn't even yours."

He shakes his ugly head.

"The old Shoggots are dead. They were a lie. We're the real, true heirs to the name."

I look at his eyes and listen to his heartbeat. What's weird is that he isn't lying. At least he thinks he isn't.

"Who are you?" I say.

"Sawney Bean."

I shake him a couple of times.

"Sawney Bean? He died three hundred years ago and a million miles away. Try again, Porky."

He laughs and grabs my arms.

"I'm Sawney and I'll eat your guts for lunch."

"Naming yourself after a dead cannibal might scare some people, but you're just a clown to me. Now tell me again why I shouldn't drop you out a window?"

"King Bullet," he says and points to his tag on the wall.

I look at it for the first time. He's painted a crude skull with a target on its forehead. A pointy crown floats a few inches above the skull. It jogs something for me.

"Yeah, I've seen it around town. Is it supposed to mean something to me?"

"It should," says Porky. "He's the one who did it. Killed off the false Shoggots and made us new ones in his image."

"One asshole didn't murder a whole Sub Rosa gang on his own."

He whispers, "You don't know the King."

"And you're high enough to believe anyone with a funny name and a few card tricks."

"I'm Sawney Bean. Hurt me and the King will burn all you know and love."

"If the King is so great and you're so important to him, why are you doing something as dumb as tagging my building?"

He opens his eyes wide.

"*Your* building? Nothing is yours. Not anymore."

"Let me guess. It belongs to the King."

"Everything," he says. Then he gets right up in my face. "Including you."

"You're not Sawney. You're just a little piggy. And it's window time."

I grab him by the collar, convinced I'm in charge of the scene. I've dealt with crazies before. What's one more? Only he's not the stupid one. I am. He digs in his heels and when I turn to look, he slips a little .25 automatic out of the sleeve of his coveralls. Presses it against my left cheek and pulls the trigger.

Now, a .25 caliber bullet is a tiny thing. Like a joke shop bullet. From any distance at all it's as lethal as a mosquito bite. But this prick jammed the thing right into my face. Even a little bullet from that range is going to hurt. And it fucking does. What's worse is that between the pain of the shot and the surprise, I let pig-faced Sawney go.

He jackrabbits to the stairs, but instead of running away he turns around and does a merry little soft-shoe routine. When he's done he sings "Rum-tiddley-um-tum-tay" before disappearing down the stairs. I stagger back to the apartment with a handful of blood and embarrassment.

Fuck Hollywood is at the door when I get there.

"I heard something," she says. Then she sees me and pulls me inside. "Oh god. Oh shit. What happened?"

Between clenched teeth I say, "I was mugged by Porky Pig."

She helps me to the sofa and says, "Oh man, you're delirious. What should I do?"

"Relax. I was joking."

She slaps my arm.

"That's not funny. Should I call Allegra?"

"No. Just bring me a mirror and a rag. And find me some pliers."

She gets up, but just stands there.

"What do you want pliers for?"

"The bullet. It didn't go all the way through and I can feel it against my cheekbone. I want to get it out. To do that, I need some needle-nose pliers."

"That's so metal."

As she runs off to get my stuff, I go to the side table and find a bottle of bourbon. It tastes good going down, but the .25 tore the inside of my cheek, so the liquor burns like a blowtorch. Still, I take another pull and in a minute Fuck Hollywood comes back with the rag and a mirror.

"I'm sorry," she says. "You gave all of Vidocq's tools to Allegra. We don't have any pliers."

I hold up a hand.

"It's okay. Just give me the other stuff."

I drop back down onto the sofa and wipe away as much blood as I can with the rag. I'm not much to look at the best of times, but now I'm considerably worse. Not only do I have a fresh hole in my face, but because the gun was pressed up against me, the skin around the wound is burned. And he didn't even shoot through She-Ra, so I have to go on wearing this stupid thing.

Fuck Hollywood hovers over me like a distraught mother hen.

I say, "First off, you sit down."

She sits on the sofa right next to me.

"Second, thanks for all this stuff, but I'm not getting us coffee."

"Stop joking," she yells.

"I know someone with tools I can borrow."

"You need to go to Allegra."

I shake my head.

"This is too humiliating. Shot by a junkie in a pig mask. And it was my fault. I'm going out again to take care of things."

"What should I do?"

I take some cash and shove it into her hand.

"Get us some coffee and I'll see you later at Bamboo House of Dolls."

"You can't go in today." She's shouting again.

"I've been there in worse shape than this. Please just get some coffee and we can laugh about this later."

"Okay," she says and balls up the money in her fist.

I toss the mirror onto the coffee table and get up, holding the bloody rag to my face.

"Be careful when you go out," I say. "I think Sawney Bean is gone, but keep your eyes open."

"Okay."

"There's a little 9mm in a box under my bed. Take it with you. If you see anyone around here in a pig mask, don't ask questions. Just shoot them."

"Okay."

"Are you even listening to me?"

"A little."

"Maybe you should stay here until I get back."

"No," she says. "You've taken care of me for a week. Go take care of you right now."

"I'll see you later at the bar."

"I'll go in early and tell Carlos what happened."

"Try to stay calm," I say as I shove She-Ra into my pocket. "Things are going to be okay." But I'm not 100 percent sure who I'm trying to convince, and even as I step into a shadow for Max Overdrive I have a bad feeling I'm wrong.

I COME OUT in the alley near the overflowing dumpster and trip over a pile of empty boxes. It's getting fucking ridiculous out here and swarms of flies are having spring break on the remains of someone's half-eaten burrito. Technically, I could have come out inside the shop, but I don't do that anymore. Why is complicated and annoying.

So let me remind you.

Not so long ago, I was dead. Dead and back in Hell for a year. While I was gone, Candy and Alessa moved in together. I couldn't blame her. Candy, that is. Or, I guess, Alessa for that matter. For both of them, there wasn't any way I was coming back. But I did come back, only after Candy and Alessa had set up a nice life for themselves. Then I met Janet and, well, that's where it gets extra complicated. Janet and I started seeing each other soon after I got back, and we get along really well. For a while I was seeing both Janet and Candy, which was fine for what it was. Only as much as Alessa and Janet claimed they didn't mind Candy and me getting together sometimes, they did. Janet got depressed and Alessa put her foot down and it was goodbye to convoluted modern love. In some ways I'm relieved. Trying to keep one partner happy can be hard enough. Trying to balance two with two other reluctant partners is a full-time fucking job.

Still, there's a big hole inside me where Candy used to be.

Janet is great and I care about them a lot, but they're not the beautiful monster I lost because I was arrogant enough to think no one could get the drop on me. Of course, I can never say any of this to Janet and even thinking it makes me feel guilty as hell. And all of this is just a long way of saying that when I go to Max Overdrive these days, I don't pop in through a shadow. I go in through the front door like any other asshole customer.

Leaving the flies to their party, I go around to the front and start inside. But the door is locked. I can't see anything through the glare on the glass, but I knock a few times. I can just make out some movement inside and eventually the door opens a few inches. It's Kasabian. He takes one look at me and tries to slam the door shut again.

"Put on a mask," he yells.

"I can't."

"Why not?"

I take the rag from the side of my face and show him the bullet wound.

"Christ, Stark. You're a goddamn calamity."

"Thanks, Miss America. Now open up."

"Go to Allegra."

"This is too embarrassing. Now open the door or we're both going to need a doctor."

He lets go of the door and runs a few feet away.

"Fine, come in, but don't get too close."

I go inside, keeping my distance. Ever since he got his body back, Kasabian has turned into a health freak. I mean, the man even eats vegetables. Plus, I can't smoke around here anymore. I guess I can't blame him. I mean, what shitty timing—

getting hands, legs, and lungs back for the first time in years, only to find yourself stuck in Plague Town. And there's plenty to be paranoid about. I mean, no one even knows what the virus is yet. For some people it's just a bad flu, but others never heal right. The bug does something to their brains. They get amnesia. They get violent. They get better, they die, or they get weird. It makes me feel a little sorry for Kasabian and I hate that.

He grabs a second surgical mask from behind the front counter and holds it over the one he's already wearing.

"Seriously, why are you even here?" he says. "Shouldn't you be in the hospital?"

"Hospitals ask too many questions and this is too stupid to bother Allegra with. You still have the toolbox? I need a pair of pliers."

"I'll get it. It's in the back. You stay right there. Don't touch anything!"

I take the rag from my face and check it. I'm still bleeding. The blood isn't going to stop until I get the slug out of me. The whole right side of my face, numb a few seconds ago, starts aching and burning. I press the rag back to my cheek and when I do, I catch a whiff of something. Spackle and paint. I look at the back of the shop and see holes in the wall and plastered-over areas.

When Kasabian gets back, I say, "You redecorating?"

He drops the toolbox on the counter and opens it up.

"Some customers did it for us. A couple of guys start arguing and all of a sudden it's *Riot on the Sunset Strip*."

I dig around in the box for a minute until I find the needle-nose pliers. They're old and dented and have seen better days.

But I test them and they seem to work all right. Kasabian makes a face.

"Aren't you even going to clean them or something? You're going to get an infection."

"Darn. I forgot my autoclave."

"Wait there, asshole." Kasabian heads to his room.

He comes back a minute later with a roll of paper towels and a bottle of twelve-year-old Macallan.

I say, "Since when did you start drinking Scotch?"

He pours a capful of the stuff onto a paper towel and rubs it all over the pliers.

"It's this new body. Bourbon, beer—all of that stuff tastes funny."

I look at the bottle on the counter.

"At least you're drinking good stuff."

"Damn right. I'm treating my body a lot better than I used to. You might consider doing the same."

"I didn't shoot myself."

"I don't care."

When he's done, Kasabian puts the clean pliers on the counter, grabs the Macallan, and steps back, making sure to keep at least six feet between us.

I hold the rag under the entry wound to catch any blood that comes out. Then I slip in the pliers, which isn't that bad. But when I spread them to grab the bullet, let me tell you, it does not feel good. I let out a little involuntary groan and Kasabian backs up a couple more feet. Even though I can feel the slug on my cheekbone, it's slippery enough that I can't get hold of it. With all the probing around blood is flowing down my face. A lot more than I counted on. I pull out the pliers and take a breath.

"That's disgusting," says Kasabian. "Can't you just—?"

"Hoodoo it out? You know I'm no good with subtle stuff. I'd probably just blow my face off."

"It's a thought. You know, burn the field so a new crop can grow."

One more breath and I slide the pliers back into my cheek.

Kasabian says, "What about Ray? He's good with healing magic."

"I can do this."

When the blood starts again Kasabian turns away.

"Oh shit. I'm going to be sick."

Finally, I can feel the teeth on the pliers get hold of something rigid. I clamp on it tight and slowly pull out the bullet. When it's clear of my cheek I hold it up like a magician and say, "Ta-da!"

"Hi, Stark. I didn't hear you come in. What are you boys up to?"

It's Candy. She's coming down the stairs from the second-floor apartment. When I didn't see her in the store, I thought she was out. Me and Kasabian freeze like kids caught snorting Mom and Dad's coke in the garage. The moment she sees the pliers and all the blood she shouts at me.

"What the fuck are you doing?"

She's not wearing a mask, but she still rushes over and checks out my face and the blood that's soaked through the rag.

"Kas, get the first-aid kit," she says.

He holds out the extra mask to her.

"You're not wearing a—"

"Now!" she yells.

While he scurries off to get the kit, muttering, Candy stays with me. Before she can ask me what I did to myself I hold up the pliers with the bullet.

I say, "It wasn't my fault. There was a pig in the building."

"A pig with a gun," she says.

I nod. "And a paint-by-numbers set."

She takes the pliers from my hand and sets them on the counter.

"Stop talking. It makes the bleeding worse. Also, I don't want to hear your perverted farm animal fantasies."

"It wasn't a fantasy, baby. The pig and me, we danced."

She puts a finger to my lips.

"Hush. The doctors will be here soon with a straitjacket and, if you're good, ice cream."

When I open my mouth to say "pistachio," she clamps her hand over my mouth and yells, "How's it coming, Kas?"

He runs back and dumps the first-aid kit on the counter, then scurries away. Candy pops the top, grabs the whole gauze roll, and shoves it onto the bleeding wound.

She says, "Is that a new coat?"

"No. I've had it for months."

"Good. It's covered in blood. You're going to have to get it cleaned."

"Goddammit."

"Look on the bright side. You didn't bleed all over my clean floor," Kasabian says.

"Your floor was always my utmost concern."

Candy pulls the bandage away long enough to get a good look at the wound.

"You've had worse. At least the bullet went in clean and didn't come out the back of your head."

"I was just telling Kas about how lucky I am."

"Next time I don't care if you get shot or your balls are stuck in a wood chipper," he says. "You don't come in without a mask."

Before I can say anything, Candy pours hydrogen peroxide on the wound. The sting shuts me up quick.

"You're not bleeding too badly anymore," she says. "But take it easy until your face heals."

"I will," I say.

Candy tears off the little gauze that doesn't have blood all over it and bandages it to my face.

"Good. No more partying with pigs for a while or you'll start bleeding again."

"Thanks, doc."

Alessa—sensibly masked—comes downstairs and over to the counter. She takes one look at me and says, "What the hell did you do to yourself?"

"He says he got into a fight with a pig," says Candy.

"It looks like the pig won."

"It was a draw," I say. "But next time I'm coming home with pork chops."

Alessa hands Candy a mask and says, "You forgot again."

Candy puts it on.

"Thanks."

Leaning in, Alessa looks at me closer.

"That really does look nasty. Are you sure you're okay?"

Not that long ago I would have assumed she was being sarcastic, but she's been a lot nicer to me ever since I gave Kasabian his body back.

I say, "It's too early for this shit. I've been better."

She looks at the repairs in the back of the store.

"So have we."

"Kas told me what happened."

"We've talked about going mail order or just leaving people's discs outside. It was probably a bad idea, reopening this quickly."

"We all wanted it," says Candy.

"We were going stir-crazy," Kasabian says.

Alessa nods.

"I know, but with the number of nutjobs who've been coming in, we might have to rethink it." She looks at me. "If we get anyone as crazy as Stark's pig in here, I don't know what we're going to do."

"Yeah, but locking people out isn't going to stop the break-ins," says Kasabian.

I look at Candy.

"You never mentioned that."

"No one's gotten in yet," she says. "Mostly they try the side door onto the alley. I suppose we're lucky there's so much garbage."

I say, "I still have some money left. I can help you get an alarm system."

Alessa lays a hand on Candy's shoulder and says, "Already taken care of. It'll be here tomorrow."

"Great. I can at least put some wards around the doors and windows in the meantime."

"Thanks. That would be cool."

She hands me the paper towels.

"But before you do it, you've got blood all over your coat. Clean up a little or people will think we're the crazies."

"Good idea."

I clean up as best as I can, then go out and around to the side door. Tossing the bloody paper towels onto the garbage heap, I bark a little Hellion hoodoo and all the flies explode like disgusting little fireworks. After that, I can work in peace, using the black blade to cut runes and sigils all around the side door. I do the same thing to the front door, and chisel a little dust off the brick building next door, laying it out in a line under the doormat. When I'm done, I put the knife away and go back inside.

From behind the counter, Kasabian gives me a look.

"You're still not wearing a mask."

"You got any extras down there? Plain ones?"

"Nope."

With my back up against the wall I don't have any choice but to put on She-Ra.

Kasabian lights up when he sees the mask.

"You've never been prettier."

"Give me a fucking break. I'm walking wounded."

"Then this will make you feel better," he says and puts a bag on the counter.

"What's this?"

"A lollipop for being good and putting on a mask."

I look inside the bag and see a few discs.

"New special stuff?"

"Choice titles and you're the first to see any of it."

To keep Max Overdrive afloat, the store has a special arrangement with a friendly witch who gets Kas copies of movies and TV shows that almost came off, but didn't happen in our reality. I look at the first disc.

"*The Third Man.*"

"With Cary Grant and Noël Coward as Harry Lime."

"I don't like the sound of that."

"I know, but they were the producer's first choice."

The next disc is *Death Wish.*

"With Jack Lemmon instead of Charles Bronson," Kasabian says.

"Now that sounds amazing."

"It is."

The next is a box set of something called *Collector's Item.*

"Never heard of it."

"It's from 1957. A TV series where Vincent Price and Peter Lorre are crime-solving antique collectors."

"Be still my heart."

"You'll love it."

"Thanks. This is a lot better than getting shot in the face."

"By a pig."

"I'm going to find that guy and drag him in here just so you can all see I'm not insane."

"Too late for that," says Candy. "Looking good, She-Ra."

She holds up her phone and shows me Fuck Hollywood's photo.

I say, "I was ambushed."

"Of course you were."

She reaches behind the counter and brings me one more disc.

"This won't be out until next week, but we trade some stuff with a record store in Glendale. It's Skull Valley Sheep Kill's new album, *Club Katabasis*."

"Damn. I've been waiting for this. Thanks."

"Thank you for magicking up the shop."

She gives me a hug and my stomach suddenly feels like it's in free fall. Just touching Candy, I'm sick with a longing that I can't stand. I take a step back, thank everybody one more time, and get out of there as fast as I can.

I COME OUT of a shadow across town near Janet's apartment, a few blocks from UCLA. It's a tony area, but like the rest of the city, you wouldn't guess it at first glance. Stripped cars. Garbage on the curbs as high as anywhere else. Tags on every flat surface, including the garbage piles. That's how long they've been there. Gangs never seen in this area before hustling for territory.

More trash and a wet stain on the steps into Janet's building. I press the buzzer and the front door pops open. Inside, all of the mailboxes are broken. Letters and packages are scattered everywhere. I kick through the junk and find a few items with Janet's name on them and take them with me inside.

Her apartment door is unlocked when I get there. Dammit. Their. Janet is nonbinary and even after all this time, I still occasionally screw up their pronouns. At least I didn't say it out loud. I go inside and Janet is there sipping tea.

"Hi. Sorry I'm late. It's been a weird morning."

They put down the cup hard enough that it sloshes tea all over the kitchen counter.

"Oh my god."

I hold up a hand.

"It's not as bad as it looks."

They take my face in their hands, turning me this way and that.

"What happened?" they say.

"I had a run-in with a psycho. I deserve the bullet for getting so sloppy."

"He *shot* you?" Their voice gets louder. "We need to get you to a hospital."

"I'm fine. I got the bullet out before coming over."

"By yourself? Come here and sit down. I want to take a look at you."

"I'm okay."

"You're an idiot is what you are."

"That too probably."

They push me down and take off the bandage. Whatever it is they see makes them frown.

"Dammit. You're still bleeding. Just getting out the bullet isn't enough. You know that, right?"

"It'll be fine by tonight."

They ignore me. "Hold the bandage to your face. I need to get something."

"It's really not necessary."

"I know. You're a fast healer and all that other macho bullshit. Just sit there and be quiet."

Janet comes back a few seconds later with something about the size of a tube of lipstick.

They say, "Move the bandage."

I drop my hand with the bandage to my side.

"What is that?" I say.

"Stop talking and hold your face still. I don't want to have to do this twice."

They pinch my cheek hard enough that it hurts.

"Excuse me, but ow."

"Be quiet, baby. This is all your fault."

They put something over the bullet hole. It stings a little and now that part of my face feels stiff.

Janet says, "There. That will close the wound long enough to get you some proper care."

"What did you do?"

"Stop moving your face around. For your information, I superglued the damn wound closed. My uncle used to do it when one of my redneck cousins got hurt deer hunting. If you don't move around too much it will hold for a while."

I talk through gritted teeth, trying not to move my face.

"How long do I have to sit like this?"

"Not too long. It sets pretty quickly."

"So. Redneck cousins."

"Yep. Piles of them."

"But you were never a country mouse."

"Nope. A city mouse all the way."

"Lucky me."

Janet smiles.

"Damn right, lucky you." They take my face in their hands and inspect the bullet hole. "I guess that's a new scar for the collection."

"I just get prettier and prettier."

"I think so."

They lean down and give me a peck on the lips.

I say, "That's it?"

"Until you get that hole in your face fixed."

"I'll think about it."

I pull their mail from my coat pocket.

"Here. You missed this."

Janet glances at it and tosses it on a table.

"Thanks. I guess I rushed inside when I got home."

"Did something happen?"

"Nothing to me. One of my neighbors was shot last night right out front."

The stains on the front steps.

"A woman downstairs said that they didn't even rob him. Just shot him and danced before someone called the cops."

I take Janet's hand.

"You're lucky you live near the college. LAPD doesn't even bother with Hollywood anymore."

"Lucky me. Woo-hoo."

"I didn't mean it like that."

"I know. I'm just tired of being scared all the time."

"I saw the tags outside. More than the last time I was over."

"There are more every day," they say.

"Have you seen a particular one—a skull with a target and a crown?"

"I haven't really been looking, but no. Why?"

"One of them is who shot me."

They squeeze my hand.

"You have to be more careful."

I pull Janet down onto my lap.

"Don't worry about me. Or yourself. I'll take care of you. If you want, you can move in with me for a while."

They kiss the cheek that doesn't have a massive hole in it and get up.

"Thanks. But I can't. All of my work is here. I can't just haul my equipment across town. Your place isn't big enough."

They're right. The apartment is Frankenstein's lab of synthesizers, wires, and computers. It *might* all fit it in my place, but only if I got rid of the furniture. And the shower. And Fuck Hollywood.

I go over and put my arms around them.

"Listen—all this shit that's happening? It's all typical L.A. craziness, just amped up by how the virus has fucked the city and the cops pretty much taking a powder. Hell, some of what's happening might be LAPD itself. They're screaming for more money and they love chaos. It makes them look good when they fix anything. Like someone starting a fire and then putting it out. Instant heroes."

"You really think so?" Janet says. "I mean, I see gang signs everywhere. All over school. Ambulances. Even city hall and cop cars too."

"There's your answer."

Their eyebrow goes up in a question.

"Camouflage. Cops tag their own cars and scare everyone. After that, they can get away with anything they want."

They shake their head sadly and go into the kitchen to wipe the spilled tea off the counter.

"You're taking all of this really well. You got shot. Someone gets murdered outside. There are rats and flies everywhere and you sit there telling me it's all an illusion."

"That's not what I meant. It's all real. It's just that in this town it's old news."

"Not for me it isn't. I'm scared."

I shut up for a minute and try to think about things from Janet's point of view. Hell, any normal person's point of view. Maybe the filth, the bugs, and the drive-bys don't bother me because I spent all those years in Hell. It's chaos there 24/7. I'm too used to crazies and bodies in the streets. Civilians aren't like that. Most of them have only seen a riot on TV. They've never felt or smelled raw animal fear. Now L.A. is a suburb of Hell and I keep expecting people to just roll with it. I need to change my thinking if I'm going to take care of myself and my friends.

I follow Janet into the kitchen.

"Come and stay at my place. Just for a couple of days. Me and Fuck Hollywood will feed you all the pizza you can eat."

They take my hand and kiss my ragged knuckles.

"I have to work. The Luis Buñuel festival is this weekend. I'm scoring *L'Age D'or* for an online concert."

"Okay. Then why don't I stay here?"

They think about it for a few seconds.

"That might be nice."

"I can do some hoodoo to keep the apartment and the building safe."

"That would be nice."

"Can I have a better kiss now?"

They come over and plant a *very* nice kiss on my lips. Then pull me into the bedroom, where we don't break any furniture, but we do pretty good. Afterward, they put on more of the damn superglue so I'm not allowed to talk for a while.

Still, through gritted teeth, I say, "What's happening with Brigitte?"

Before the epidemic, Janet married Brigitte so she could stay in the country. The two have been dealing with Immigration ever since. They even lived together in Janet's cramped apartment for a couple of weeks to get used to how they'd interact as a couple. They're completely prepared for an Immigration interview whenever it happens.

"Absolutely nothing. We might have a Skype meeting with an official in a couple of weeks, but they've had to reschedule twice. They keep losing people too."

"Fuckers. Brigitte should have her green card by now."

"I agree."

"How's she taking it?"

Janet rests their head on their hands.

"All right. Frustrated. Scared sometimes. But mostly all right."

"Let me know the moment you hear anything."

"Of course. Hey, you want to hear some of the music I wrote for the show this weekend?"

I look at the clock.

"I do, but I'm late for Bamboo House of Dolls. Play it for me when I get back?"

"Of course."

They put a fresh bandage on my face and I kiss them one more time.

"See you tonight."

I GET TO Bamboo House around three, a little before it opens for the afternoon crowd. Charlotte and a crazy ex-pat Brit in a top hat who calls himself Babadook are out front flanking the door. They're hired muscle Carlos called in a few weeks ago to keep the crazies and the no-mask crowd outside. Between them they have enough meat to build a Brahma bull, but, like a lot of giants with nothing to prove to anyone, they're sweet as apple pie. Charlotte, an aspiring MMA fighter, gives me a little finger wave when she sees me. Babadook puts out his grizzly bear–size hand to shake. Before he lets go, he pulls me in a little bit.

"Oi. You got any of those funny cigarettes of yours? The ones that smell like a yak's ass combusting?"

I take out a couple of Maledictions. He's the only civilian I've ever met who likes them as much as I do. I've never told him where they come from because he'd probably want to meet Samael or go to Hell with me on a shopping spree.

He accepts the cigarettes and says, "Cheers, mate." Then, "What's up with your face? I mean you're an ugly bloke, but today you're top-drawer hideous."

Charlotte rolls her eyes.

"Jesus, Babadook. He doesn't look that bad."

"Are you kidding? My dog died when he saw Freddy Krueger and he isn't half as homely as this geezer."

Charlotte and I can't help but laugh. Babadook is always like this. I don't know if he used to be a bouncer or a street hawker, but he could talk the stripes off a zebra, then hug it if it cried.

"It's okay, Charlotte," I say. "To answer your question, Babadook, I had a disagreement with a bullet."

They both perk up at that.

Charlotte says, "Really? Can I see?"

"Yeah. Give us a peek, Elephant Man."

"Maybe later. I have to get inside."

Charlotte claps me on the back as Babadook tugs up one side of his surgical mask and lights a Malediction.

"Oh no," she tells him. "Change places with me. If you're going to smoke those things, you're going to stand downwind."

He bows and they switch.

"Always happy to accommodate a lady."

I head inside while Charlotte, an ex-smoker, goes into great detail about what Babadook is doing to his lungs.

These days, I work part-time at Bamboo House with Carlos. Sometimes I do little jobs for Thomas Abbot, the head of all Sub Rosa business in California. But he hasn't given me many jobs since the thing with a rogue angel named Zadkiel. I tried not to kill her, but she tried even harder to kill me, so I didn't have any choice. Before she died, she said, "I've done something awful." I sometimes wonder if the virus is her gift to the city. Anyway, until something big comes up, I'm slinging drinks with Carlos. Sometimes playing bouncer. The epidemic hit Bamboo House hard, so mostly I'm there to bring in customers. Hell, sometimes I'll even take selfies with people who aren't too obnoxious about it.

Fuck Hollywood, with her Mohawk plastered straight up, is busing the few occupied tables. When she looks up, I say, "Is tonight the night?"

"A hundred percent," she says.

The plan is that after we close up tonight, we're murdering her ex's skateboard, her last connection to Buzzard. It will be good for her. A ritual death. Cut him out of her life completely.

The bar is about a quarter full with Lurkers and civilians. We could fill the place twice over, but social distancing and all that garbage. Mostly, people come in for to-go drinks. The rest sip their cocktails and beers under their masks through straws. No one is sure any of this is legal, but the cops are too busy causing trouble to bother with a few wayward martinis.

A pretty woman in black lipstick and big round sunglasses to match comes up to the bar. Trickster tattoos cover her toned arms.

"Yuzu-sansho sour, please," she says to me.

"I don't know what any of those words mean."

Carlos says, "I've got it, you savage."

Carlos does the cocktails. I mostly pour beer and shots.

With the shades, the woman looks like a starlet trying not to be recognized. When Carlos gives her the drink, she flashes a million-dollar smile and slides the cash across the bar to me.

"Keep it," she says.

Her phone number is on a small piece of paper under the bills. I smile, wad it up, and throw it in the trash with all the others. It's nice to be well thought of by someone, but life is complicated enough right now.

I keep the tip, though.

Things continue on in their ordinary way for most of the night. Me and Carlos deal with drinks and Fuck Hollywood takes care of any food orders. Everybody is masked and so well behaved it could be Sunday school.

The place gets about half-full when the evening crowd shows up. Half-full is all Carlos will let in these days. Really, for a day that started with getting shot in the face, it's turned into something pleasant. And I get to hear Janet's music later.

It's somewhere around nine when something happens outside. The whole bar hears it. Screams. A couple of gunshots. Then people burst through the door and rush inside, getting as far from the front of the place as possible. Fuck Hollywood is young and wild enough to think she's bulletproof. She runs to the door to see what's going on.

When she doesn't come back, I feel for the black blade in my boot and pull the Colt from my waistband at the back. I have the gun out when a couple of L.A.'s finest come in wearing surgical masks. The first cop is dragging Fuck Hollywood with him by the hair.

But there's something wrong with the cops. Their uniforms don't fit right. They're torn and spotted with dried blood around what look like bullet holes. And then there's the fact that the second cop is carrying two severed heads—Charlotte and Babadook—over to the bar, where she drops them. The cop pulls down the surgical mask and surveys the room. The cop is a woman—teeth stained black and with large, ugly hooks through both cheeks. The wounds look recent, and infected. It's obvious she's a Shoggot, which explains the ill-fitting uniforms. She and the other creep stole them from some cops they killed. Smart. Even these days, people open their doors for cops. Her name tag reads "Despentes."

I look at Fuck Hollywood. The other cop still has her by the hair.

"You okay?"

"I think so. I don't know."

Officer Despentes looks at the 9mm in my hand and grins. She says, "Two Shirley Temples, darling."

I point the pistol right between her eyes.

"Outside. Right now. Just you, me, and Deputy Dawg over there."

The cop holding Fuck Hollywood by the hair pulls down his mask.

He's even uglier than Miss America over here. His nose is gone. Like it was hacked off. There's just a wet void in the middle of his face. And the face. It's melted and waxen, like someone stuck it into a fryer for a few minutes. Still, Jason Voorhees–ugly as the guy is, Fuck Hollywood squirms around a little to get a better look at him.

She says, "Buzzy?"

"Miss me, baby?" says the cop.

It's Buzzard, the worthless skate rat. I wonder if this was his idea. He's got the same crazy eyes as Sawney Bean. Did Fuck Hollywood leave him because he was always this crazy or is he just another brain turned to clam chowder by the virus?

"Let her go," I say to Buzzard.

He yanks her hard so that when she yells, he can put the barrel of his Glock into her mouth.

Murmurs from around the room.

I say, "I swear to god, kid—"

Despentes drums her fingers impatiently on Babadook's head.

"How about those drinks, handsome? Also, lay the gun on the bar."

"I wouldn't piss in a teacup for you."

"Stark," says Carlos, a warning in his voice.

I look at Fuck Hollywood's frantic eyes, then back to Despentes.

"What was it you wanted?"

"I wanted Shirley Temples. But now I'm bored."

"There's the door."

"No," she says, pouting. "I want to play a game."

"People come here to drink, not play games. I'll make you your drinks."

She pulls her pistol. It's an older one. A revolver. She points it at Carlos.

"I want to play, or I'll make more of these."

She elbows Charlotte's head off the bar. It rolls across the room to the crowd, which rears back, pressing itself even harder against the back wall.

"What kind of game?" I say.

She swings the revolver around, points it at me for a second, pops the cylinder, and empties the bullets.

"What happened to your face?" she says idly.

"Which time?"

"The new one."

"I got shot."

"Let's see if we can even you out with one on the other side."

She puts one bullet in the cylinder, spins it, slaps it closed, shoves the gun in my face, and pulls the trigger.

Nothing.

I say, "I guess it's not your night. Maybe you should have your drinks and leave."

She swings the gun over at Carlos and pulls the trigger.

Nothing.

"Fuck," she screams. "This game isn't fun. Let's play another."

She opens the gun's cylinder and puts in a second bullet.

Points at Fuck Hollywood for a second. She's quietly crying while Buzzy grins like a demented clown. Eventually, Despentes sights down at the crowd behind them.

She pulls the trigger one more time and when nothing happens, she goes nuts, yanking the trigger again until she's fired both bullets. One goes high and hits the edge of an old X poster. The other shatters a glass hula girl light fixture next to the starlet in sunglasses.

"That's more like it," Despentes says.

As she loads more shells into the revolver, Buzzard pulls the Glock out of Fuck Hollywood's mouth to point at something.

"Look," he says, and never says anything else because I've thrown the black blade and it's sticking out of his forehead like a goddamn handle on a goddamn skillet. When he crumples onto the floor Despentes fumbles and drops her bullets. But she's fast. Before I can grab her, she dives onto the floor and grabs Buzzard's Glock. Starts firing wild, shooting up the whole room. People hit the floor screaming. I stay put as she gets to her feet and runs out the front door.

No one moves or says anything for what feels like a full minute. Then, as people are slowly getting up off the floor and remembering how to breathe, Despentes comes back in with a balloon on a string. Everyone hits the floor again.

The balloon is in the shape of a 9mm bullet. She lets it go and it floats to the ceiling.

"A present for you, sweetheart, from King Bullet. I'll tell him all about you."

She aims her gun at the ceiling, sings, "Rum-tiddley-um-tum-tay," and fires.

The balloon pops and what looks like about a million

cockroaches falls out. Maybe she meant for it to happen or she's just stupid, but the effect of the bug attack is pretty dismal because they're all dead. Choked on helium.

Despentes screams one more time and empties the Glock rounds into the bar, not even trying to hit anybody, just leaving her mark on the place. When she's empty, she takes off outside. There's the sound of a siren and a car peeling out.

The moment she's gone, I jump over the bar and go to Fuck Hollywood. She's already up and kicking dumb, dead Buzzard's body over and over again with her big boots. I pull her away and sit her down at one of the tables.

When I go back to the bar Carlos says, "What are we going to do about all these bodies? LAPD will shut this place down forever."

"Let me handle the bodies."

"What about them?" he says, looking at the crowd.

"They just want to go home." I look at the terrified mob scattered around the room. "Isn't that right?"

A lot of nods and murmurs of agreement.

"Then here's how it is," I say. "From now until the sun goes cold, nothing happened here tonight. This is for your benefit. LAPD will never believe you know nothing about how the two real cops in those uniforms died. And they're not in the mood to be patient or forgiving. Understand me?"

More murmurs and nods.

"Now go home and forget everything that happened tonight. But come back tomorrow because everyone here tonight gets a free drink. Right, Carlos?"

He looks at me for a second, then says, "Yes. One drink on the house."

"Now all of you, scoot. Go home and be smart and be quiet."

I don't have to tell them twice. The place clears out in under a minute until it's just me, Carlos, and Fuck Hollywood.

Carlos says, "So, what happens now?"

"First, I get rid of Charlotte and Babadook."

"Man. I liked them."

"Me too, but focus. While I'm gone, I'll need you to hose off the sidewalk. Can you do that?"

"Yeah. Sure." He nods toward Fuck Hollywood. "What about her?"

With her traumatized eyes, she looks like she's gone somewhere far away and might never come back.

"Leave her for now. She needs to process this. I'll talk to her later."

"Good. I have no idea what to tell her." He heads out back for the hose.

Neither do I, which is why I'm dealing with the corpses first.

Fortunately, when I get out front there's no one on the street. I drag Babadook's and Charlotte's bodies into a shadow and come out in the Angeles National Forest. There are open mass graves ready to be filled in. I lay them out with their heads in place. When I'm done, I stand at the grave rim and say a few words of Hellion hoodoo. They sink into the sod until there's no trace of them.

Take care, you two. I'm so sorry things ended this way. But Heaven is open to you now. Go through the gates and don't look back. We'll take things from here and make sure the crazy fuckers who did this pay for it.

I go back to the bar, and I'm not so careful with Buzzard's body. I drop him down south in the dump. Let the cops or whoever is left for this kind of thing deal with him.

When I get back to Bamboo House the place is locked down tight. Carlos sits at a table with Fuck Hollywood, a martini and a glass of water sitting between them. Neither has been touched. I pull up a chair and sit down with them. After a moment she looks at me.

"You killed Buzzy."

"Yeah. I'm sorry."

"Don't be sorry. I'm glad you did it."

Carlos says, "That guy who was here tonight, he wasn't the guy you knew. The virus, you know, it messes with some people's minds."

Fuck Hollywood shakes her head.

"I know. But Buzzy always had a little bit of a mean streak. If he got sick, it just let it out more. That was him tonight."

I say, "You still want to do what you told me at home?"

"Yeah. More than ever."

Fuck Hollywood takes the skateboard she stole from Buzzard out of her backpack.

"I don't have any lighter fluid, but I have Everclear. That should work," says Carlos.

"Okay," she says.

He grabs the bottle and we all go to the alley behind Bamboo House. Fuck Hollywood pours Everclear over the skateboard and I hand her my lighter. She holds it to the rear wheels and the board bursts into flames. And the tears start to flow. Sobs and sobs from deep down inside her. Fear and love and anger all mixed together.

As we watch the board go up Fuck Hollywood says, "I loved you, you fuck."

We stand quietly until the board turns crispy at the edges. Fuck Hollywood looks at me.

"You killed him. Kill this for me."

I bark some Hellion and the board flares bright as the sun for a second. Then it's just melted plastic and ashes.

She says, "I guess I'm free now. Huh?"

"If you want to be," says Carlos.

Wrapping her arms around herself, Fuck Hollywood says, "I do. I used to be so afraid of being alone. But then all the guys I was with turned out to be, well—" She looks at me. "You met him."

I once had to throw Buzzard out of Bamboo House for threatening her.

I say, "You were smart to get out. Even if it did hurt."

She takes Carlos's and my hands. It's technically against epidemic rules, but this isn't a moment to get fussy.

"Thanks for being my friends." And looks up at the drifting smoke. "I like it out here. It's so quiet and calm. I come out here sometimes when things are too much inside."

"It is nice," I say, even though the place is a garbage-strewn shithole.

She wipes tears from her eyes.

"A friend of a friend might have a room I can move into," she says.

"Cool," I tell her. "But there's no rush. We like the same kind of movies. Stay as long as you like."

She hugs me and looks at the ashes of the skateboard one more time.

"Bye, Buzzy. You know, I thought he was the one."

Carlos says, "We all have someone like that in our past. The one who got away."

I flash on Candy's face, but push it away as quickly as it appeared.

Fuck Hollywood looks up at me.

"You too?"

"Me too?"

"Who's yours?"

"I'll tell you about it sometime. But not tonight."

"Okay."

We all go inside. Fuck Hollywood hugs Carlos and I take her home through a shadow.

She flops onto the sofa and says, "You going to see Janet tonight?"

"I was. But are you going to be okay? I can stay if you like."

"I'll be fine," she says and lies down. "I'd actually like to be alone tonight."

"Sure. But call me if you need anything."

"I will."

I grab a few things and when I go back to check on her, Fuck Hollywood is asleep. Adrenaline crash. It's going to be a bad few days when she wakes up. I'll need to keep an eye on her.

I step into a shadow and come out in front of Janet's place. Their music is playing when I get up to the apartment. They're excited and try to pull me into the bedroom. I shake my head and tell them what happened at the bar tonight. We go to bed, but just lie there wrapped around each other, Janet's movie music playing softly in the other room. We fall asleep that way and I dream about a beautiful black-eyed monster holding my hand and saying, "It's just us. The funny little people who live in the cracks in the world."

IN THE MORNING, Janet goes back to work making the final tweaks on her music and I go outside with my coffee to smoke. I finish my second Malediction and get out my phone. Hit Abbot's number. It takes a few rings, but he finally picks up. His voice is thin and raspy.

"Stark. It's good to hear from you. How are you doing these days?"

"I'm all right. But you don't sound so good."

"I'm just over a round with the virus. Listen, I've hardly seen anyone in weeks. Why don't you come over and we can talk about whatever you want?"

"Give me a few minutes and I'll be there."

I take my coffee cup back upstairs and tell Janet that I'm going out.

"Will you be okay while I'm gone?"

"I'm not going out and I'm sure not opening the door for anyone but you."

I give them a kiss and head out through a shadow.

These days, Abbot lives in a broken-down shed on a vacant lot in Westwood. Sub Rosa aesthetics can seem funny to regular people. Civilian blue bloods like to show off their money with giant estates and palm trees that punch holes in the sky. Sub Rosa are the opposite. The more the outside of their place looks like a garbage heap, the classier they are. Abbot's place looks like a storage crate fucked an outhouse and they had an ugly baby.

I knock on the door a few times and a bodyguard the size of a pickup truck comes out. It's Matthew, a guard I met once before. A real tight-ass, but not dumb. He looks me up and down and clearly isn't impressed with the freshly healed gunshot wound in my face.

"Where's your mask?" he says.

I take it out of my pocket and put it on.

"Sorry."

"Don't take it off inside. The Augur still isn't himself."

"Got it."

He looks at me suspiciously.

"That's it? That's all you're going to say?"

"What else do you want?"

"You usually have some smartass comeback."

"I'm too tired for that shit right now. Aren't you?"

"Most definitely. You'll find a chair when you get to the Augur's room. Sit in it and don't move it any closer to him. Understood?"

"He's still that fucked up?"

He holds the shack door open for me. "Just follow the rules and everything will be fine."

Inside, the hovel changes into something more like a scaled-down Versailles. Marble everywhere. Crystal chandeliers. Classy furniture and a wall of windows that look out over the Pacific.

Matthew takes me to Abbot's office and points to the lone

chair in the room. A fancy upholstered antique that I'm pretty sure I'll break just thinking about.

"Remember what I said."

"Don't get close to Abbot and never bet on an inside straight."

"There's the asshole I was waiting for."

The moment Matthew leaves, Abbot looks up from his work.

"Hello, Stark," he says. Then waves his hand. "Come closer."

"Matthew said to stay over here."

"Matthew is a little too protective. Come closer so I don't feel quite so much like Typhoid Mary."

The closer I get, the shittier Abbot looks. His hair is long and he seems weak and frail. He was never a big guy and it looks like he lost twenty pounds and his surgical mask droops on his face. With his bony cheekbones, when he smiles he looks like a well-dressed corpse.

"I'm glad to see you in a mask," he says.

"I'm not. I hate these things."

"Speaking as someone who caught the virus and almost died, better safe than sorry."

"You look like shit, so I'm guessing it's as bad as people say."

"It's worse. Not only did I have influenza symptoms, but the fever swelled my brain. I don't remember much of it, but I had to be restrained and sedated for days. And this was in a private Sub Rosa clinic. I don't know if I would have survived in a civilian hospital."

"Goddamn. But you're okay now?"

He leans on his elbow and opens his hands.

"Finally. It was touch and go for a while."

I look at him sitting there like he wants to fall over, but is working to convince himself he's a whole person again. It makes me want a cigarette. If I was as sick as him, all I'd do is drink and smoke until Samael or one of his flunkies came to take me away.

"I heard the virus hit Sub Rosa, but you're the first person I've talked to about it."

"It's been a bad few weeks for everyone. We've lost some good people."

"Months," I say. "It's been months."

"Yes. Months. God. I hate to think of all the wasted time."

I sit back in the chair and cross my legs and say, "Relax. L.A. would be falling apart with or without you. I doubt you could have made much of a difference. There's just too much happening at once."

"I'm not convinced that's true. I'm convening whatever part of the council is well enough to work and seeing what we can do to pull the city back together."

"Let me know if I can help."

He looks at me, a little surprised. I'm a little surprised too. But I really hate L.A. on its last legs like this.

"I'll remember that," he says. "But I have a feeling you're not here to bring me a get-well card."

"I had one, but my dog ate it."

"You don't have a dog."

"I did, but my other dog ate that one."

"And what happened to that dog?"

"The cat ate it."

"Maybe I should send *you* a get-well card. Why are you really here?"

I lean forward with both feet on the floor.

"I want to know everything you know about King Bullet."

Abbot raises his eyebrows a fraction of an inch.

"You've met him?"

"Some of his people. One of them put this hole in my face. Another killed two friends and almost killed a third."

"I'm sorry."

"I'm going to nail his skin to my living room wall when I find him. But first I need to know where to look and what to expect when I get there."

Abbot scribbles something with his pen.

"I'll tell you what I know, which, unfortunately, isn't much more than you, I bet."

"I'll take anything you have. Start with a name."

"King Bullet. That's all anyone knows. He's new to the city and no one has been able to trace his whereabouts before that. Not through fingerprint records or location rituals."

"What about the cops? Don't they have facial recognition tech?"

Abbot waves a hand vaguely.

"King Bullet wears a mask at all times. And he changes it often enough that no one local has been able to get a line on him. I even checked with our Federal contacts. They're not faring any better than we are. One thing he's become notorious for is stealing the clothes of the people he's killed and wearing them until he kills again."

"That might explain the cops in Bamboo House." I think for a minute. "Did he really take over the Shoggots and kill the Sub Rosa clan?"

"Killed them and assimilated their hangers-on. He has a

small army at this point and he's making moves on the rest of the gangs in L.A. Join or die."

The word "army" is alarming. I was hoping he wasn't this organized. It's one thing to go after a small-time crime boss, but a cult leader is something else.

"Is there anything else you have that might be useful?"

Abbot thinks for a minute.

"Remember the knife Audsley Ishii used to kill you?"

"Of course. Samvari steel and it hurt like hell. What about it?"

"Samvari steel is very rare on Earth."

"So, where did he get it?"

"The Shoggots. The original clan, that is."

"I sort of felt bad for a minute, but now I'm happy to see them gone."

Abbot says, "I only bring it up because if the previous incarnation of the Shoggots had access to powerful objects like that, they might still have them."

"See? Now that's useful information."

"You're still on salary, but I'll pay you a bonus if you look into King Bullet for the council."

"Why don't you just send your own enforcers?"

"We have. But our people have to behave within certain parameters. You, on the other hand—"

"I get it. How many did you lose?"

Abbot falls back against his chair. He looks more exhausted than ever. Just talking is taking all of his energy.

"Three," he says. "And two are missing."

I look at him.

"Do you think they might have gone bad?"

"Joined King Bullet's mob? Don't tell anyone that I said this, but we're investigating that possibility."

"A friend of a friend, a kid named Buzzard, went a little psycho and joined them. You think that might have happened to your lost sheep?"

"That's one avenue of investigation."

I wish I had a cigarette more than ever.

"I'd say tell me what they look like and I'll keep an eye out for them, but the way Shoggots cut themselves up, I don't know if a description would help."

"Probably not," Abbot says. He looks at me hard. "Are you keeping safe? This newer strain of the virus is the one that's affecting people mentally."

"You don't have to tell me. I'm immune, but I've seen the results."

Abbot looks like he's on his last legs, but he keeps going. I generally hate to like bosses, but I like him.

Abbot says, "But it isn't just outward violence. It's self-harm too. The local authorities are keeping the numbers out of the press, but suicides and self-mutilations are skyrocketing. And I know what you're going to say. That the Shoggots have always mutilated themselves."

"There is that."

"But this is different. Shoggot scarification is directed and controlled. And limited to their small numbers. This is widespread. And what I'm talking about are dangerous compulsions such as autophagia."

"What the hell is that?"

Abbot has a short coughing fit and gets it under control only after a long sip of water from a glass on his desk.

"Autophagia is a rare syndrome in which a person develops a powerful drive to consume their own flesh. Often, it will start with the lips. Then they'll attack their limbs. Then—"

I hold up a hand.

"Okay. Stop right there. I saw too much of that kind of thing Downtown. You really think that's happening here?"

"I've seen the evidence. I know you're strong and recover quickly, but you need to be on guard. This virus is new and if it can affect me, it might be able to affect you too."

"You don't think this is some kind of weapon, do you? I remember an old story where the army or someone sat offshore and blew cold germs into San Francisco to see what would happen."

"We've looked into it and it seems highly unlikely that it's a weapon."

The next thing I say, I say quietly.

"I haven't told many people about this, but a few months ago I killed an angel who had a grudge against me. I've been wondering if this might be some kind of plague she called down before she died."

Abbot gives me a look.

"Are you saying that you think that what's happening might be partially your fault?"

I put up both hands at that.

"No. I just mean—"

He looks away wearily, then turns back to me.

"You know angels better than I do."

"That's the thing," I say. "I keep trying to figure out what's going on, but I don't really think this is her. It doesn't feel right. The epidemic is bad, but it's not like she called down the apocalypse, and that's what I think she meant."

Abbot relaxes, his body going slack. Maybe at relief because of what I said or maybe his energy is about to run out.

"I'm glad to hear you say that. Being connected to the epidemic, well, I think the guilt would be overwhelming."

"Yeah. It would." I say it like I'm all confidence, but I'm not. "One more thing: Have you or your people heard anyone say something like 'Rum-tiddley-um-tum-tay'?"

He frowns.

"No. What is that?"

"Both times I've run into King Bullet's people they kind of sang it, almost like a nursery rhyme."

He makes another note on the piece of paper.

"I'll look into it," he says. Then his body goes limp. He puts a hand to his forehead. "I'm afraid that's all I can give you right now. I'm very tired. Let's call it a day, all right?"

I get up and drag the chair back to where it was. I don't need Matthew giving me grief right now. I am seriously not in the mood for more bullshit.

"Sure. Take care of yourself," I say.

Abbot raises a listless hand to me.

"Thank you. Stay safe. And wear your mask."

I turn as I'm heading for the door.

"What do you think I'm wearing now?"

Abbot wipes sweat from his forehead with his hand.

"I know you well enough to know that you'll take it off at the first opportunity. The hospitals are full, Stark. Don't go wasting a bed because you don't want to be a grown-up."

"I'll take that under advisement."

"And you'll look into King Bullet for me?"

"That's the plan. But I've got my own people to look after too. If I have to choose, I'm choosing them."

Matthew walks me outside. I offer him a Malediction, but he waves it off.

"Things are bad enough without getting cancer too," he says.

"It's never too late to develop bad habits."

He just stands there like a brick wall. Finally, he says, "The Augur looks bad, huh?"

"Worse than I've ever seen him."

"Me too."

"It looks like he's well taken care of."

"He is, but listen. I don't like you. You're a pain in the ass, even when you think you're playing the good guy."

I check his eyes and listen to his heart. He doesn't seem like he wants to start a fight.

I say, "And your point is?"

"The Augur likes you," he says. "He was happy you called. So call more. He lost some good friends to the virus. He needs to be around people he likes."

I listen for microtremors in his voice. He's telling the truth.

"I'll keep in touch."

"Good," says Matthew. "Now get the hell out of here. People see your ugly ass hanging around, it brings down property values."

I light a Malediction and walk away, making sure to get some smoke in his face first.

I'm sorry Abbot doesn't think the virus is some spook lab weapon. That means the odds are it's some natural fuckup in a cold germ that's let it run wild. Any alternate explanations are too much. Mostly, I can't begin to think about being somehow connected to the epidemic. Not with wrecking the city and killing all these people. Even I can't fuck up that badly.

Can I?

Before going back to Janet's place I stop by the apartment to check on Fuck Hollywood. She's curled up on the sofa watching a Godzilla marathon on TV while eating yet more pizza. She's wearing what I'm pretty sure is my Skull Valley Sheep Kill hoodie, but I don't say anything. In all, she looks a lot better than she did last night at Bamboo House.

I say, "How are you feeling? You feel up to going into work today?"

"There is no work. The place is closed today while Carlos and Ray patch the bullet holes in the walls."

"They need help?"

Fuck Hollywood offers me a piece of pizza, but I shake my head. She says, "Carlos said for us to stay home and be safe." Then she turns back to the TV.

She's held it together pretty well, but it feels like she's made of cracked glass. One false move and she'll fall apart.

"I'm going to find King Bullet and take him out," I say.

She nods.

"Good. Thank you. But please be careful."

That last she says with a lot of tension in her voice.

"I always am."

"Yeah right," she says, taking a long pull straight from a two-liter bottle of Coke.

"I'm heading to Janet's for a while. Call me if you need anything. Promise?"

She burps and it sounds like the roar of a tiny T. rex.

"I promise."

"And don't get pizza on my hoodie."

Her head falls back against the sofa.

"You are so old, Grandma. There are washing machines now. We don't have to beat things on a rock down by the creek."

I go out through a shadow and come out at Janet's place. It smells good inside.

They say, "I got Indian food delivered."

"I thought you weren't going to let anyone in."

"I told them to send Jimmy. I know him."

"That's good, but wait until I'm here next time. Okay?"

They make a face and say, "I know you're right, but I wanted to have something nice for when you got back."

"Thank you," I say and we kiss.

They put out jasmine rice and three containers of food. It looks and smells great. I scoop a bit from the first container onto my rice. It's just some kind of cheese sauce and spinach.

"Saag paneer," they say.

"It's just spinach?"

"And spicy sauce."

"What's the other one?"

"Aloo gobi. Potatoes and cauliflower in a turmeric curry."

The third dish looks more promising. Little lumps of what I hope is chicken on skewers.

They say, "The other one is paneer tikka. Cheese cubes grilled like tandoori chicken."

"Why couldn't we just have tandoori chicken?"

"This is healthier."

"Chickens are healthy, otherwise they wouldn't give you chicken soup when you have a cold."

"That's mostly chicken broth."

I say, "Lamb is healthy. And they're cute."

Janet smiles a little.

"Going without meat for one meal won't kill you."

I look over the food.

"This might. Spinach and cauliflower aren't vegetables. They're punishment. They're the solitary confinement of food."

Janet sighs.

"Fine. Then just have the paneer tikka."

I put a couple of skewers on my plate and eat it with the rice. It's actually not as bad as I thought it might be, but I can tell that Janet is annoyed with me.

They pause between bites, wipe their lips on a paper napkin, and say, "Someone tried to get in while you were gone. They said they needed help. They said they were a neighbor. I didn't let them in the building."

Janet's voice is thin and tense, and their heart rate is up.

"You did the right thing," I say.

They set down the napkin.

"But what if they really needed help and I left them out there?"

"If it happens again offer to call 911 for them."

"I did that."

"What did they say?"

"Nothing. I heard them buzzing other apartments."

"That's it then. It was a hustle. They were just trying to get into the building."

They push their food away and say, "I'm so tired of being scared. I don't even want to take out the trash."

I look into the kitchen and there are two bulging plastic garbage bags.

"I'll do it," I say. Any excuse to get away from cauliflower and cheese lumps.

I grab the bags and while I'm heading for the door Janet says, "Please be careful. I don't know what I would do if you got hurt taking out trash I'm too afraid to touch."

Everyone keeps telling me to be careful when all I want to do is protect them.

It's a little exhausting.

"It'll be fine. I'm armed to the teeth."

"I know. But still."

"You sit tight and have more gloob."

"Aloo gobi."

"Right."

I go downstairs and add Janet's trash to the mounds of other bags lining the curb. Next door, a guy in a trench coat and mask that covers most of his face presses a buzzer. He's big and I can't get a look at his face to see if it's scarred. I reach under my coat and get a grip on the na'at. I'm not letting down my guard again with anybody. But a minute later the door opens and a blond woman comes out. She's smiling. The big guy takes off his mask and they kiss. His face is fine. The blonde looks over and notices me staring. Then the guy looks over as the blonde takes his hands and pulls him inside.

Great. Now *I'm* the street creep.

After last night, I can't help being on guard, but looking for killers behind every mask is no way to think. As easy as it would make things, not everyone is the enemy. I've got to keep my head on straight. Take care of Janet, Candy, and the rest of my friends. They're all that matter.

When I get back upstairs, Janet is already clearing away the dishes and I'm trying to figure a way to sneak out for a burger later. We settle down and I show them the special versions of *The Third Man* and *Death Wish* Kasabian gave me. When they're over and I turn the lights on, Janet is frowning in thought.

"I don't get it," they say.

"Don't get what?"

"I just don't get the attraction of these weird movies you show me. I mean, if they were supposed to happen, they would have happened, right? And they'd be better than the versions of the movies we already have."

"Yeah, but isn't it interesting to see into other worlds and get a look at things that might have happened and maybe even should have happened?"

"I guess," they say.

I'll admit it. My stomach is knotted up and not from just the food. How can you not like seeing something great like David Cronenberg's *Frankenstein* or Alejandro Jodorowsky's *Dune*? Candy always loved the otherworldly movies—

And I stop myself right there. What am I doing comparing the two of them? That's not fair to anyone. And Candy is gone. I need to stop this shit. Janet is the one I have to concentrate on and if I have to watch my funny little movies alone back at my place with Fuck Hollywood, I can do that. It's not such a big sacrifice. I need to get a fucking grip. Take the movies back and not go to Max Overdrive for a while. Get Candy and the place out of my head for a while.

"Are you okay?" says Janet. "You looked like you were a million miles away."

"Nope. I'm fine."

"I'm sorry I don't like the movies. I just don't see the attraction."

"That's fine. We can look at other things. Don't worry."

"Good. Because I like watching movies with you."

"Me too," I say, but my stomach is still in knots. Then, to change the subject, I add, "I think I'm going to go after the boss of the guy who shot me. King Bullet."

Janet looks at me, their face tense with concern.

"Please don't. I don't want you to get hurt again."

"I was sloppy last time. That won't happen again."

"I know, but still, please don't."

I put an arm around them.

"I might not have a choice. Thomas Abbot pays my salary and he wants me to. And I want to know more about the King. For starters, what the hell does he want?"

Janet just sits there, arms crossed, body tense.

"Don't worry," I say. "I'm not running out tonight. If I do the job, I'll do some prep work first. Try to get more information about him." It's only half a lie. Abbot gave me enough to get started. I figure if I start kicking at this anthill, something interesting is bound to come out. But not tonight.

They take a breath and let it out again.

"I know this is the kind of thing you do—dealing with people like King Bullet or whoever—I just wish it wasn't."

For all my promises, tonight isn't going great for us. First the food. Then the movies. And now this, because they're basically asking me not to do something fundamental to my life. I don't let myself think of Candy. No more comparisons. Just stay here in the moment with Janet and say something, anything, to make them feel better.

"It's going to be all right."

Well, that was nothing. I'll need to try harder than that.

"How is your work going?"

That wasn't much better, but I'll take it right now.

But the distraction seems to help. Janet relaxes a little and says, "It's okay. I'm pretty much ready for the show."

"It's in an hour, right?"

"That's right."

"What can I do to help?"

They look a little sad again.

"Just kiss me like you mean it."

So I do. I try to anyway. I don't think I've ever been so conscious of a kiss before. How do you kiss someone trying to convince them that the kiss is real? So, I kiss her a little harder and longer and hope for the best.

When we part, I must have done something right because they're almost smiling. They touch my hair and run their hand down along the scarred line of my jaw. Then one more peck on the lips.

"Okay," they say. "I need to start getting ready."

"I'll be over here staying out of your way."

They fire up their laptop, check their keyboards and the mixing deck. Run the beginning of the movie back and forth a few times to make sure that the music and images sync up properly. Then they get dressed. A long-sleeve black men's dress shirt and a brocade corset over tuxedo pants. They're a total knockout.

About a half hour before the concert, faces begin popping into the Zoom app on the large monitor behind their bank of instruments, giving the audience a good look at both Janet and the film.

Finally, it's showtime. I dim the lights in the apartment. I don't know how many people are in the audience, but the Zoom screen is completely full. Janet does a short introduction and launches into *L'Age d'Or*.

Janet is riveting for the movie's sixty-minute running time. I've seen the movie before, so I just watch them. They're intense, sexy, and perfect in their choices for music, sometimes matching the scenes and sometimes playing against them, creating a weird emotional contrast. I've never seen Janet do a whole solo concert before. It's something they were born to do.

When the last frames of the movie fade away, the sound of hoots and tinny applause from several dozen people comes from the speaker on the big monitor. Janet takes their bows and waves happily to the audience as, one by one, the listeners blip off the screen. It takes a few minutes for everyone to exit the app and Janet smiles and waves to people the whole time. They're happier than I've ever seen them.

Finally there's only one woman left on the Zoom screen. It looks like she's crying quietly.

She says, "Thank you so much. You don't know how much that meant to me."

"I'm really glad you enjoyed it," says Janet.

"My name is Maggie and *L'Age D'or* is my favorite film."

"It's one of my favorites too."

"I'm in L.A. You are too, I think?"

"Yes, I am."

Maggie smiles and wipes her eyes.

"Then you'll understand me when I say that I didn't want to leave without seeing the movie one more time."

"Oh? Where are you going?"

"I don't know. But somewhere better than this."

"I don't understand," says Janet.

"Thank you again."

Then Maggie puts a Smith & Wesson .357 Magnum to her head and blows her brains out.

The Zoom screen stays open, a blank portal to an empty room. I pull Janet away and turn off the monitor. Their hand is clamped over their open mouth. They don't make a sound when I put my arms around them, but I can tell they're on complete overload, body rigid and screaming and screaming on the inside. I lead them into the bedroom and get the corset off before laying them out on the bed. Soon the stiffness leaves Janet's body and they start to cry. I bring them tea with bourbon in it and they choke it down. It relaxes them a little, but the crying never completely stops. I sit next to Janet in bed, just holding them. The crying seems to go on all night.

Around four a.m. I'm startled awake by the sound of someone struggling for air. Janet is only half-conscious as her body convulses with deep, racking coughs. When they're finally fully awake they look at me and take my hand.

"Oh god. You don't think it's—"

"No. I don't."

"You need to get away from me."

"Forget it. If it's the virus, it's too late for that. I'm taking you to see Allegra."

THE CLINIC DOESN'T open until six, so we have a tense two hours to sit around and drink coffee while we're waiting. The moment the clock hands hit twelve and six, we put on surgical masks and I pull Janet into a shadow.

We come out in the strip mall where Allegra has her little clandestine hospital. The mall was always a shabby place with a cut-rate nail salon and third-rate pizza, but boarded up and with piles of trash outside it looks like the end of the world. In case Allegra is alone and in the back of the place, I bang on the clinic's door with my fist. A minute later I hear a lock being turned—and then there's a gun in my face.

And it's not an ordinary pistol. It's a Devil's Daisy. A Hellion weapon. Very rare here in the world. Daisies are twisted things, like gnarled tree roots, and they will kill you fifty ways dead. I've only ever seen big rifle-size ones, but this one is small. Pistol-size. And a frowning Allegra has it right in my face.

A second later, when she recognizes me, she lowers the Daisy.

"Fuck, Stark. It sounded like you were trying to knock the door down."

"Sorry. I just thought you might not hear me."

"I heard just fine," she says, still a little annoyed. Looking past me, she says, "Hi, Janet."

"Hi. What is that?"

I say, "It's called a Devil's Daisy. Kasabian tried to kill me with one of those once. Where did you get it?"

Allegra looks at it and makes a face.

"I found it in Vidocq's things."

"Have you had to use it?"

"Not yet."

Janet leans against the door and goes into a coughing fit. Allegra pulls them inside.

"That doesn't sound good. I need to take a look at you."

I follow them in, locking the front door behind me.

They head straight to the exam room and Janet sits on the table and Allegra removes their mask.

"You aren't wearing a mask," says Janet.

"I don't need to anymore. I've hit myself up with so many magic herbs and tinctures and elixirs that I could dance my way through the Black Death."

I say, "That's great. Can you give that stuff to Janet?"

Allegra listens to Janet's heart and feels under their chin for swelling.

"Only if I wanted to kill them."

I say, "What do you mean, 'kill them'?"

Allegra glances at me.

"I've been building up my system over months. Some of Doc Kinski's old mixtures helped build up my immunity, and I found more ideas in Vidocq's books. But a few of those things, man, they almost murdered me. That's why I can't just give it to anyone like a spoonful of cough syrup."

She has Janet lie down and puts a series of what look like small brass coins on their body from their throat to their stomach. Almost immediately, the coins begin to glow. Two turn red and the one by their heart turns black.

"Is that bad?" says Janet, trying to angle their head so they can see what's going on.

"Please try not to move." Allegra uses an eyedropper to put a small amount of a golden liquid on the black coin. After a moment it lightens to its original brass color. Allegra smiles.

"Congratulations," she says. "You have a cold."

"That's all?" says Janet, brightening.

"That's all. Get some bed rest. Drink a lot of fluids and have some soup. You also might try relaxing a little bit. You're coiled up inside like a rattlesnake."

After Allegra gathers the brass coins Janet sits up.

"I'm fine. I mean, everyone is tense these days. Right?"

"Yes, but tension plus your cold isn't doing your immune system any good. Let me give you some pills that might help."

Janet furrows their brow.

"I don't like pills."

"You just saw someone kill herself," I say. "That's going to make anybody tense. Why don't you just try the pills for a few days?"

"You're right, but I never want to sleep again after that."

"I can imagine. But you need to sleep if you're going to get better," says Allegra. "Take one of these a day for a week and see how you feel."

She hands Janet a plastic pill bottle and looks to me.

"How are you with your PTSD meds? Still taking them, right?"

"Sure. I just don't know if they're helping."

"You'd know if they weren't. I'll give you more before we leave. Enough to tide you over for a few weeks."

I hadn't expected that.

"Does this mean you're shutting down the clinic?" Things must have gotten bad here if she's thinking of closing. She was always dedicated to it, but now with Vidocq gone, it's pretty much become her life.

She gives me a quick, tight nod.

"I don't have any choice. I've only been seeing a few humans and Lurkers that I already knew well. After the last time one of them attacked my assistant, Fairuza, I can't handle it anymore."

"What are you going to do with yourself without your patients?"

She gives me a rueful smile.

"I have no idea. Watch TV? Take up needlepoint? Why? Do you have any suggestions?"

"You could work part-time with me at Bamboo House of Dolls."

She laughs.

"I don't think I'd be a very good barmaid."

"Think about it. And if you're nervous at home, you can always stay at my place. You know it's safe. Crowded, but safe."

Allegra puts a few bottles and some of Kinski's strange medicinals into her shoulder bag. When she gives me my psych pills she says, "I have Vidocq's tools. He showed me how to make my place safe. Besides, he used to live at your place. *We* used to. There are too many memories there."

"Okay. Keep that Daisy with you all the time. And call me if you need anything."

"Thank you."

I try to think of something else to say. Something to keep her from just brooding about the world, alone in her apartment. But I don't have anything to offer her. If I can't take care of my friends on this basic a level, how can I take care of anyone?

It's hugs all around, then we walk Allegra to her car and I take Janet home, wondering and worrying about when I'm ever going to see Allegra again.

Back at Janet's place, I get them to take one of their pills and, after not sleeping much last night, it knocks them right out. When I'm sure they're out and breathing right, I go through a shadow to Max Overdrive.

I TRY THE front door, but it's locked. Kasabian lets me in and gets six feet between us.

"What's wrong with you? You look like someone sold your pet canary smack and it OD'd."

I put the movies from last night on the counter.

"Janet didn't like them."

Kasabian shifts his shoulders uncomfortably.

"Didn't like them how?"

"Didn't like them didn't like them. They said they didn't see the point of watching movies that never happened."

"That doesn't sound right," he said, and there's a tiny hint of something like sympathy in his voice.

"I know."

"I guess it's good they watched them with you at least."

"And they fed me weird food. All spinach and cauliflower and cheese."

"Did they?" he says and now the sympathy is gone, replaced with a knowing little smile.

"What's that about?"

"Nothing. It just explains why you're like the good boy who didn't get a cookie. Tension. A little trouble in paradise?"

I stand up straighter.

"I didn't say that. Janet just needs some regular movies."

Kasabian scratches his chin.

"Forget it. I'm just fucking with you. I haven't touched a woman since dinosaurs walked the Earth. Go look for something. *Mi casa es su casa* and all that crap."

I wander back to Musicals and wonder for a minute if Janet would like something stupid like *Xanadu* or *Roller Boogie*. But I shove them back into the display bin because I don't want to die of a disco aneurysm. I grab *Urgh! A Music War*, but put that back too. I don't even know if they like punk or new wave bands, which I know is a strange thing not to have figured out by now. I guess we've mostly been listening to their music and I haven't heard a single X song. Finally, I decide to play it safe and grab *Singin' in the Rain*.

When I bring it up front, Kasabian taps the disc on the counter a couple of times and looks at me.

"Have you actually made it all the way through it?"

"Janet likes music."

"Yeah. But have you—"

"I tried a couple of times. There's a lot of—"

"Merriment. I know. Your brain rejects that stuff on principle. Stay here, dummy."

I wait up front like some asshole whose mom is picking

out his suit for prom night right in front of all the mean girls from school.

Kasabian is back in a minute with *How to Steal a Million* and *Roman Holiday*, a couple of sweet and dumb Audrey Hepburn romantic comedies. He drops a third disc on top. A movie I've never heard of.

"It's *They* by Anahita Ghazvinizadeh," he says. "There's a nice kid in it. Smart. Sweet. Nonbinary."

I look at him like he just turned into a three-legged unicorn.

"Did you just actually go out of your way for someone?"

He tosses the discs in a bag and says, "Not for you I didn't. For Janet. They need people smarter than you looking out for them."

"Thank you. I'll tell Janet you found it for them."

He looks away, annoyed that I caught him being a human being.

"You're lucky I even let you in," he says. "They're installing the alarm later today. I'm sick of all these freaks. I'm pushing Candy and Alessa to shut down for a while. Just until things blow over."

"Do you have the money for that?"

"We have some in the bank. I mean, it would help if we knew how long we'll have to hide in a cave with the Morlocks. But I had a *great* idea."

There's something about the way he says "great" that makes me suspicious. He picks up the discs and points to them like a magician pulling a mangy rabbit out of a hat. I say, "Don't you fucking dare."

"We should start a secret streaming service with all the special movies."

I slam my hand on the counter.

"Goddammit, Kas. You *rent* movies. On disc. People have to leave their homes to get them. Interact. Be people."

"But people aren't people anymore," he shouts. "That's the whole fucking problem. I got my body back just in time to die because some maniac brains me with a pipe. I can't even go to Donut Universe anymore."

"If you're that scared, make a list and me and Janet will bring you things."

He looks at me appraisingly for a second.

"You asshole. Do you even know what's going on in the world?"

"I've been a little busy."

"They burned it last night," he says. "The crazies burned Donut Universe to the ground. Danced and sang until there was nothing left."

"Oh shit. I've got to tell Janet." But how? I think about them at home, knocked out and dreaming of Maggie and the gun.

Kasabian shakes his head.

"That's where you two lovebirds met, isn't it? They aren't going to take it well."

"No. Probably not. Maybe I shouldn't tell them."

"Good. Lying is always the best solution in these situations."

"I don't know what to do."

"Problems at home and no more apple fritters."

"You're being a prick again."

He makes a face and says, "Sorry. I just keep wondering when they're going to come for us."

"No one is coming for you. You're right to lock the place

up. In the meantime, I'll throw on some Downtown hoodoo that no civilians can break."

"Yeah? Maybe we might survive after all. If you don't fuck it up."

"I'm good at this stuff."

"You're good at wrecking things. Not fixing them. You said so yourself."

I say, "I'll lay down something simple where if anyone tries anything funny they'll blow themselves up."

That makes him happy.

"I like that. Yeah. Do that one."

"I'll do it on my way out."

Kasabian puts my discs in a bag, but can't resist taking one more shot.

"It must be depressing using the door these days just like any schmuck."

"It is a little weird."

"Candy's not here if that's why you really came by."

"It's not. In fact, you might not see me for a while. I'm going to try staying away."

"Finally, you say something smart. And you know what's funny?"

"What?"

"If you can't come in for movies anymore, you're going to be the first customer for our streaming service."

"Fuck me."

What kills me is that I know he's right. While I'm absorbed in my agony, he puts three more of the special discs on the counter.

"Here's something to tide you over. Kubrick's *Napoleon*. Ken Russell's *Dracula*. Ridley Scott's *Blood Meridian*."

I pick them up and look them over.

"These should last a while. Okay. I take back what I was thinking about you."

He ignores me and says, "How about this as a name for the streaming service: Faster Pussycat Watch! Watch!"

"It's a little long."

He frowns.

"I know."

"How about L'Age D'VHS."

"That doesn't completely suck. I'll write it down."

I say, "Drive-In Death Wish."

He says, "Black Funday."

"UFO Slumber Party."

"Barbarella After Dark."

"Doomsday Cocktail Lounge."

"The Devil's Betamax."

"Netflix and Kill."

"VHS Murder Zombies."

"The Good, the Bad and the VCR."

"Video Harakiri."

He puts the extra discs in the bag, looking a little smug.

"When we get the streaming service running, I'll send you info on how to hook up."

I head to the door.

"Like I said: don't rub it in."

I GO BACK to Janet's place and let myself in. Sure enough, they're asleep. I didn't get much shut-eye myself last night, so I lie down with them. I manage a couple of hours, but then I'm wide awake with all kinds of ugly noise in my head.

Abbot talked about Samvari steel and how Audsley must have gotten it from the Shoggots. A big part of me wants to brush it off with a "fuck you" to all of them. But I can't. Audsley got what he deserved—ripped apart by Candy when she'd gone all Jade. But the Shoggots. They're responsible for everything wrong with my life. If they hadn't given Audsley the knife I wouldn't have died and Candy wouldn't have moved in with Alessa full-time. I'd still be at Max Overdrive with her.

What makes it worse is that I know I'm a bastard for even dwelling on this shit. I should be taking care of Janet and not obsessing over what might have been. But I can't get the idea of the life I could have had out of my head.

I know the original Shoggots are gone, but some small part of them survives through this new bunch of freaks. I don't have any choice. If I'm going to continue with this new life I'm trying to grow into, there's only one thing that makes sense.

I'm going to kill every single one of the them.

JANET SLEEPS ON and off all day. I bring them soup, crackers, and tea. Turn on their music. It's mostly soundtracks, which makes sense. Writing them is what they want to do when they graduate. A lot of the music is good. Max Richter. Jóhann Jóhannsson. In the Nursery. Ennio Morricone. By the time I turn on Lustmord's *First Reformed* soundtrack it's dark out and they're sleepy again.

I kiss Janet on the forehead and they smile.

"Listen," I say. "I have to go for a little while. Abbot wants me to do something."

They nod sleepily and kiss my hand.

"Come back soon. And be careful."

"I will. Listen, maybe I should call Brigitte to come over and keep you company. I'll tell her to bring her gun so you'll feel safe."

"No, no," they say, half-awake. "I don't want to get her sick."

"That's nice of you."

I take out the Colt and hold it up for them to see.

"I'm putting this on your bedside table in case you get scared."

"You're so sweet."

"I'll be back as soon as I can."

Janet mumbles something I can't understand and is out like a light. I lock the door and add a little hoodoo before I leave.

I shadow walk to the basement of my apartment, where I keep the Hellion Hog under a tarp. Push it into the freight elevator and ride it up to street level. Then hit the gas and blast off the loading dock like a goddamn cruise missile. After the last few days it feels good to have wind on my face and exhaust in my lungs and to not give a shit about anything but motion. I mean, I'll care about things again in a few minutes, but I need this moment of blind motion. Lane splitting. Running lights. Skidding along empty sidewalks all over town. Hell, there's little enough traffic on the streets that my worst behavior is barely noticed except for some lunatic cabbies hardcore or desperate enough to keep working, and masked street kids who've taken over the avenues on their skateboards and BMX bikes. And, of course, there's LAPD surveillance cams. But they can go fuck themselves at the best of times and right now, they can fuck themselves and Mount Rushmore too.

What I'm doing isn't exactly what Abbot asked me to, but it's in the same neighborhood, because even in Plague Town there are still places where people want to go. And considering how much Shoggots like to fiddle about with the citizenry, if I look hard enough and long enough, I bet I'll find some in the act. Then I'll peel their skin off until they tell me exactly where to fucking find King Bullet.

I take a quick pass through Hollywood, but without tourists and the theaters closed, it's Death Valley with neon. On a hunch I head for some of the more, let's say, livelier parts of the city. Places with junkies looking for a fix, pickpockets looking to get lucky, and thieves in the act or after it, looking to spend some of their filthy lucre. And, yes, even tourists. Midwest dummies who booked their trips before the shit tsunami hit, and who would rather face the wrath of God than lose the deposit on their hotel rooms.

I hit downtown first. Then Chinatown. Then Hyde Park and, finally, I go all the way out to Venice Beach, but don't see a single untoward act. Not even a goddamn jaywalker.

Please, Mr. Muninn, if you're up there and still in business, send me a carjacking or a Shoggot necromancer playing three-card monte for people's souls. After all these miles I'll even take drunks shoplifting beer at a corner bodega. Just don't send me home revved up and looking for trouble with nothing to show for it but funny looks from solid citizens because I'm wearing She-Ra.

But no. Muninn doesn't come through with even a single

tagger. After a couple of hours, I'm so frustrated I'm tempted to beat myself up and call it a night. I mean, if King Bullet has been cherry-picking the best and brightest from gangs all over town, where are they? They must have a hangout somewhere in L.A., but fuck me if I have a clue where.

I'm pretty much ready to give up and head back to Janet's when I decide to make one final stop—Skid Row. It's a sad place. Over the years, and depending on the mood of whatever mayor or police chief was in power, the city has ignored the place, tried to clean it up, or, more recently, just used it as a dumping ground for the homeless and mental patients no one wants to deal with. I suppose it's like any other skid row in any other big city, but this one has been almost cleaned out by the virus. It seems to me that a fucked-up neighborhood like that might be just the kind of real estate brain-dead Shoggots would enjoy.

I make a circuit around the perimeter of Skid Row, turn inside on South Central Avenue, and roll up and down the maze of largely empty streets. Even the cars are gone. Stolen or hauled away by the city for unpaid fines by owners who are probably long dead. People have been dumping trash and other junk there, so the whole neighborhood is like a landfill and I have to dodge piles of plastic bags and broken furniture overflowing from the sidewalk into the street. A small homeless encampment is spread out along San Pedro Street, but there's a body sprawled halfway out of one tent, so I don't think anyone is home.

But near the corner of Fifth Street and Crocker, I get lucky. On one side of the street is an old clothing warehouse and on the other is an appliance repair shop that hasn't seen the light of day since zoot suits. Between them, some poor slob is getting worked over by two guys with what look like a baseball bat and a chain. That's heavy firepower for a mugging, but not for a couple of Shoggots out for a night on the town. The guy on the ground is definitely hurt. He isn't even moving anymore.

I kill the engine and park the Hog around the corner on Towne Avenue. Creep back to Fifth and Crocker behind mile-high piles of garbage, dodging rats and the occasional half-eaten corpse they haven't finished with.

I stick to the shadow of the warehouse, and when I get near enough to the beating, I take out the na'at, extend it seven or eight feet, and use it like a sword, stabbing it into Chain Guy's back hard enough that it comes out his belly. Bat Boy doesn't notice until his pal falls on his face, trying to hold his guts in. He looks around, but by then I'm back in the shadow of the warehouse. I twist the na'at's grip, and it loosens from a rigid sword and turns into a whip. I swing it over my head a couple times, advancing on Bat Boy. The whip wraps around the head of the bat, so I'm able to snatch it out of his hand. Another couple of steps and I get the whip around his throat. With one good pull, I jerk Bat Boy off his feet so he falls and cracks his head on the dirty street. Retracting the na'at, I run to the victim on the ground and flip him over.

It's a mannequin. I look back at the clothing warehouse and spot at least ten more mannequins in the street, all smashed to pieces. What the hell are these two idiots doing out here murdering dressing dummies?

I go to Bat Boy and turn him over. From the tattoos on his hands and chest it looks like he's in one of a handful of

Eastern Bloc gangs. Hit men and human traffickers mostly. Chain Guy has similar ink. Fuck them both. They weren't killing anybody tonight, but I won't shed any tears for either of them. But what the hell were they doing all the way out here?

Maybe this is all they have left. They both stink of booze and their eyes are all pupil from the ton of meth they've been smoking. Did King Bullet and his crazies chase them out of their old territory so that they had to hide in No Man's Land and take out their frustration on some innocent prom dress dummies? Chain Guy is extremely dead, so I leave him in the street, but Bat Boy has some life in him. I'm going to want some answers, so I drag his carcass farther down the block into the light. I bark some healing hoodoo at him to try to close the gash in his scalp. I don't need him dying on me until I get to question him.

Soon, his eyes flutter open. He stares at the sky for a few seconds, trying to get his brain moving again. So I start with the easy stuff first.

"Who are you?" I say.

Before he can answer, we both look over at the clothing warehouse. There's a flickering light behind the windows on the ground floor. A fire. And it's spreading fast. I pull Bat Boy to his feet so I can walk him back to the Hog and away from the flames.

That's when the explosion hits us.

Bat Boy goes flying through the front window of the appliance repair shop and I'm blown the other way onto a three-legged sofa that stinks of mildew and rat piss. Flaming debris covers the street. Piles of burning clothes and mannequin heads and arms. But the explosions keep going, high over our heads. Red. Green. Silver. Purple. Fuck me. It's a fireworks display.

Roman candles and bottle rockets bounce off my arms and head as I dive for cover. The clothes were just a front. The warehouse was really an illegal fireworks factory. And about a million dollars' worth of inventory is going off all at once. Buildings are burning all around me and Bat Boy. Did one of these shitheads drop a match or a lighter in the warehouse when they were stealing mannequins? Looking back at the place one more time, I realize that it's unlikely either of these two did anything. On one intact wall of the warehouse someone has painted a skull with a crown over its head. This was one of King Bullet's parties. Before I can figure out why he'd want to set off a Skid Row Fourth of July I hear a siren and spot an ambulance heading this way. I still want some answers from Bat Boy, so I flag it down. Let them take him away and I'll question him in the hospital.

A couple of masked EMTs jump out of the back of the ambulance and I yell, "In there," pointing to the appliance repair shop. They haul a gurney inside and in no time at all, they wheel Bat Boy into the street. The gurney folds up as they shove it into the ambulance. I go over to find out which emergency room they're taking him to, but realize he's not going anywhere. Inside, Shoggot EMTs are having a grand old time working over Bat Boy with hammers and knives while singing their creepy little "Rum-tiddley-um-tum-tay" song.

I start to pull them off when I hear something roar from behind me. I turn and there's another Shoggot with a chainsaw. He's round and, along with the scars, has a big walrus mustache like the rich guy from the Monopoly game. I back away from the ambulance. Sorry, Bat Boy. I have my own skin to worry about.

Wannabe Leatherface thrusts the rotating blade at me. Swings it over his head while singing the Shoggot ditty, then charges me. I don't like chainsaws. I don't like rotating blades of any kind. They remind me too much of the House of Knives Downtown. So I start for the na'at, which should be enough to take on Leatherface, but then say fuck it and manifest my Gladius. The burning blade slices through the chainsaw like it isn't even there. As the motor sputters out, I kick Leatherface in the gut, doubling him over. Bent and wheezing for air, he's easy to drag into a shadow.

WE COME OUT by Johnny Ramone's gravesite in Hollywood Forever cemetery. A four-foot bronze statue of Johnny in full rock-star guitar-playing position sits on a stone pedestal. It's a weird sight in daylight, but at night there's something slightly malevolent about the thing. As if Johnny, who was a stone-cold prick when he was alive, might decide to haul off and lobotomize you with his bronze Mosrite guitar.

The quick trip across town seems to have had an effect on Leatherface. He falls onto the manicured green lawn and looks around. My first impulse was to beat him to death and leave him up there on Johnny as a warning to the other Shoggots to back off. But seeing him scrabbling around in the dark, I get a better idea.

From flat on his back, he looks up at me and says, "We'll

cut you into giblets and eat you for dinner." When he tries to get to his feet, I tear off his surgical mask and slap him hard enough that he falls back on his ass. Stick a finger in his face and say, "Play nice."

He looks puzzled. I don't think anyone has tried to talk to him in a long time, because he seems genuinely confused by the concept.

Finally, he says, "Who are you?"

I say, "No one important. Who are you?"

He has to think about it for a few seconds. Sort through a lot of mental detritus before he comes up with something. No, this guy hasn't chatted in a long time.

"Billy?" he says. "Billy Boop."

I look at him trying to figure out what the name means. The only Billy Boop I ever heard of was a cartoon character from the thirties.

"Are you Betty's little brother?" I say.

He sits up when I say it.

"You know her?"

Yeah. This guy thinks he's celluloid and nothing more.

"I've seen all her movies."

"Me too," he says. "Why did you kidnap me?"

"I wanted to talk and you didn't seem interested with that chainsaw in your hand."

"I guess not. But you hurt me."

He whines like a child. I'm going to have to take it slow with little Billy here.

"I'm sorry. But I was just anxious to talk to a Shoggot in the flesh."

"The flesh," he says and laughs an idiot's laugh.

I kneel down next to him.

"Do you know King Bullet?"

Billy shakes his head. Points between my eyes and says, "King Bullet knows you."

Damn, I hate these crazies.

"Who is he?"

That's another puzzler. Billy stares at the blank sky. Finally, "Father. Brother. The Devil. He is the bang and we are the bullet that blasts a hole in the world."

"What do you want?"

"Everything," he says and giggles. "The city is nearly ours. The children of the Devil and one true Eve. The plague will cleanse the streets. Then the world."

More Shoggot delusions. This guy swallowed all the Kool-Aid.

"How did the father call you? Why?"

Billy makes a sour face.

"I was a Mad Motherfucker. Outfit from Santa Ana. Then worked for the Russians. My whole crew. We had power, but we were nothing. Dealt drugs. Hits for pocket change. Endless war with the Bloods, Norteños, the Angels. King Bullet changed all that. He holds out his hand, offers family and enlightenment."

Billy holds out his hand like Jesus himself offering me a cookie.

I say, "What happens to the people who don't want Nirvana?"

Billy puts a finger gun to his temple and makes like he's pulled the trigger.

"Bang."

I grin at him. I want whatever this loon has in his head.

"When the King pulls the gangs together, what does he give you?"

"Purpose. Vision," he says firmly.

"What if I want to join up?"

He turns his head slightly and eyes me with suspicion.

"Who are you with?"

I shrug.

"No one. I'm on my own. But it's getting me nowhere. I thought I was all I needed. But now that I've seen what you can do, I want to be part of something bigger."

"Yes," he says and puts a hand on my arm. "You're never alone with the King."

"Do you think he'd take someone like me?"

Billy stares at me, finally getting a look at the scars on my face.

"Maybe. You almost look like one of us already. How did you get those scars?"

"Fights. Hits. I won plenty, but I lost plenty too."

"The King never loses."

"Would he have someone like me?"

"Maybe," Billy says, removing his hand from my arm. He's more relaxed now, like he doesn't even remember that I dragged him here.

"Your face is good," he says. "We can help you finish the transformation."

"Yes. Good. Where would I find someone who can help me?"

Billy scoots back a couple of feet. Looks at me suspiciously again.

"How do I know you're not lying?"

Hell. I was hoping it wouldn't come to anything like this. But I take out the black blade and hand it to him.

I say, "Help me. Start the change."

He weighs the knife in his hand. Looks at me.

"Really?"

"Do it."

He's a little tentative as he jams the blade into the skin of my forehead. The pain is immediate and sharp, but I've been through worse. I can't see what Billy is doing, but he's smiling as he goes, so I guess he's turning me into a real beauty queen. He cuts for a minute or so. Blood flows down into my eyes. I have to wipe it away with the back of my hand. Finally he's done.

Wistfully he says, "You're beautiful. On your way to being one of us."

"How do I go the rest of the way?"

"Only the King can do that."

"King Bullet himself?"

"Yes. Only he can bless you and bring you into the family."

"How do I meet him?"

I wipe more blood from my eyes.

"That's a secret," whispers Billy.

Now it's my turn to look hurt.

"You said I'm almost changed. How can I become one of the family if I don't know where to go?"

He puts his hands over mine.

"A child of the bang and the bullet?"

"Yes. That. How can I become worthy of the bullet?"

Billy looks away, the rusty gears in his head slowly grinding together. He reaches up and wipes some of my blood onto his fingers. Puts out his tongue and tastes it.

"Tomorrow night," he says. "At city hall. The King, all radiant death, will be there. New converts will pledge their lives, take the bullet into them, and become part of the flock."

I don't like the sound of that.

"What does 'take the bullet into them' mean?"

Billy grins his mindless grin again. Touches his heart and bruised gut.

"That you'll have to wait for or you won't understand."

I wipe more blood onto my hand and hold it out for Billy to shake. He does. Gleefully.

"I'll be there."

"Brother."

"Brother."

He thinks for a minute.

"You never told me your name."

I stand up and say, "Sandman Slim."

Billy's face changes. All the beatific goofiness of the last few minutes transforms into animal anger.

Through gritted teeth he says, "He said you were here."

"Yeah? What else did he say about me?"

"That you are nothing and that he will obliterate you."

I look out over the cool black water of Sylvan Lake.

"I doubt that."

"I am the bullet that does his will!"

Billy lunges at me with the black blade, but I knew it was coming, so I knock the knife out of his hand easily. Billy scrabbles after it, but I pull him back over to Johnny.

He sits at the base of the grave marker with his knees pulled up to his chest and mumbles, "What have I done? What have I done?" He pulls out handfuls of his hair and chews his lower lip until he's bitten off a good-size piece—which the sick fuck swallows.

I get in close, hoping that I can squeeze a little more information out of him.

"What will King Bullet do to you when he finds out what you've done? I don't think he's the forgiving kind."

Billy shakes his head.

"The Devil doesn't forgive. The bullet doesn't heal."

I'm down on my haunches next to him. With a scream he launches himself at me again and knocks me onto my back. I'm ready for him to attack or run away, but he doesn't do either. Instead, he turns around and bashes his head into the corner of Johnny Ramone's gravestone two or three times, until there's a dent deep enough that he can pull away a part of his skull, exposing his brain.

I know I should do something, but this is fucked up even by my standards.

Yelling "The bullet does not heal!" he digs his fingers into his head, pulling out bits of brain matter. And like he did with my blood, he shoves it all into his mouth and swallows. Still crying, he bangs his head against the stone a couple of more times before I can grab him and pin his arms to his sides.

"Stop it," I shout. "Stop it!"

"I am the son of the Devil. A child of the bullet."

He bites down on my hand hard enough that I loosen my grip. Free now, he runs headlong into the stone pedestal and I swear I can hear his head crack like a pterodactyl egg. He slumps to the ground, but his lips are still moving.

I lean in close to listen. It takes a few second before I understand that he's trying to sing.

"Rum-t . . . rum-tid . . . rum-t . . ."

Soon, he slumps over, leaking whatever was left of himself all over the lawn. I tear off one of his sleeves and wipe Billy's brains off Johnny's gravestone. It's the least I can do. Literally the least for an asshole like Johnny.

When I'm done, I toss Billy's body into Sylvan Lake. Once I've put away the black blade, I clean more blood off my forehead.

Yeah. I really do hope I'm immune to this shit.

I SHADOW WALK to where I left the Hog and ride it to Janet's apartment. She buzzes me in, but when I get to her door, some last trail of blood blinds me for a second and I knock the door open as I stumble inside.

A gunshot. Something blasts past and hits the wall behind me. I hit the floor and roll, clearing my eyes and pulling the black blade to gut the shooter.

Except it's Janet. They're standing there with the Colt pointed right at me. I still have the knife in my hand. I don't move.

Finally, they relax and collapse onto a chair.

"God, Stark. You scared— What happened to you? I thought you were one of them."

I kneel next to them and put away the knife.

"I'm sorry. I told you I had to do something for Abbot."

They look at me.

"And you come back like this. Could you have warned me or something?"

"Yes. I should have. I'm sorry. I just wanted to get back to you."

They look at the floor.

"This is the second time you've shown up with half your face gone. I think I'm going to be sick."

"Just relax and breathe."

They lean over in the chair. I put a hand gently on their back.

"Can I have my gun back?"

They let go and it tumbles to the floor. I put it in my coat and say, "It's not like I planned on getting hurt when I went out."

Janet sits up, pushing their hair from their face.

"I know. I just got scared."

They cough a couple of times and look around for something.

"Where's my phone? I have to call work and tell them I'm not coming in tomorrow."

Shit. I forgot about that.

"Why don't you let me do it?"

"Why should you do it?" They look at me for a minute. "Is there something you're not telling me?"

"Go back to bed. We can talk about it tomorrow."

"What's going on?"

When I don't answer, they put a hand on my shoulder.

"Stark?"

"It's gone. Donut Universe is gone. Burned to the ground."

They pull their hand away and cover their face. They begin to cry, quietly at first, but it soon turns into deep racking sobs, which triggers a coughing fit. I've never seen Janet more miserable. I put my arms around them and hold them for a minute. They lean on my shoulder and hug me back.

But when Janet moves back and starts to kiss me, they turn away.

"You have blood all over your face."

With everything going on, I hadn't thought of that. I quickly wipe away what I can with my sleeve.

"Don't bother," they say. "It's all too much."

"I'll go clean up."

"No. Go home. I love you, you know. But I can't look at you right now."

"Okay. But let me make you some tea or something first."

They lower their head.

"Please. Just go home. I need to sleep and I can't sleep with you here like that."

I stand up and say, "I'm sorry about everything. I'll call you tomorrow and bring you some soup. This will all be healed by then."

Janet takes my hands and kisses them. Then goes into the bedroom and shuts the door.

I get the bag from Max Overdrive and go through a shadow into my apartment.

Fuck Hollywood is passed out on the sofa with *Godzilla* roaring on the TV. I turn it off and go into the bathroom to wash my face. When I clean all the blood off I can finally see what Billy carved into me: Betty Boop. Sure. Why not? It makes as much sense as anything else that's happened in the last few days.

In the bedroom, I strip off everything in case I got some of Billy's brains on me. I'll take a shower later. Lying in the dark, I close my eyes but can't sleep.

I can't really blame Janet for anything that happened tonight.

Donut Universe was the one steady thing in their life. They liked the place and they had friends there. Plus, like Kasabian said, it's where we first met.

Things would be bad enough for Janet with the city falling apart, but being with me, I bring the chaos home every day. And blood. Too much blood. I have to be more careful. But if I'm going to get close to King Bullet how can I guarantee that? I don't want to lose Janet over something as stupid as a bad guy Abbot or his boy scouts should be taking care of.

It's starting to feel like the bad old days, when I first escaped from Downtown. Maybe I'm better off on my own. Janet is sick of me. Donut Universe is gone. In its own way, so is Max Overdrive, which means Candy and Kasabian and too many memories to count. At least I have Bamboo House, though if King Bullet's muppets come back that might go down too.

I hope the new scar won't scare Fuck Hollywood too much. Hell, she might laugh when she realizes what it is. It's nice having someone around, but the more I think about it, it might be better for everyone if she took the room in her friend's apartment. Then I'd be on my own with no distractions or fear.

What would Vidocq say right now? Hell. It's been only three months and I'm having trouble remembering his face. What would he tell me right now? It doesn't matter. He's gone. Another ghost in a city of ghosts.

I miss you, old man, but I have to work this one out on my own. That means, not what would Vidocq say, but what do I say?

And the answer is nothing. Nothing at all. My mind is

a blank and my face itches as the skin knits back together, already healing from Billy's artwork.

All I know for certain is that if I'm going to ever get back something like a life someone is going to have to kill King Bullet. If not Abbot, then me. And if it is me, I don't know how much of me will be left at the end. I'll probably end up on my own, whether I want it or not.

IN THE MORNING, I stumble out of the bedroom without bothering to shave or even comb my hair. There's only one thing in the world that I want: coffee.

Fuck Hollywood is on the sofa eating a bowl of cereal.

"Morning, sunshine," she says. "You're looking perky today."

I bump into a chair and stop in my tracks.

"Goddammit. I forgot to get coffee."

"I got some," she says cheerily.

"You're my hero."

"I know."

I make a pot, and she slides down the sofa so I can sit. There's some kind of astronomy show on the TV. We're whizzing all over the solar system at warp speed. I point to the set with my cup.

"You like this stuff?"

She starts to talk and almost dribbles milk all over herself. Finally, she swallows and says, "Stars and planets and shit? Sure. Don't you?"

"Sometimes I feel like I've seen too much of the universe and don't want to see one more inch."

"Aww. Someone needs a burping."

"Stars are nice sometimes. We buried Vidocq under the stars."

"Yeah. Candy told me."

"There aren't any stars in Hell. I guess I missed them there."

She looks at me funny and says, "Where? What did you say?"

I shake my head.

"Never mind."

Fuck Hollywood puts down her cereal and pushes my hair back off my forehead.

"Did you get hurt again?"

"You can still see it?"

Squinting, she says, "A little." She looks harder and makes a face. "Is that—Betty Boop?"

"Shit. Well, I can't go out until this is done healing."

She grabs her phone and holds it up to take a picture.

"Come on, Betty. Smile pretty for me."

"Please don't."

"Come on."

I put a hand on her phone and lower it.

"Seriously. Not today."

"Are you all right? Your stupid head aside."

I take a big gulp of the coffee and scorch the back of my throat.

"I don't know," I say. "What do you do when you feel like you need to do something, but doing it might hurt someone you care about?"

"What kind of something?"

"Part of it's revenge. Which I know isn't exactly noble. But there's something else. I might be able to help save the city from the people who came into the bar the other night."

"That's a good thing. What's the problem, then?"

"What if I lose Janet?"

She crosses her legs and turns to face me.

"That's a tough one. But why do you have to save the city? Don't you have super-duper magical friends who can do it?"

"That's the problem. They won't. At least not yet, and I'm afraid they're going to wait so long that there won't be anything left. At least not for civilians."

"Who are civilians?"

"You. Regular people. If the virus doesn't get you, I'm afraid the crazies will."

She clutches a pillow to herself.

"Can we please not talk about them anymore?"

"Sorry. But what if no one else is going to stop them?"

"So, to save Janet you might have to lose them."

"Something like that."

Fuck Hollywood blows out a long stream of air like she's winded.

"Dude. I have no idea. But I think if Janet found out that you could have stopped those people who killed Charlotte and Babadook and didn't, they'd be pretty pissed."

I pick up the coffee and drink some more.

"I think you're right."

"And what about everybody else?" she says, getting more animated. "Are you going to let Candy and Carlos get hurt? *Me?* You said you'd take care of me."

I put an arm out and she slides down to lean on me. With Buzzard gone, I don't know who else she has in the world.

"I will take care of you. You and everybody else."

She shrugs.

"Then I guess that's your answer."

"I guess it is."

She gives me a quick peck on my unshaven cheek and sits up. Instead of reaching for her cereal she rubs her hands on her legs.

I say, "You okay?"

"Yeah," she says, looking at her hands. "I just feel weird. Like I itch all over. My skin is crawling. Maybe it's the new soap we're using at the bar."

"I'll save you from the big things, but you'll have to handle dry skin yourself."

Shaking her hands out, she says, "I'll get some hand cream on the way to work."

"That means we're open today?"

"Yep. Normal hours and everything."

"But no muscle outside."

"Carlos gave up on regular security. I think he's hoping you'll handle it."

I drink the last of my coffee and go back for more.

"No problem. I have some things to do, but I'll be there."

She gestures to her forehead.

"What about Betty?"

"I'll do some healing hoodoo and hope I don't explode my head."

"If you go out, don't forget your mask."

"I won't."

Fuck Hollywood goes back to her cereal and stars. I finish

my second cup of coffee, then go in to brush my teeth before calling Abbot. He picks up on the second ring.

"Hello, Stark," he says. His voice still sounds weak. "Have you thought over my proposition to look into King Bullet?"

"Damn. Jumping right to business. The Council must be nervous."

"We are. Things are quickly going from bad to worse. King Bullet and his Shoggots have taken over some city services. Many of the police precincts. Most of the transportation system. Do not get on a bus for any reason."

"What I hear is that I should steal more cars."

"I said nothing of the kind."

"I can read between the lines. Don't worry. It's our secret."

"Dammit, this is serious."

"Calm down. I did look into King Bullet, at least some of his asylum fodder."

He coughs a few times and says, "Did you learn anything useful?"

"A couple of things. It turns out that autophagia thing you were talking about is true."

"What do you know about it?"

"Just that after Billy, my Shoggot friend from last night, realized he'd given me some of his secrets he ate his own brains."

There's a pause for a couple of seconds.

"Stark, half the time I don't know if you're making these things up just to test me."

"I'm telling you. It happened. The good news is that he said a couple of things before he checked out. This King Bullet asshole says he wants the city. Why, I don't know. But he's got some serious Charlie Manson–level true believers working for him."

"He does at that. And on that score, we have important new information too: not all Shoggots are scarred. The ordinary ones are the groups working into city services, and worse. We think they might be in the utilities companies, which means that, conceivably, they could black out the city."

"That's great fucking news. Are they anywhere else?"

"We think they might be in some of the local hospitals."

"I might be able to confirm that. Billy and some of his friends were dressed as EMTs. They had an ambulance and everything. The question is, now that you have all this new information, are you and your people going to do anything about it?"

Abbot sighs.

"Sadly, the Council is still hesitant."

I don't say anything for a few seconds, trying not to shout. When I feel like I'm under control I say, "They're always hesitant. It's just like with the people stuck with the ghosts in Little Cairo."

"Understand, we can't just charge and make a spectacle of things. We have agreements with civilian leaders to get only so involved with day-to-day life in the city."

"Day-to-day life is falling apart and you're not doing anything to stop it."

I'm about to shout at the useless bastard when something clocks and my stomach tightens.

"God, I'm stupid," I say. "You told them you'd talked to me about dealing with King Bullet, didn't you?"

"I said that I'd asked you to look into the situation."

I run my fingers over Betty on my forehead.

I say, "You're not sending in your people because if I fix things, it looks good for you. But if something happens to me, I'm just some expendable stooge. And don't tell me it's the Council doing it and not you. If you wanted to overrule them, you'd find a way."

When Abbot speaks, his voice has the officious tone of a junior high principal.

"They think, and I have to agree, that we need more information before we act."

"Sure. What's a few more dead civilian nobodies and my donut shop when you have your mansions to look after?"

"What donut shop?" he says. "What are you talking about?"

"And even if the crazies turn off the power, you can hoodoo your lights and air-conditioning back on like nothing happened."

"Look," he says, and this time he sounds pissed. "If you had something solid that I could take to the Council. Some way that we could get to King Bullet himself. I know that they'd listen to reason."

"Because they're always ready to jump in and help the little guy, right?"

I think about what Billy said—King Bullet's party at city hall tonight. Should I tell him about it? Back when the ghosts were running wild in Little Cairo, the Council was ready to hang me out to dry and nuke every civilian in the neighborhood. Would they do the same again? Go scorched earth on the meeting, taking out me and any poor asshole office workers pulling the late shift downtown? Can I trust them enough not to do it again?

I say, "King Bullet is hosting a party at city hall tonight. That might be a good time to introduce yourselves."

He doesn't say anything for a minute.

"Abbot?"

"I'm here. It's just that city hall is a problem."

"What are you talking about?"

"We can't just go charging into the center of civilian power without an understanding first."

"What the fuck does 'understanding' mean?"

"The Los Angeles city fathers have always been wary of the Sub Rosa community treading too closely to them. For the Council to go on an armed mission, we'd need permission. And that requires negotiations."

"Well, call the mayor and tell him what's going on."

"It's not simple."

This again. I can't fucking believe this shit.

"You wanted something solid and I gave it to you, but you still won't do anything."

"Can't—"

"Won't."

"Of course, you could be our unofficial representative at the site."

And there it is.

"You are so useless. Fine. I'm going in and doing things my way. Unofficially, of course."

"Thank you. I really appreciate it. Call me when you get back."

"Fuck you."

I hang up and stand there for a minute, thinking bad thoughts. Is Abbot being straight with me? I'm handing him Public Enemy Number One and he's worried about stepping on some city hall shitheel's toes. Abbot and the Council have always held back when they want me to do something hardcore. What do they want more: King Bullet gone or for me to disappear? Maybe tonight they think they can get a package deal. Let us do each other in while they kick back and drink Chardonnay. I don't know. I've got to think about this. I thought Abbot was a stand-up guy, but how well do I know him outside of the few deals we've made? He's the Augur. Power is his business. Everything else is secondary. Including me and a load of nine-to-five civilians downtown. I need to think about this more. But mostly I've got to watch my back. If something happens to me, what happens to Janet and Candy and the others?

I pop some PTSD pills.

I have to make another call, but I smoke a Malediction instead. Giving myself a few minutes to calm down. When I finish and toss the butt out the window, I dial Janet's number. Brigitte answers.

"Hello, Jimmy. How are you?"

"I'm okay. Is everything all right over there?"

"Everything is fine. I'm just staying with Janet for a few days. We're practicing for my Immigration interview."

"That's great. Good luck. But why are you answering their phone?"

When she speaks, she does so quietly.

"Jimmy, I'm afraid that Janet doesn't want to talk to you right now."

That stomach-tightening feeling again.

"Did they say why?"

"No. I'm sure things will be fine. They just need a little time and quiet right now."

"Is this a brush-off? Is 'time and quiet' a way of saying they don't want to see me again?"

"No. It's nothing like that," says Brigitte, so calmly and reasonably that I don't believe a word of it. "They're just exhausted after what happened the other night."

"The suicide or me?"

"They didn't say. Does it matter?"

I want to say something, but my throat is dry and I've run out of words.

Brigitte breaks the silence.

"Janet loves you. Don't doubt that. Just give them some time. I'll be here to make sure they're taken care of."

"Do you have your gun with you?"

"Of course."

"Good. Take care of them for me."

"I will."

"And take care of yourself. If either of you need me—"

"I understand. But I should go. Goodbye for now, Jimmy."

"Tell them I— Dammit."

This time, I'm the one talking when the phone clicks off.

I sit there on the bed feeling foolish and angry and completely confused by the world. After the craziness last night, I thought that today I might get a day off from the shitstorm. But, if anything, the situation is even worse.

At least I have that pile of movies from Max Overdrive. If

Fuck Hollywood moves out, I get the feeling I'll be spending a lot of time alone for a while.

LATER IN THE afternoon, the healing hoodoo has worked and my head remains blissfully unexploded, so I head over to Bamboo House of Dolls. Just before I leave, I remember to put my mask on.

Fuck Hollywood is already inside with Carlos and there's a line of early birds forming outside. Some of them aren't wearing masks. They're happily smoking and talking. After all these weeks they don't give a fuck anymore and I can't blame them. I feel the same way. Of course, half of them will be coughing up their lungs by the weekend, but they'll have a good time tonight. Or, rather, a good time somewhere else. There's no way I'm letting them into the bar.

It's a quiet afternoon checking IDs, chatting up the regulars, and posing for the occasional always-annoying selfie. But things are easy and smooth and no one tries to cut the line. How well behaved we've trained our customers to be. I guess when you see enough murders while sipping a piña colada you learn to listen.

Things go on like that beyond sundown and into the evening. Right after I let Kasabian in, a couple of people down the line start coughing. The crowd parts around them, trying to get some distance.

I say, "Coughers can go home. No coughers inside."

One of them steps out of line. A young sharp-dressed guy. Frat boy. Tech bro. Maybe just a general nuisance with money. He says, "It's just allergies."

"Go home, take a pill, and try again tomorrow. You're not getting in tonight."

The nuisance heads my way, followed by three friends.

When he gets to me, he pulls his mask down to talk.

I reach out and pull the mask back up on his face. That doesn't help the situation, but I don't need him spewing all over the rest of the crowd.

He snatches the mask off completely and says, "We came all the way up from Santa Ana to see this shithole and we're not leaving without having a drink."

"Santa Ana? Why don't you go back down south and sneak a pint in Disneyland? That'll make you feel edgy too, Beaver Cleaver."

The crowd laughs, but Beaver doesn't. He looks like he wants to take a swing at me. And why not? He has three friends backing him up. One of them is skinny, with ropey muscles on his arms. That guy is stronger than he looks in his flashy clothes. His dark eyes look a little funny. Is he high or is he a little crazy? I look back at Beaver. His eyes are fine. His heartbeat is up a little. From fear or excitement? Normally I can tell from his sweat smell, but he's got on so much cologne I can't get a reading. It can't be on purpose, can it?

I look back at Crazy Eyes and the two other guys. They're all ready for a fight. Ready to bum-rush me when Beaver gives the word. Which makes me wonder something bad. The trouble we had with the Shoggots the other night? What if this is round two and these boys are the pretty ones without scars that Abbot talked about? There's no way I'm going to let them make the first move.

I shove Beaver back into two of his friends, grab the na'at, and form it into a whip. Snag Crazy Eyes around the neck and pull him to me. There's one good thing. He's capable of being surprised. His heartbeat jumps to around a thousand a minute. That's good. A fear response. But his eyes are crazier than ever. I tighten the na'at around his throat a little and say, "Tell the King and his toadies they're not welcome here."

Beaver yells, "What are you doing? Are you nuts? Let go of him." But he's all talk. He doesn't move an inch away from his other friends. That's another good sign. Shoggots might be murderous, brain-eating piss weasels, but they're not cowards. Maybe I read these boys wrong.

Still, though.

Crazy Eyes is starting to look a little frantic. Not breathing will do that to you.

"Please," he squeaks at me.

"What's your name?"

"Ronald."

"Show me your ID."

He fumbles in his jacket for a few seconds. I keep a good eye on him. The moment I think he's going for a weapon, I can use the na'at to snap his neck. But he gives me his wallet and I don't have to kill him. I flip it open to his driver's license.

"What's your last name, Ronald?"

"Topor."

I look at Crazy Eyes hard and say, "Did the King tell you to come back and finish what started the other night?"

His weird eyes dart around like they're trying to escape his skull. This guy is high. He's also on the verge of tears. Next to his driver's license is a student ID. This is no Shoggot. I loosen the na'at and put it away. Close his wallet.

"I don't know about your friends, but you're underage, Ronald."

I throw his wallet down the street.

"Fetch. And don't come back."

Beaver picks up Ronald's wallet and points at me.

"You're crazy, man. I'm calling the cops."

"Please do. I'm sure LAPD would love to meet some fresh-faced dummies like you."

The four of them wander down the street, cursing and throwing around bags of trash. Once they're far enough away that I'm certain they're not coming back, I stick my head in the bar. Come back out and say, "Sorry, everyone. We can only let a few people in at a time and the place is full. You're going to have to wait a little while for someone to leave."

There're a lot of disappointed noises from the crowd, but no one budges. The bar can hold more folks, but I'm sick of looking at people without masks and being jumpy about who might or might not be a Shoggot, so I go inside to cool off.

CARLOS SETS A drink on the bar when he sees me. I look around the room for anybody getting too close to anyone else, but it's all good little drinkers tonight. Kasabian brought a plastic straw with him so he can keep his mask on while he drinks Scotch. Carlos points to him with a pint glass.

"I was telling him about those fake cop *pendejos* from the other night."

Kasabian does a theatrical shudder.

"I had to make him stop. The whole cutting-off-heads thing. It's triggering for me, you know?"

I lean on the bar and sip my bourbon.

"It was extra triggering for Charlotte and Babadook," I say.

Kasabian rubs his neck.

"Poor schmucks. What a lousy way to go."

Fuck Hollywood comes by with a tray full of empties. Her hands look red and raw from scratching.

I say, "Did you get your hand cream?"

"I'll get some on the way home."

"I'll go with you."

"Cool."

Carlos touches my arm.

"What was that song the cop sang? You know. The one who got away."

"They sang a song?" says Kasabian. "Like a song song?"

I touch my face where Sawney Bean shot me.

"She sang it and so did the crazy in my building. I mean, it's not much of a song. Just a line or two."

"No way. You two are fucking with me," Kasabian says.

Carlos says, "I can't sing for shit. You sing it to him, Stark."

"What makes you think I can sing?"

"When I sing, birds die. It's a terrible thing. You don't want to hear it."

"Fine." I take a gulp of bourbon and half-sing, half-mumble, "All I ever heard was 'Rum-tiddley-um-tum-tay.'"

Kasabian gives me a funny look.

"Sing it again."

"No. Now you're fucking with me."

"Seriously. One more time."

"If you laugh, I'm taking your head off again."

He looks at me.

"Triggering."

I say, "Sorry," and say the stupid line again.

He gets thoughtful for a minute, then he says, "I know that from somewhere. Some old English movie. It's a music hall song. I can't remember who sang it. Helen something? Helen Trish? No. Helen Trix."

"Do you know the rest of it?" says Carlos.

"A bit. But I can't sing either."

"You don't have to sing it," I say. "Just say the words."

He takes a breath and thinks.

"Rum-tiddley-um-tum-tay,
Out for the day today.
Nobody cares what people think or say.
Our little lot's okay,
In our little tin-pot way.
Rum-tiddley-um-tum-tay."

Fuck Hollywood heads out back with a garbage bag, gnawing on a broken fingernail.

"What the holy fuck does that mean?" says Carlos, making a face at Kasabian.

Kasabian says, "I told you. It's a dance hall song. Everything is about being happy and what a good time everybody is having."

"I guess it makes sense," I say. "'Nobody cares what people think or say' sounds like them."

"And the 'our little lot's okay' part," says Carlos. "They're having a party while we're just trying not to breathe the wrong way."

"Do they wear masks?" Kasabian says.

I think about it for a minute.

"Yeah. The ones I've seen."

"So they must be scared too."

"Maybe. Maybe it's camouflage. Or who dies and who doesn't is just part of the game. The way they decorate their masks, it's like Halloween in the psych ward."

I leave Carlos and Kasabian talking and go back outside to let a few more people inside. Everyone waits their turn, wears their masks, and, in general, behaves themselves until closing.

After he's locked the door, Carlos looks at the tables. They're overflowing with glasses and beer bottles and napkins.

"Where's Fuck Hollywood?" he says. "She's really falling down on things tonight."

He goes back to the kitchen and comes out shrugging. I knock on the restroom door and yell, "You in there? Are you okay?"

Kasabian says, "The last time I saw her she was taking the trash out back."

I head outside with Carlos and Kasabian right behind me. I should have taken the trash out. If there was a Shoggot hiding out here and they hurt her, I swear I'll use every bit of arena magic I know to make them suffer. Then drag them to Hell and throw them in Tartarus—the Hell below Hell—forever.

I find her crouched on her haunches, her head down, by the dumpster. She's talking very quietly to herself. When I'm a few feet behind her I say, "Hey. Are you okay?"

Her head pops up when she hears me.

She says, "It's so good."

"What's so good?"

That's when I see the blood on the ground around her. I rush over and she holds up her hands. Her face and lips are covered in blood. She's gnawed off half of her left pinkie and is working on the flesh between her index finger and thumb.

"Help me," she whispers. Then dreamily, "It's so good," and bites herself again.

I grab her and pull her head back from her hand. She doesn't resist, but she comes away with a little more flesh between her teeth. When I get my arms around her, she collapses against me.

She says, "Help me. It's so good."

When Carlos sees us, he curses and runs back inside for the first-aid kit. Kasabian just stands there like a stunned deer saying "Oh god," over and over.

I spot something on the ground by Fuck Hollywood's foot.

"Kas, get over here."

He creeps up on us like he thinks we're snakes. I point to something on the ground by the dumpster's front wheel.

"Get that."

"What is it?" he says.

"Don't think about it. Just get it and give it to me."

He reaches for it, still in that scaredy-cat "Will this bite me?" way that's beginning to piss me off.

When he reaches it, he says, "I can't."

"Yes, you can. Just get it and hand it to me."

Slowly, he kneels down and picks up Fuck Hollywood's pinkie. He tries to hand it to me, but shudders like he's going to throw up. At least he has the brains to throw the finger to me before he runs down the alley to spew up all of his expensive Scotch.

When Carlos gets back, he puts antibiotic cream on her wounds and wraps both of her fucked-up hands in layers of gauze.

"No!" yells Fuck Hollywood. "It's so good. Let me go." If Allegra was here she could shoot her up with a sedative. All I can do is whisper some hoodoo and knock her out. She'll wake up with a hell of a hangover, but it will keep her down for now.

Carlos pulls out his keys.

"I'll drive her to the hospital."

"No. We can't trust them anymore."

"Then what?"

"What about Allegra's?" says Kasabian.

"She closed. Fuck it. I'll take her back to my place and figure out something from there. You're coming with me," I tell Kasabian.

He looks a little panicky.

"Why me?"

"Fuck him," says Carlos. "I'll go and call Ray. Maybe he can do something to help."

"Great."

"Then what do I do?" Kasabian says.

Carlos tosses him the keys to the bar.

"You close up."

"How do I do it?"

"You know how to lock a fucking door, right?" shouts Carlos.

"I can do that."

I pick up Fuck Hollywood. It feels like she weighs nothing.

"I'm sorry I can't help more," says Kasabian. He folds his arms over his hands. "It's—all that blood. I just can't."

"I get it. You just got your body back," I say. "Go lock up the bar and go home. Tell Candy I might call her later."

"Why?"

"Just fucking do it," I shout.

He runs off as I grab Carlos and pull him into a shadow.

AT MY PLACE, I carry Fuck Hollywood inside and put her in bed. Me and Carlos stand over her doing nothing like a couple of witless gargoyles.

"What the fuck happened to her?" Carlos says.

"It's called autophagia. The virus does it. She probably got infected when goddamn Buzzard was breathing all over her the other night."

He puts a hand on her forehead.

"What do I do? I don't know how to help her."

"You call Ray. He helped me when I was sick."

"Right. Good idea."

He gets out his phone as I dial Candy.

It takes a few rings for her to answer and her voice is unsteady with sleep.

"Stark? What's wrong? It's the middle of the night."

"I'm sorry. Can you come over to my place right now?"

"What's wrong?" she says, sounding sharper.

"Fuck Hollywood is hurt bad. But we can't take her to the hospital because there might be crazies there. Can you come over?"

"Sure, but why me? Shouldn't you call Allegra?"

"Because I have to go out and I need a stone killer to protect everyone in case the wrong people show up. Can you do that for me?"

"You know I can," she says, wide awake.

"Call Allegra when you get here. See if you can get her to come over with her doctor gear. And tell her to bring her Devil's Daisy."

"How about you? Are you okay?"

"Not even a little."

"I know I can't stop you from going out, so take care of yourself."

"I'm not the one who needs help."

"Yes, you are," says Candy. "I've heard you like this before. You're about to explode. Whatever it is you're doing, let me come along and help."

"I need you here more. So does Fuck Hollywood."

I hear her breathe for a few seconds, trying to figure out a way to stop me from going out. A moment later she says, "Okay. Go. But don't do anything too stupid."

"This might be the smartest stupid thing I've ever done."

"That's not comforting. Just go and come back alive."

"I promise."

I make sure I have the black blade and check the na'at. Pop the cylinder on the Colt to make sure it's fully loaded. Then I whisper some hoodoo and put on a glamour so no one will recognize me.

Carlos looks up from *Fuck Hollywood* and lurches back from the bed.

I say, "Calm down, man. It's me."

"Goddammit. Tell me when you're going to do that shit. I hate that fucking Steve McQueen face you always use."

"Sorry."

A little bit more hoodoo adds scars and burns to my glamour face so I'll fit in with the other Shoggots.

I check the time. It's well after two in the morning. Billy didn't say what time the party was starting at city hall. I hope I'm not too late.

I go to the bathroom, find my little first-aid kit, and give it to Carlos.

"There's not much left, but there's some gauze and hydrogen peroxide to clean her wounds. But try not to do anything until Allegra gets here."

"Ray is on his way over."

"Great. Listen, I'm sorry I drag you into this shit all the time."

Carlos gives me a look.

"What?"

"Just shut the fuck up, motherfucker. This is family stuff. We take care of our own. Right?"

"Right."

I'm just about ready to leave when my phone rings. It's Janet.

"Hi," they say. "I hope it's not too late."

"No. It's fine. I was up."

"Listen. I thought that maybe you could come over so we can just, you know, talk."

"That sounds great, but I'm just walking out the door to a thing."

"What kind of thing? Oh god. Are you going out to get hurt again?"

"I hope not."

"You never tell me what these things are until afterward."

I check the time again.

"I'll tell you all about it later."

"Please stay safe," they say. "And please don't come over here all bloody again."

"Don't worry about that."

"Then go and get over here when you can."

"I promise."

Janet hangs up and I just stare at the phone for a moment.

What the hell am I doing? Being dead was awful, but it was simple. I miss it sometimes. Which reminds me.

I grab my PTSD pills off the bedside table and pop two. I'm only supposed to take one, but I'm not sure of the last time I took one.

"How is this my life?" I say.

Carlos looks at me. "What? I missed that."

"Nothing. I've got to go. Thank Ray when he gets here."

"What did I just tell you, motherfucker?"

I nod to him and shadow walk across town.

AND COME OUT a block from city hall. The lower four floors of the building are burning, and from the look of it, the flames aren't going to stop there. Stragglers like me, late for the festivities, run or jog down North Main Street to catch the show's finale. We have to work our way through a jungle of abandoned vehicles on the street and sidewalk. Cars, both civilian and cop. Taxis. City buses. Ambulances. A couple of eighteen-wheelers. Even an ice cream truck.

The small park in front of city hall is an inferno. Burning leaves swirl upward while flaming palm fronds drift by on the breeze like snakes made of fire.

I finally reach the mob outside city hall. Almost everyone is masked. Some with simple surgical types over their ears. Other have tied bandanas around their faces. A lot of the crowd—men and women, young and old—have decorated their masks with blades, feathers, bones, and animal skin. There are costumes too. Horrible clowns. Wild-eyed cowboys. Nurses grimy with blood and dirt, like they'd been sleeping in the street. Soldiers and priests too, though I'm not sure if these last two were costumes at all.

It's part Halloween, part metal show, and part pagan rite to some forgotten blood god. I remember Abbot told me that the virus can get into your brain and turn you strange. I just never imagined how many would be hit with it or how strange they would get. And he was right about something else too. Not all of the Shoggots are scarred. A fair number are as fresh-faced and normal looking as Mr. Rogers in his sweater.

After all the shit I've put up with, I'm not staying in the cheap seats with the other losers. I lean into the crowd and muscle my way up close to the front.

And there he is—King Bullet himself. He must have been talking for a while because the crowd is pretty wound up.

"—we, born of plague, of demons and angels, the scum of the universe, possess a beauty *they* will never comprehend.

Who among the unmarked can understand perfection? You, my children, my children, will dance on the burning grave of this world."

The King is wearing a scorched and tattered Armani suit. I wonder what happened to the poor slob he stole it from. Like most of the others, he wears a mask. It looks like the front half of a human skull. The lower jaw is missing, but the upper teeth are all gold to match the twin gold narco gang .45s he has in holsters strapped around his waist. There's a single neat bullet hole in the skull's forehead. Circling the top is a sort of crown made of bullets held in place with barbed wire. In his hand he holds something impressive enough to be a Hellion weapon. But it's not. It's a kpinga, a large throwing weapon from central Africa. Three curved metal blades curl out from a central shaft with a grip wrapped in copper. It's a wicked-looking weapon in anyone's hands, but King Bullet holds it easily. He gestures with it. Points into the crowd like an orchestra conductor and uses it to pull the crowd along as he yammers.

He points away from the crowd, into the city, and says, "None of them are worthy. None of them will embrace the bedlam of the stars and madness of worlds beyond this. None but you. The chosen."

The King is flanked by two flunkies with AR-15s. The guy in the pig mask I recognize as Sawney Bean. The woman might be the fake cop who came into Bamboo House, but I can't be sure.

The mob looks wild, but King Bullet isn't through with them yet.

He says, "Existence is an open maw. Its teeth are white

and sharp and once inside, nothing escapes. Existence is hungry. It must eat. It must drink. Will you let it devour you?"

"No!" they scream back.

"Will it drink you like wine?"

"No!"

He throws up his arms.

"I am the bang."

The mob chants, "We are the bullet that blasts a hole in the world."

King Bullet's mask leaves his mouth exposed. He smiles down at us in our bones and blades and leather getups, a benevolent father handing out gifts on Christmas morning. He smiles to himself as his speech gets fancy.

"We few, we happy few, we band of horrors. For they today who shed their blood with me shall be my brothers, my sisters, my blessed beasts. Now. Go forth and make creation weep."

As the mob fans out to rip downtown apart, a handful of police vans and BearCat armored personnel carriers rolls up on the scene. It's the frazzled remains of LAPD and the county sheriff's department coming in with their usual brilliant timing. Hit the crowd when it's already in a frenzy and out for blood. Good plan.

To give them some credit, the first volley of rubber bullets and tear gas drives back the Shoggots in regular surgical and industrial masks. But it doesn't slow down the ones in gas masks. They surge the overeager John Wayne cops who came in riding on the BearCat running boards. But before they can drag all of the cops away, the ones on their feet open up with shotguns and rifles, easily cutting down the front line of Shoggots and driving back the others.

For a few seconds it looks like a successful massacre and like the Shoggots are falling apart before they really got started. However, the cops' gunfire at street level doesn't stop the crazies who climb up the backs of the vans and personnel carriers and jump down on them. The cops fall fighting, but they fall. The BearCats pour on the tear gas as more armored cops come in from the sides of the plaza, firing their rifles. King Bullet is in the middle of the fight, killing cops with his kpinga, using it like an ax to crack open heads.

I can punch hard and I heal fast, but that doesn't do a damn thing against the choking fumes in the street. My eyes burn, my nose runs, and I can't stop coughing. But I have to keep going. I claw my way through the madness, trying to get close enough to King Bullet to snap his neck.

Cops and sheriff's deputies pour on gunfire and rubber bullets from two sides of the plaza. But there are too many Shoggots, and when enough crazies get behind them, they start going down too. And while the Shoggots are psycho, they aren't dumb. They grab the rifles lying by the dead bodies and turn them back on the cops. City hall sounds like goddamn World War III.

I'm just a few yards behind King Bullet when a couple of moron sheriff's deputies jump on me, knocking me to the ground. They must have run out of bullets, but decided to go down fighting. It's admirable in a brain-dead sort of way. One of them works me over with a truncheon while the other pounds me with heavy leather SAP gloves.

I could take out both of these clowns with my hands, the na'at, or the Colt, but I kind of feel sorry for the idiots and don't want to kill them. If I can turn off their lights long enough, maybe they'll stop fucking hitting me and lie still long enough that the King and his attack dogs will think they're dead and leave them alone.

I swing one of my legs out and knock the truncheon cop off his feet. The problem is that he falls on top of me instead of the other way. Once he's there, he joins in with Mr. SAP gloves, punching me in the back of the neck and kidneys as hard as he can.

A minute or so of this and I start getting annoyed. I need to get these fucks off me. I need to get up. I need to get rid of them and get to King Bullet.

Fuck this nice-guy shit. I swing an elbow back and catch the cop who fell on me on the side of his head. I spin and manage to grab the prick's gloved hands long enough to punch him in the fucking throat. All of a sudden, I'm not the only one gasping for air. But before I can get up and knock them silly so they don't get shot, they get shot. Once each in the back of the head. I look up and see Sawney Bean above me, one of King Bullet's narco .45s in his hand. He gives me a "you're welcome" wink and heads straight back into the fight.

That was too goddamn much. There's no way in this world or the next that I can owe that crazy little shit monkey *any-thing*. I'm tempted to run after him and pull out his spine just on general principle, but I need to get to King Bullet first. Lucky me, when Sawney's done being my hero, he makes a beeline back for the King. I follow, playing the grateful dog, knocking cops and crazies out of my way as I go.

In the distance, the cop vans are all on fire. The crowd has pushed burning cars around the remaining BearCat on all sides, penning it in. It's going to get hot in there soon. Eventually, the cops inside will have to run for it or boil like lobsters.

Overhead, helicopters swoop down over the plaza, lobbing flash-bang grenades and rifle fire down at us.

And I've lost King Bullet in the crowd. I'm running around like a chicken trying to find its head, when I spot him standing on the cab of an eighteen-wheeler. He's holstered the .45 and slung the kpinga from his belt. As one of the choppers makes a low pass over him—as if it wants to blow him off the truck—he raises both arms in front of him. Something like a boiling black mist pours from his hands and into the air, enveloping the helicopter.

That's not good news. Maybe the rest of the Shoggot crazies are just brain-fried civilians, but King Bullet is definitely Sub Rosa. How does Abbot not know that?

It's only a few seconds before the chopper is literally ripped apart in the air like an immense brat tearing apart a giant child's toy. Twisted pieces of plastic and metal veer off in every direction as the helicopter rains down on the cops and crazies.

While groups of Shoggots drag cops away to toss them into the burning park, others steal their weapons and shoot at a low-flying chopper trying to drive the crazies back with prop wash. The Shoggots stand their ground and get a couple of hits on the helicopter. It spins into the sky at a crazy angle before the propellers give out and it crashes down on the Triforium sculpture a block away. Fuck it. One less piece of eyesore municipal art.

I pull the Colt and take out a couple of crazies as they crash into me. Toss their bodies back at some cops looking as wild and out for blood as the Shoggots themselves. I guess I can't blame them at this point, but I can't let them get in my way. I have to coldcock a couple of the grabby ones. I'm too close to King Bullet now to let anyone get in my way.

He's got his back to me as he shoots with his left hand and swings the kpinga with the right. Killing with both hands like that, he's an impressive fucker, but even Sub Rosa don't have bulletproof skulls, so looks aren't going to get him anywhere.

A smell hits me when I'm just a few yards away. It cuts right through the stink of the tear gas. A bitter vinegar smell that gets stuck in the back of my throat. King Bullet might look like Elvis on a killing spree, but I don't think he bathes too often.

Sawney Bean is still at King Bullet's side. He smiles at me like an old friend when he sees me with the Colt, but his expression goes dark when he realizes who I'm aiming at. The little Porky Pig creep throws himself at me just as I pull the trigger. My shot goes wild and takes down a crazy in a bloody Easter Bunny costume who's swinging an ax around like a furry berserker.

King Bullet turns when he realizes Sawney isn't there anymore and his eyes lock on me. Just as I pull the Colt's trigger, he hits me with the same black whatever the hell it is he used to take down the chopper.

I learn two things real fucking fast.

First, even though the black beam looks like mist, it's just a kind of pulsing black light.

Second, there are *things* in the light.

They had hand teeth and claws and they're hungry and cold. They rip at my coat and face. I blast away with the

Colt, but it doesn't do any good. Hands grab my arms and pull in opposite directions. I scream at the strain as they try to tear me apart. I bark some Hellion hoodoo and ignite a blast overhead that sets the surrounding air on fire. The claws loosen just long enough for me to throw myself free of the black light.

King Bullet is just a few feet away and his stink fills the air. His cool-as-hell Elvis demeanor falters for just a second when he sees me. I don't think anyone has ever crawled out of the black light before. The Colt is empty, so I put it away and pull the black blade. The King smiles when he sees it.

"It's you, isn't it? The monster who kills monsters. I've wanted to meet you for so long."

I'm bleeding and way beyond chatting right now, so I throw the blade at him. The fucker doesn't budge, but catches it midair and throws it back at me. I reach out to grab it, but I'm shaky from the black light fight, so my aim is a little off. Instead of catching the blade, it goes right through the palm of my right hand. The King laughs like it's the funniest god-damn thing he's ever seen.

He says, "Come on, monster. You can do better than that."

So I do.

I bark more hoodoo and the plaza rumbles like a 6-point quake. The ground opens up all around King Bullet and in each filthy fissure, spinning steel blades—like the guts of a woodchipper—wait for him to fall. But he's fast and strong. He drops to his knees, but keeps his balance well enough so that he doesn't slip into the grinding blades. Instead, he blasts me with the black light again. This time I don't hesitate. The moment I feel the hands, I hoodoo up a swarm of Hellion hornets. Big fuckers, with pincers like little bear traps. I don't know if they'll stop whatever lives in the light, but they'll sure distract them.

I'm feeling pretty good as I roll out of the black light. If this is the best King Bullet has to offer, I'll take him down fast.

But it's not all he has, and I'm too dumb to realize that the bastard is behind me, swinging down the kpinga. He buries one of the blades deep in my back, tearing muscle and cracking a rib or two. I can't help screaming, but when he pulls the blade out to pig stick me again I roll out of the way and manifest my Gladius.

With a hole in my back, I'm not at my best. I swing the blade in his direction, but I'm a little hunched over from the pain. He sees that I'm hurt and shoots the narco .45. I catch two of the shots with the Gladius, but a third gets through and hits me square in the chest. I slam down onto my back and the Gladius goes out. I just lie there like an upside-down turtle trying to right itself. King Bullet comes over like he just won the lottery and stands by my shoulder. I manifest the Gladius again and swing it at his legs. He dodges it easily and does the one thing I hadn't counted on—the prick walks away. Before he disappears into the chaos of bodies, he spins on his heels and sings to me.

"Rum-tiddley-um-tum-tay."

If he says anything else, I don't hear it because what feels like fifty Shoggot crazies lands on me and start dragging my carcass to one of the burning police cars. But before they can stuff me inside, I bark more hoodoo.

Spiders, big and fat and with red glittering eyes, pour from inside my coat, from the cuffs of my sleeves and pants. A whole vicious army of ugly, poisonous fuckers.

The Shoggots drop me and I land flat on my back on the street, which does wonders for the kpinga wound in my back. My vision goes black from pain for a second. When I can see again, I roll into a shadow under one of the burning cars . . .

. . . and come out in my apartment. Technically, I roll into it, try to get up, stumble, and go down flat on my face. Candy is there with Alessa. She gets up and starts over to me, but I hold up a hand.

"Don't get near me. I was with King Bullet and his crazies. I don't know what kind of germs I have all over me."

Allegra is also there. She puts a hand up to her face.

"What's that smell?"

"Tear gas." I start to get up, but lie back down again. "There was a little bit of a riot. Voices were raised. You know the drill."

"No. I don't know the drill. Your clothes look like shit and— Are you bleeding again?"

"A little probably. I got shot."

"Goddammit."

"And stabbed."

Candy is still hovering over me.

"Let me at least help you up."

I drag myself to my feet.

"No. No one gets near me until I clean up."

"Hurry your ass," Allegra says. "I want to see those wounds."

I look over at the sofa.

"How's Fuck Hollywood?"

"Stable. I gave her some herbs that I hope will help with the eating compulsion."

"'Compulsion.' That's a good word. The whole city's going nuts and King Bullet is responsible. I'm sure of it."

As I head to the kitchen, Allegra says, "Go straight into the bedroom when you're done. I'll treat you there. Not everyone needs to see your blood."

I get a garbage bag and bring it into the bathroom. Strip and stuff all my clothes into it and tie it tight. Then I get in the shower.

Standing there is torture. Every part of me hurts, not just the bullet hole and stab wound, but the million little cuts and tears from the things in the black light. And what the hell kind of trick was that? Mason was as powerful a dark Sub Rosa piece of shit as I've ever known and I don't think even he could have pulled that off. What does King Bullet know that the rest of us don't?

I have to sit on the edge of the tub for a minute. As the adrenaline in my system winds down, the holes in my chest and back start to get to me. I have to hold on and breathe for a while until the dizziness passes.

When I can't take the water anymore, I put on an old robe I pull off the back of the bathroom door and take the bag of clothes straight to the garbage chute in the hall. The landlord has painted over the King Bullet graffiti with a single coat of cheap white paint, but I can still see the fucker through it like a smug ghost.

Once I've dumped the trash, I head back to the bedroom and drop onto the mattress. Allegra is waiting and gives me a what-the-hell-is-wrong-with-you look. She comes over and pokes at the kpinga wound in my back.

"Ow, goddammit," I say.

She ignores my whining and says, "Flip over. I want to get a look at that bullet wound."

I roll onto my back and she lets out a sigh.

"Jesus, Stark. What, did you get hit by a cannon?"

"A gold .45. If you're going to get shot, a gold .45 is the classy way to do it."

She uses one of Doc Kinski's contraptions to examine my chest. A little gold box with tiny spiked wheels that—I think—lets her get a look inside me. It takes a while, but she actually grins a little when she understands that I'm not about to croak.

"Here's the crazy thing," she says. "You got shot in the chest, at what looks like close range."

"All true."

"But there's no exit wound in your back. And from what I can see, the bullet isn't lodged anywhere inside you."

"You mean that asshole has some kind of magic bullets that disappear? Fuck that guy."

She says, "No. I think the bullet went out of the stab wound in your back. What a crazy bit of luck, right?"

What a goddamn egomaniac. King Bullet is one prancing show pony show-off.

As she bandages my hand I say, "That wasn't luck. He knew what he was doing. He was sending me a message."

"What kind?"

"That he's better than me. That he's going to kill me and he's going to have fun doing it."

Allegra puts a cold purple salve on the bullet wound and says, "You really know the best people."

"Don't I just? Tell me more about Fuck Hollywood. Can you do something about her finger? Reattach it or something?"

"I've done what I could. Her little finger is back in place. Whether it will work properly or not, I don't know. Her wounds were extensive."

"I already killed the guy who infected her. That means when I take out King Bullet we'll be almost even."

"I don't care about that. Roll over so I can work on your back wound."

I do it and feel a stabbing pain in my side.

"I think he might have cracked a rib."

"It's not cracked, but he did nick one. There's not much I can do for it. Do you want some painkillers?"

"You have painkillers and you didn't give me any before now? Gimme. Everything you've got."

She gives me a look.

"You can have one pill now and one tomorrow. After that you have to suffer and think about your sins."

"That would take all year and I don't have time."

"Then just grit your teeth and try not to move around too much for a few days."

"Will do. And thanks."

"You want to thank me? Put on some damn pants and come into the living room. People are worried about you."

"Give me a minute."

After she goes out, I lie there, waiting for the pill to come on. While it does, I gather my thoughts.

So, that was King Bullet. He seems nice, in a Charlie Manson meets P. T. Barnum kind of way. What else did we learn tonight, children? He fights mean and he smells bad. And he likes the sound of his own voice. Plus, he has access to some peculiar hoodoo I've never seen before, even Downtown. And the bastard figured out who I was. Like he was waiting for me. Every part of me wants to find him fast and finish him, but I'm in no shape for that right now. Probably even tomorrow. But soon. Something started tonight and there's no stopping it. One of us has to go.

I get dressed and head into the living room to reassure everybody that I'm in one piece. Honestly, what pisses me off the most right now is that the King cost me my coat. Luckily, Fuck Hollywood still has my old one. Yeah, it has a million holes and some of my dried blood on it, but it's in one piece and will hold my weapons. I'll just borrow it for now and give it back to her when she's well again. And she will be well, if I have to march into Heaven and drag Mr. Muninn down here to perform a miracle.

Everyone has a million questions that I don't want to answer. You get shot enough times, it's the last thing you want to talk about. And anyway, I already told Allegra what happened. She can fill them in so I don't have to fucking repeat myself. I go into the kitchen and call Janet. They're still up, so I go right over.

When I get there, I'm a little nervous because of what

happened earlier. But they pull me right inside and kiss my bruised face and raw knuckles.

I say, "I'm sorry for coming over so messed up again."

"It's okay. I had a feeling you might be. At least you cleaned up first."

"I'm not going to be worth much of anything tonight."

They smile and put a hand on my cheek.

"You want to tell me about what happened?"

"Only if you want to know."

"I do. What you do still scares me, but I want to know all of you."

They make coffee and I tell them about Fuck Hollywood getting hurt—though I leave out how—and then the riot. They actually listen. They get scared a few times and get a little teary when I tell them what King Bullet did to me. But they listen. They tell me about being scared of me sometimes and I listen too. We talk until I can't talk anymore, and I fall asleep in their bed with them beside me. It feels good.

In the morning, Janet makes breakfast and I make coffee. Afterward, even though they feel like crap because of the cold, they go back to work on their music. With Donut Universe gone, it's the only thing they have to fill the days.

I say, "I can stay here today if you want."

They blow their nose and shoo me away.

"No. I'm gross and you'd be bored watching me poke at my laptop all day," they say. "Besides, I know you want to check on Fuck Hollywood."

"Yeah. I kind of do."

"Then go. We'll catch up later."

I start to kiss them, but they sneeze.

"Go," they say. "I don't want you coming down with this."

I kiss their hand and shadow walk back to the apartment.

ALLEGRA IS CURLED up asleep in a chair. Fuck Hollywood is just waking up and gives me a weak smile. I put a finger to my lips to tell her not to talk. Then I shake Allegra gently. She slowly opens her eyes and glances at Fuck Hollywood, who waves back. There's a compression glove on her right hand, but she can use it. However, her left hand is mummy-wrapped in gauze and bandages.

After Allegra inspects the dressings she stretches and says, "I'll stop by tonight to change that wrapping. Other than that, you look good."

"Thank you so much," says Fuck Hollywood.

I take Allegra back to her apartment through a shadow. She unlocks the door, but doesn't go right inside.

"Keep an eye on her for a while. If there's anything odd about her mood. If she tries to scratch or get her bandages off, call me immediately."

"You think she's still sick?"

"I think she's in as good shape as can be expected. But we don't know how the virus works. Just because she's okay now doesn't mean she might not relapse."

"You're a lifesaver."

"I'm going to want to have another look at you too. How are you feeling?"

"Honestly? Worn the fuck out. I itch, which means I'm healing, but I should be farther along. I think King Bullet might have put some hoodoo on his kpinga. I might be stuck with this sliced-up hand for a few days."

"Want me to check it now?"

"No. I want to get back. Are you okay? I mean, with the clinic closed."

She shrugs. "You know. Restless. Angry. Sad. Fairuza is coming over later and we're going to drink ourselves stupid."

"Good plan."

"Promise that you're not trying any heroics today."

"Don't worry. I couldn't steal a Milk-Bone from a Chihuahua."

"Good. I'll call you later."

I head back to the apartment and Fuck Hollywood is sitting up, trying to work the TV remote with her fucked-up hands. I try to help her, but she shoulders me away.

"I'm a big girl, Dad. I'll get it."

"You do that. I'll make coffee."

When I get back a few minutes later, she's watching an anime about some guy with a reptile head and his friend, an ass-kicking woman with a dumpling shop. It looks like fun. She mutes the sound when she sees me.

I say, "Can you hold the cup okay?"

She takes it with her right hand and holds it up.

"I'm fine. See? And, honest, you don't have to baby me. I'm feeling a lot better."

I sit down next to her on the sofa.

"Exactly what the hell are we watching?"

"*Dorohedoro*. And don't ask me anything about it, because I'm going to make you watch it from the beginning."

"You're the boss."

We watch the show for a few minutes, just letting the images wash over us. But I can tell Fuck Hollywood is restless.

"Are you okay?"

She looks at me.

"It's okay if you want to go out," she says. "I'm really feeling a lot better."

I blow on my coffee.

"I think I'll hang around for a while. It feels like every muscle in my body got kicked in the balls."

She stares at her injured hands for a few seconds.

"Me too. Allegra told me what I did."

"Do you remember any of it?"

"Bits and pieces. It's weird to think about. I mean, I know what I did was horrible, but I also remember not being able to stop because it felt so good and right. Creepy, yeah?"

"Not really. After what I saw last night, I can imagine any kind of craziness getting stuck in people's heads. The way a lot of those Shoggots cut themselves and each other up . . ."

She touches her forehead.

"Is that what happened with you and Betty Boop the other night? Someone did that to you?"

"Yeah."

"Because you wanted them to?"

"No," I say. "I needed information from him and it seemed like the fastest way to get it."

Fuck Hollywood thinks for a minute.

"You get hurt a lot trying to help people."

"I'm just clumsy."

"I meant it as a compliment."

"Oh. Thanks."

"You really are lousy with people being nice to you."

"It's easier getting punched."

"All those scars you have from trying to help people."

I take a gulp of coffee. The reptile guy just swallowed some suit-and-tie guy's head. I like this show.

"I'll have more scars before this is over, so it's best not to think about it." I look at her. "Do you hurt? Allegra gave me a pain pill. You can have it."

She shakes her head.

"I'm okay. She gave me one too. But see? You were going to hurt yourself to help me."

I watch the show and ignore the comment. Fuck Hollywood stares at her hands.

"This morning, Allegra said that my pinkie looks good and will probably heal up okay. Not a hundred percent, but pretty okay. She had these big clunky chunks of something like cloudy stones. Like big opals."

"It sounds like divine light glass."

She laughs a little at that.

"Is that like holy water? A priest blesses it and suddenly it's magic."

I set down my cup. "Nope. It's part of one of the vessels that God used to make the first stars."

"Get out of here."

"It's true. One of the vessels broke. The glass fell to Earth and created life. Including us."

"You're fucking with me."

"I'm not. We're one gigantic cosmic mistake."

Fuck Hollywood stares off into space for a minute. Eventually, she looks at me.

"That's kind of cool when you think about it," she says. "I mean, if we're just a mistake it means that anything nice we do is special. Any music or paintings or movies or people we love. They're all special because we're not even supposed to be here."

"I never thought of it that way before."

"All that punching addled you, boy."

"I wouldn't be surprised."

"Are you going out later?"

"I don't know. Maybe I'll just stay here if you want to do something."

"That's okay. It's just that on TV earlier they said the governor is sending the National Guard into L.A. And there's a curfew. No one's allowed out after eight or before six."

I think about the scene last night.

"I wouldn't want to be one of those National Guard guys going up against the crazies. I don't know how many there were last night, but there are just going to be more and more."

"Didn't a lot get shot?"

"As long as there's the virus there will be more crazies."

"That's scary."

"It is," I say.

"There was something else too. What's the name for what I did? What I have?"

"You mean autophagia?"

"That's it. The TV said that other people have it too. Like, a lot of people."

"You'll be safe from all that here."

She looks at her hands, not as reassured as I'd hoped.

I say, "If there's a curfew, maybe I should go out and get us some food now before it's all gone."

Fuck Hollywood looks around for her phone.

"I'll order us a pizza. A couple of pizzas. Don't know how long we're going to be locked up."

"Absolutely no pizza tonight. I'll get some burritos and tamales and things."

I put my empty cup in the kitchen and Fuck Hollywood says, "It's going to be all right, right? I mean you're coming back."

I go over to the sofa.

"Of course I'm coming back."

She looks uncomfortable.

"My friend who had the room I was going to rent? With the way things are, she doesn't want new people around."

"It's okay. Stay here as long as you want. This is your home now too."

"Thank you."

She grabs me in a hug and I wince at the pain in my back.

Letting go, she says, "They really messed you up last night, didn't they?"

"I've been worse. But I'm not wrestling any gators today."

"Did you really get shot?"

"Yep."

She looks a bit sheepish and says, "Can I see?"

I pull up my T-shirt so she can see the half-healed wound.

She stares for a minute and says, "That is so metal."

Now I laugh.

She says, "I'll find something for us to watch while you're out."

"Nothing with guns. But something with gore."

"I'm on it."

I head to a little bodega a block away where they sell hot food and get double orders of everything. They have big bags of sour gummy worms at the counter, so I get those too. They seem like something Fuck Hollywood might like.

When I get back, she's found a station playing *The Abominable Dr. Phibes*.

"Perfect," I tell her, tossing her the worms.

She tears into the bag happily.

For all of its baroque gore, *Dr. Phibes* is a fairly straightforward movie. Back from suspended animation, using biblical plagues, Phibes goes after the doctors who let his wife die. It's not just murder. It's the retribution of an angry god, making the unworthy pay for their sins. Naturally, he fails in the end and doesn't kill all of the doctors. Even gods can't be right all the time. Phibes's sin was wrath, but he gets away by going back into suspended animation. And so the world waits to see if God will return and what sins we'll be judged for down the line. Of course he does a year later in *Dr. Phibes Rises Again*. This time, after all the murders, he gets away with the secret to eternal life with his beloved wife. Us sinners should all be so lucky.

I wonder who King Bullet thinks he is. Sinner on a rampage or god on a killing spree? In the end, it doesn't matter. I've killed nefarious Sub Rosa before and I can do it again. I just hope I don't get beaten up as ugly as his Shoggots.

By the end of the movie, Fuck Hollywood is asleep. She's got a lot of healing to do, so I leave her that way and go into the bedroom to call Candy.

"Thanks a lot for coming over and taking care of everybody last night."

She says, "How's Fuck Hollywood?"

"A lot better. Allegra says that her hand should heal pretty well."

"That's so great."

"How are you doing?"

There's an annoyed exhalation of air on the line.

"The fucking alarm company refuses to install the system," she says. "Not after the riot last night. Chickens."

"Do you need any help? I mean, I'm absolutely no good at those things, but I can bring snacks."

"It's okay. Alessa and I got all the sensors in place ourselves. Kasabian wouldn't even help. He thinks if he gets on a ladder he'll fall and be paralyzed."

"Or he's just lazy."

"I don't think that's it. He's working on getting the system online, but is having trouble. Want to come over and help him? He won't let Alessa or me do it. I think he could use some guy company."

"He's desperate enough for me?"

"Don't talk like that. And yes, he is. Come right over," she says and hangs up.

I check on Fuck Hollywood and she's still out like a light. Before leaving I whisper some hoodoo so that if she wakes up, I'll know it and can come back. I put on my mask and go straight to Max Overdrive. I hate that there are nervous butterflies in my stomach, but there's no denying it.

As usual now, the front door of the shop is locked. And they've installed a second dead bolt. I knock a few times and Kasabian opens the door. Then he goes back to the laptop open on the front counter. He stares at me until I lock the door, before poking at the computer again.

I point to the machine.

"Need any help?"

He doesn't look up.

"No. Go hit something with a hammer. This is brain work."

I hold up my bandaged right hand.

"No hammers. I'm out of commission for the day."

"How about your left hand?"

"It's fine."

He hands me a thick computer manual.

"Good. Hold this. You're my book stand."

He goes back to ignoring me. Just poking at the laptop and cursing quietly.

I try to look over his shoulder.

"Do you have any idea what you're doing?"

"Of course."

"Because you've been typing the same thing over and over for five minutes."

"You've been here for only one."

"I'm just assuming."

He says, "I'm looking for the sweet spot."

"Hurry up. The manual is getting heavy, what with my encumbrances."

"Get your ass kicked again?"

"Got shot."

"Is that all you do now? That and moon after Candy?"

I look at him hard.

"If you ever say that where another human being can hear, your head's going to be back on a skateboard so fast."

"Candy would love you if you did that."

"Just push the right buttons, for fuck sake."

He pokes at the keyboard for a minute and throws up his hands.

"Yes!" he yells like he just cured cancer. He even smiles when he looks at me. "Remember my streaming service?"

"You mean your betrayal of all movie rental shops ever? I remember."

"I'll have Disney Voodoo Riot up and running in a couple of weeks."

I look at him.

"That's the name you're going with?"

"What? You don't like it?"

"It's fine. I'm sure when the Mouse finds out about it he'll be amused too."

"Disney will never find it. We can run the server from the same place we get the movies. There's no way to trace it because it's not in this plane of existence."

I have to smile at that.

"You bad man."

He laughs quietly.

"The worst. This is going to be my mark. I know I'm third-rate as a magician, but I always had the best movies in L.A."

"And the way you'll know if you've made it big is if no one ever knows it's you?"

"Exactly. I'm the man who makes things happy behind the scenes, but no one knows. I'm Dr. Mabuse."

"That's great. Just remember: Dr. Mabuse ended up in the nuthouse."

Kasabian makes a face.

"Always with the negative waves, Moriarty."

I shake my head. "You aren't Donald Sutherland."

"And you aren't Clint Eastwood, so just hold the damn book while I finish."

Another minute or so of his slow, uncertain poking and then little red lights go on all around us as the alarm system comes online.

He pulls out his bottle of Macallan from beneath the counter.

"You can stay and have a drink if you don't talk," he says.

My phone vibrates. There's a new text.

"Jimmy, I know you're having fun and games with your movie chums, but we need to talk. Meet me at Musso & Frank's nowish."

I read the text over a couple of times, trying to decide if it's real.

"No time for drinks," I say. "I have to meet Samael."

Kasabian frowns.

"What does that guy want?"

"I guess I'll find out."

"Well, don't bring him around here. He gives me the heebie-jeebies."

"Say goodbye to Candy and Alessa for me."

"Sure thing. Coward."

"Not a word or it's skateboard time, Alfredo Garcia."

The Musso & Frank Grill isn't far from Max Overdrive, so I walk because with all the madness going on, I want to feel a little human for a minute. Big mistake.

Every masked face I pass is a potential Shoggot and it gets me jumpy as hell. I'm still hurting from the riot and the last thing I want right now is to have to mud wrestle even one crazy. I breathe in through my nose and out through my mouth, an old calming trick. It doesn't do a goddamn thing. I step into the doorway of a shuttered tourist trap selling Hollywood snow globes and T-shirts and, as discreetly as possible, move the Colt from my back and into my coat pocket, where I can keep a hand on it. I'm not saying I'm looking forward to shooting a Shoggot in the face, but I am saying that it would be very satisfying.

Someone has painted King Bullet's skull graffiti on the wall next to an Irish pub that's selling to-go drinks. There's a homeless guy hanging around outside. He's wearing two or three ragged coats and a sweat-stained Captain America baseball cap. Any other day, I might feel sorry for him, but today I eye him like he's a napping T. rex. He mistakes my look for sympathy and heads my way. Or maybe he's a Shoggot lookout and I'm going to get to shoot someone after all.

He holds out a grimy, callused hand in my direction and we lock eyes. I should be able to read him this close and know whether the homeless look is a gaff or not. But I can't get a lock on him. His mind is going in a dozen directions at once, which tracks for some of the wilder Shoggots. I keep my eyes on his, giving him my best Lee Van Cleef narrow-eyed stare. Soon, his eyes twitch away. He pulls back his hand and limps behind a parking meter, like he thinks I won't be able to see him there.

Great. I just scared some poor asshole who's having enough trouble clinging to reality. He doesn't need me glaring at him like I think he's a rabid dog. Feeling like a heel, I take a twenty from my pocket and hold it out to him. It takes him a moment to come away from the safety of the parking meter, snatch the bill from my hand, and go back into his imaginary hiding place. One more day I've ruined. One more brain I've bruised when I didn't need to. King Bullet is deep in my head and I want him out. Maybe getting drunk on Samael's dime will help me start.

Musso & Frank's is old Hollywood. It's been on Hollywood Boulevard for more than a hundred years and I hope it makes it for another hundred. Frankly, with its red upholstered booths and classy look and feel, the place is a little intimidating for someone like me who grew up heating frozen macaroni in the microwave because Dad was gone and Mom had been at the box wine all afternoon. So, when I find Musso & Frank's door closed, I consider turning around and leaving. But it opens a moment later and a red-jacketed waiter in a black surgical mask ushers me through the front of the place to the back room.

Samael is there, checking his phone and sipping a martini. He smiles when he sees me and waves me over.

I say, "I thought this place was closed because of the virus."

"Not for me it isn't."

"And why is that exactly?"

"Years ago, a few of the staff sold me their souls."

"But you're not Lucifer anymore."

"They don't know that and we're going to have a lovely meal because of it."

The waiter comes back with menus and a martini for me. I hand it back to him.

"Can I get bourbon?"

Samael gestures for the waiter to set the glass down.

"Drink your martini, Jimmy. It's a classic."

"I don't like martinis."

I wait for him to say something clever, but he just ignores me until he's looked over the menu.

"I recommend the steak tartare as a starter."

"Raw beef? I'd rather eat my own leg."

He shakes his head sadly.

"Not a politically correct joke in an age of autophagia."

"I wasn't making a joke and I'm not eating that stuff."

He takes a breath.

"Then try a lobster cocktail."

"Is it cooked?"

"Exquisitely."

"Okay then."

"Soup?"

"I hate soup."

"Of course you do."

I skip all of the middle stuff on the menu and go straight to the steaks.

"If you're paying, I'll get the filet mignon."

"Get the lamb chops."

"I like filet mignon."

"That's because you have the palate of a twelve-year-old. Trust me. You'll be happier with the lamb chops."

I set down the menu harder than I needed to.

"I want the filet mignon."

He finishes his martini and takes mine. Then he gestures for the waiter.

"We'll have the steak tartare, a lobster cocktail, the French onion soup, house salad, and two orders of the lamb chops."

"Goddammit."

"Ignore him. He thinks the Last Supper was nachos and Twinkies."

The waiter beams at us both and heads back to the kitchen. Samael looks me over.

"I take it from your slight hunch that your back is injured and the bandage on your hand tells me that things didn't go quite your way with King Bullet?"

"It might not be so bad if I'd had backup. Fucking Abbot and his blue bloods. I think they want me dead."

He eats the olive from my martini and says, "You're stronger than any of them and you have powerful friends. Therefore you pose a threat. Of course they want you dead."

I think about that for a minute.

"It's not like I don't want to murder King Bullet and feed him to the coyotes," I say. "I just don't want to go after him without a plan or backup."

"All perfectly reasonable. By the way, would you like to know why I invited you to lunch?"

"Yeah. Why am I here?"

"That friend of yours. What was her name? The wayward angel a few months back."

"Zadkiel. And she wasn't my friend. I never heard of her until you told me to find her."

"And then you killed her."

"Only after she tried to kill me."

Samael looks around for the waiter.

"I could use another martini. How about you?"

"I'll pass. And what's the story with Zadkiel? I mean, I have my suspicions, but I want to hear it from you."

"Oh? What are your suspicions?"

"Before she died, she said 'I've done something awful.' I think she might have meant the virus. She sent it."

"Interesting," he says. "But I don't think so."

"Then what did she do?"

"She ripped a hole in the universe."

I look at him for a minute, waiting for him to go on, but he gets distracted looking for the waiter again.

I say, "What the hell does that mean? Ripped a hole in the universe? How?"

"She was the Opener of the Ways. She opened a door that even Father didn't remember being there. Tore the thing right off."

"And what does that mean? Did something go out? Did something come in?"

Samael shrugs as the waiter comes by with two more martinis. He doesn't even pretend the second one is for me, but slides both to his side of the table. Out of curiosity, I take mine back and sip it. It's like getting a mouthful of rubbing alcohol and bitters, only cold.

"Is she or isn't she responsible for people dying and going nuts?"

"It's doubtful either way. But I suspect it's possibly the indirect result of the universe going a bit pear-shaped."

I push my martini back to him.

"Can't Mr. Muninn just fix it?"

A sigh. Genuine this time.

"He's not at his best. Still recovering from battling the rebel angels."

"When he's better, will he do anything or is he still playing hands-off with the universe?"

"You of all people should know that Father isn't what he once was. He can't just reshape creation with a blink anymore. What is it you once called him?"

"A janitor," I say, feeling lousy saying it out loud.

"Exactly. Not the creator or lord of time and space, but a janitor just trying to keep the grounds clean. And honestly? There are days when he's closer to that than any of us would like to admit."

"I didn't know it was that bad."

Samael nods, looking annoyed with me.

"Now you do, so you might give the old man a break now and then."

"I was just hoping for something that might help me beat King Bullet. But I'll tell you a secret. Something that just came to me sitting here right now."

He looks at me. "You don't want to fight him again."

"Exactly. At least— No. Fuck it. I'm out. I got beaten, knifed, and shot. And for what? I didn't even lay a finger on King Bullet."

"But it sounds like you gave it the old college try."

"I sure as hell did. Let Abbot's troops handle things from now on. Why am I getting my ass handed to me if he won't lift a finger?"

"There's absolutely no reason at all."

"And if Abbot won't send in the troops it means the Sub Rosa Council has deserted L.A. And maybe that's not a bad thing."

"Maybe not."

The waiter brings Samael his tartare and me my lobster cocktail. I take a couple of bites. It's good. Very good, but I lose my appetite.

I push the food away and say, "But what if the Council just lets King Bullet run amok?"

Samael swallows a big mouthful of tartare. I feel a little sick watching.

"See?" he says. "This is what you always do and why you have a bullet hole in your chest. You can't ever leave a fight alone. But Mr. James Butler Hickok Stark, not everything is your responsibility."

"It is if it affects my friends."

"Why not at least wait a while? Maybe your chum Abbot will surprise you."

He finishes his tartare and I think I might even be able to eat again someday.

"Do you know something?" I say.

The waiter brings the soup, but Samael ignores it.

"Just that the National Guard has been pulled back to the edges of the city."

"Getting out of someone's way?"

"Who knows?"

"Finally. Good for you, Abbot."

Samael eats the top off of his French onion soup and pushes the rest away.

"You didn't finish your soup."

"I just like the cheesy bit on top. I can't stand the rest."

He waves off the salad and tells the waiter to bring our entrees.

"I'd advise you not to go charging in trying to help them," he says.

"I didn't say I was going to."

"Don't be ridiculous. You can't stand anyone having a fight without you. But let this one go. They want you dead. Just because they're going in force doesn't mean they'll protect you when the moment comes, and it *will* come."

The waiter brings the lamb chops. I'm still angry, but I take a bite of one. And it's like someone split my head open and filled it full of heavenly choirs and motel sex with Candy. But I keep frowning. There's no way I'm letting Samael know how good they are.

"Good?" he says.

"Passable."

"If you don't want yours then I'll have them."

"Touch my plate and I'll stab you in the eye with this fork."

"Good boy. We're expanding your palate quite well today, don't you think?"

I eat more of the lamb and it just gets better as I go.

Between mouthfuls I say, "So, I just sit around and wait for the news?"

"No. You go home and take care of that poor injured child in your apartment."

I look at the time on my phone.

"You're right. I probably shouldn't leave her alone too much longer. But I need to stop and pick up some food."

"Don't bother. I'm having them prepare a few items for you to take home."

"No tartare?"

"No tartare."

"And more lamb. This isn't the worst thing ever."

"I'll have them add an order."

"Then I accept your generous offer."

"Bully for me."

The waiter brings two pieces of key lime pie and it's almost as good as the lamb.

Samael says, "I miss your shop. I miss stealing your movies."

"Stop by. Kasabian wouldn't dare stop you."

"How is your lady friend, Candy?"

"She's fine."

"And your other friend?"

"Janet is fine too. They have a cold, but they're generally fine."

"I'm so glad to hear that your little menagerie is doing so well. And no complications?"

I finish my pie and put down my fork.

"If you're thinking of giving me any love life advice, I don't want to hear it. Everything is confusing enough."

He finishes and wipes his mouth. As he folds his napkin he says, "As the poet once said, 'Love has more faces than the moon.'"

"What the hell does that mean?"

"I have no idea. But it's very pretty, don't you think?"

The waiter comes back to the table with two shopping bags full of amazing-smelling food.

"And here's your goodie bag," Samael says.

"Wait. That's it? Zadkiel jimmied a lock and now you're just going back to Heaven?"

He sets his napkin next to his plate.

"I had a lovely lunch and good company. I thought you might enjoy an update. What more is there to do?"

"What if I decide to do something about King Bullet and I need backup?"

He gives me a look.

"I thought you said you wouldn't."

"Yeah, but what if I do?"

"I mean, we just discussed it."

"I know. But what if I *have* to?"

He sighs heavily, like he's in a silent movie, and hands me a small golden case he's been hiding all along. The case is a pyx and it holds one consecrated Host.

"How theatrical."

He nods in agreement.

"I thought you'd like it."

"What do I do with it?"

"If you need me, just break it in half."

I push the pyx to his side of the table.

"You know what? Never mind. I'm out of this fight."

He pushes it back to my side.

"Keep it anyway. Who knows? Maybe you'll want a snack later. Have it with a glass of red wine. It's traditional."

I reach into my pocket to give the waiter a tip and Samael glares at me.

"By everything holy and infernal, if you're about to take money from your pocket I'll destroy this sordid planet and everything on it."

I put the cash back and take my bags of food and the pyx to a shadow.

"Thanks," I say.

He smiles at me, relaxed again now that he's won the fight.

"Scoot home. I think your young ward is awake."

He's right. I can feel a tickle at the back of my head. I step through the shadow and come out back in the apartment.

Fuck Hollywood finger waves at me, munching happily on a piece of pizza. There are three more pies on the table.

"So we won't run out," she says between bites.

I show her my bags.

"Those won't all fit in the refrigerator with this food."

"Can't you magic the fridge bigger? Or make the pizzas smaller?"

"I don't think so."

She pushes a pizza my way.

"Then you better start eating."

THE REST OF the day is pretty quiet. Samael gave me a lot to think about, but I decide not to decide anything important right now. My head isn't clear enough.

Later, Janet is still sick, but also restless. I bring them to my place and put them to bed. I help Fuck Hollywood put medicine on her hands and change her bandages. Her left hand is still a mess—raw, red skin and Frankenstein stitches. Allegra said that the stitches will disappear on their own. But the sight of her injured hands has Fuck Hollywood crying again. I get the bandages and her glove back on fast and bring her pizza and gummy worms, which seems to help. So does a couple of beers. We don't talk about any of it, but watch Kubrick's *Napoleon* until the sound of explosions wakes Janet and they come out to join us.

The Battle of Waterloo is where the noise and carnage really goes wild. It's Kubrick at his most epic and baroque. Perfectly choreographed shots and sequences of mass slaughter across the Belgian countryside. The sound is ferocious enough that it takes me a few minutes to realize that some of the noise isn't coming from the movie.

A loud bang outside rattles the windows. I look outside and see impressive fires to the north. More explosions and what might be gunfire. Is this the National Guard? Is it the Shoggots just having fun? Or is this Abbot and the troops going in? Are they finally getting off their garden-party asses and going after King Bullet head-on?

I pause the movie and turn to a local news channel, but there's nothing about the fires or the explosions. I check another. Nothing. I flip through all of the local channels, hoping for some confirmation that what I'm hearing is what I think it is.

But, of course, Abbot has deals with all of the local power players, and that includes the media. If he doesn't want something on TV, it won't be there. The absence of any coverage of our mini-Waterloo has to mean that Sub Rosa heavies have gone in hard. Tomorrow, Sub Rosa hoodoo tech types will have their hands full trying to wipe the memories of as many Angelenos as possible to cover up the fight.

"What's happening out there?" says Janet.

"Things might be over with tonight. King Bullet. The Shoggots. All of it."

Janet puts an arm around me and Fuck Hollywood whispers, "Awesome." We turn off the lights and watch the flames and occasional starbursts as things explode in the sky like it's the Fourth of July, because maybe it is. A holiday. A liberation. A victory.

Like all good fireworks shows, it winds down after a while

and I put Janet back to bed. When the movie ends, Fuck Hollywood curls up under a blanket on the sofa while I wolf down a cold lamb chop in the kitchen, savoring every bite.

It isn't until I'm getting ready for bed that I notice that I have a new voicemail. It's from Abbot. I go into the bathroom to listen so I won't wake anyone. It's not the good news I was hoping for.

"Are you there, Stark? I'm a little woozy from the painkillers. I'm injured. We all are. And we failed. Miserably. King Bullet and his people were simply too much for us. We tried not to kill anyone at first. But even after I approved lethal action, there were simply too many Shoggots. And King Bullet himself. He marched through the madness like he was on his way to a church picnic. We couldn't lay a finger on him. He's strong. I'm sorry to say, maybe stronger than you. The black light he can summon—we had nothing to fight that. It was a rout. Pure and simple. But I have good news too.

"I was foolish not to tell you about this before and to ask you to help us use it, but I'm telling you now. Do you remember the Golden Vigil?"

I worked with the Vigil for a while, and not because I enjoyed it. They were a bunch of hyper-religious government spooks. God's Pinkertons on Earth, except Mr. Muninn had no idea who they were. They muscled and bullied, kept track of all hoodoo activity, and controlled as much of it as they could get away with. But their old leader, Marshal Wells, blew the job and almost killed the world. After that, Wells got put away and the Vigil was disbanded.

Abbot says, "They have a weapon that we think might be able to stop King Bullet. It was arrogant of me to think that we could go after someone like him with conventional methods. But I won't make that mistake again. The weapon has been in a government warehouse under lock and key since the Vigil was dissolved. Unfortunately, it will take some time to acquire the weapon. There are politics involved. Fools protecting their little fiefdoms while the world around them burns. But if we can get the weapon—when we get it—will you help us use it? We're not going to stop King Bullet on our own. I know that you're furious with the Council, and you have every right to be. But we need you now. We can't do this without you. Please call me."

Paperwork. Abbot gets his ass handed to him in a punch bowl and the first thing he brings up is paperwork. How many people got killed tonight? If I'd been there, would I be in one of the mass graves in the Angeles National Forest right now? If Abbot is bringing up the weapon now, it means that he knew about it before. And he was holding out on me. Was Samael right? Would Abbot or any of the others have put out a hand to me if my back was against the wall? And why does he need me to use the weapon? It can't be anything ordinary. It means he needs someone hard to kill to use it. That means if I'm lucky enough to get a shot at the King with it, I might end up dead too. Or am I just being paranoid? This whole situation is getting to me. But I can't shake the feeling that there's more going on with the Council than they're letting on.

I'm tempted to hit the Call Back button and tell Abbot to go to hell. Instead I put the phone away. Let Abbot and the Council wonder and worry overnight. Let them beat each other up over this.

Paperwork?

What the fuck is wrong with those people?

IN THE MORNING, I tell Janet and Fuck Hollywood I'm going out to pick up some bourbon, but the truth is that I just want some time to myself to think.

I walk from North Sycamore east toward Vine along the Hollywood Walk of Fame. A mile and a half of pure showbiz cheese. Celebrities' names on stars embedded in the street for tourists to gawk at and dogs to piss on. The pinnacle of L.A. success. Usually, it's good for a laugh and a way to clear my head, but today it feels like I'm walking on tombstones toward a cliff edge and a long fall down, down, down. I used to worry about landing in Hell, but now? I don't know. I imagine some kind of silent oblivion as a ghost watching my friends in trouble and not being able to do a damn thing about it.

A National Guard truck loaded with troops rumbles by. Dozens of beady eyes on me, as suspicious of me as I am of them. It never occurred to me before that this stupid surgical mask might be the only thing that keeps me from getting arrested or shot. With all the scars on my face, any one of these G.I. Joes might mistake me for a Shoggot and open fire on principle. I pull the mask up a little higher and turn away from the truck. I don't need that kind of trouble right now.

I have no idea what I'm supposed to do about Abbot. I have to call him back, but what am I supposed to say? Were you going to hang me out to dry last night? Was I going to be bait to bring King Bullet into the open? Do you want me to be bait now that you're fessing up about a super weapon in your Fortress of Solitude?

Even if the Council isn't planning my unfortunate demise, the situation feels like they want to drag me into a fight while caring fuck all what happens to me. What do I owe the Council? Nothing. Abbot pays my salary, but I can walk away. I've been broke before. I can do it again. If it comes to it, I'll loot some of these tourist shops and drag the goods Downtown and open my own store selling souvenirs to Hellions. Maybe get Wild Bill to run the place with me like we used to run his bar.

But none of that deals with King Bullet, and he has to be dealt with. A guy like that isn't going to just give up and go away. And why should he? He's winning. He has zero incentive.

More Guardsmen roll by in APCs. Cop cars and BearCats. Sheriff's department vans. I halfway expect the Boy Scouts and a gaggle of movie cowboys to ride along behind. John Wayne, Tom Mix, and the Lone Ranger. A whole dream team cavalry to the rescue in a fight they don't know they can't win.

And on top of it all is Zadkiel and her goddamn curse.

"I've done something awful."

No shit, sister. But if you didn't hit us with the virus, then what did you do?

According to Samael she ripped a hole in the universe. Was she looking for a way out or inviting something in? King Bullet? What the fuck for? To beat up cops and spray graffiti around town? That's not quite the apocalypse I was prepared for. Before you know it, Shoggots will be stealing candy apples and dunking girls' pigtails into inkwells. Oh my.

It doesn't add up. King Bullet and the virus are linked, but that's all I'm sure of. Abbot doesn't think it's a biological weapon, but I'm not so sure. The virus shows up and weakens the city. Then the King rolls into town. And he has his black light trick. That's a nice weapon. Is he some freak from the same lab that made the Vigil's toys? A psycho scientist or tech gone rogue, looking for kicks before he dies or tries to blackmail the world like some third-rate Blofeld?

In my pocket, I can feel the pyx Samael gave me. It's tempting to break the Host now, but it doesn't feel like the right time. And begging Mr. Muninn for favors won't do any good if he's laid up with war wounds. No, for the moment I'm on my own. I can't fight or shoot my way out of this—at least not yet. I'm going to sit back and watch L.A.'s best and brightest go up against the King and his minions. Let them take the hits and maybe I can learn from it.

I stop at a liquor store called Unhealthy Spirits. The sign over the door has a picture of an old cartoon moonshine jug with a ghost coming out and chasing away a preacher and a revenuer. All I have are hundreds in my pocket, so I get a bottle of Angel's Envy and leave the change for the clerk. Down the block, I step into the alcove of a shuttered bookstore and open the bottle for a morning pick-me-up. At least there's one good thing about the streets being mostly deserted.

I take a couple of big gulps before putting the cork back in the bottle, and I'm feeling better than I have all morning. Then I make the mistake of looking up. There's the damn painted skull again. A bullet hole in the forehead and a crown hovering overhead. I just can't get away from this guy. Slipping the bottle in my coat pocket, I start back home. I get a block before my phone rings. It's Candy. I check the time and answer it.

"Hi. You're up early. What's going on?" I say.

"Stark," she says, and I can already hear how out of breath she is. "He's shot. Kas got shot. And it's all my fault. The guy was trying to shoot me."

She sounds on the verge of tears, of breaking down completely.

"Hold it," I say. "Tell me exactly what happened."

"One of the alarms went off this morning. I went downstairs and there was this guy there. His face was a mess. Burned or something. He said my name like he knew me and pulled a gun. Then fucking Kas comes out of nowhere and tackles the guy. I'm still halfway across the shop, so by the time I get to them, Kas is shot and the guy's run away."

"Is he still there? I can get him to the hospital fast."

"No. Alessa called 911 and an ambulance took him away."

My gut tightens.

"Did you get a look at the ambulance crew?"

"What do you mean?"

"Like, did they seem legit? Were they weird or twitchy in any way?"

"No. They just seemed like regular EMTs. It's all my fault. Kas got shot trying to save me."

"First off, it's not your fault. Second, I'm going to make sure Kas is all right. Where did they say they were taking him?"

"L.A. County hospital."

"I'm heading over now."

"You think they might not have been legit guys? Oh shit. Did I give Kas to some freaks?"

"We'll know soon."

"Tell Kas I'm sorry!"

I step into a shadow and come out across town in Boyle Heights.

THE L.A. COUNTY hospital is huge and it takes me a few minutes to find the emergency room. Inside, it reminds me of the bad old days and the chaos of souls entering Hell for the first time—a deafening mix of animal screams, fury, and cries for help. I put on my mask and go inside.

The ER is packed with patients, nervous families, and staff. It's the usual mix of gunshots and knife wounds, but the craziness level goes way beyond that. Whole families have to hold down bloody patients with mangled faces—Shoggots in the making. Mixed in with them are patients with their hands and arms wrapped in crude bandages. Some are still gnawing on their wounds. More autophagia cases. Many of them have already gnawed off their own lips. Still, they snap at their limbs and any of the interns who try to put surgical masks over their faces. I don't know what else to do, so I get in line with all the civilians trying to talk to someone at the counter.

The line doesn't fucking move. I wait for five minutes. Then ten. After that I start running hoodoo tricks through my head. Murdering everyone is out of the question—Janet and Candy wouldn't approve. Can I make this crowd disappear? Yes, probably. Can I bring them all back? I have no idea, so maybe that's not a good option. Can I turn invisible? Again, maybe. But I still have no idea if I could make myself visible again. Phones are ringing all over the place, but none of them are getting answered, so I can't even call like a regular asshole.

I keep my eyes open for interns or staff who might be one of King Bullet's crazies, but I doubt I'll find any here. There are too many people and most of them are already scared. Where's the fun in terrifying people whose fear meter is already pegged as far as it will go?

After a couple more pointless minutes I get out of line and look for the youngest, most pissed-off, most exhausted intern I can find.

I spot her wrestling with a big guy who's already eaten one of his hands and probably his tongue, from the look of the blood coming out of his mouth. I run over to them and hold him down until a couple of linebacker-size orderlies come by and take over.

The intern brushes some blond hair from her face with the back of her hand. Her scrubs are soaked with sweat and her eyes are red with exhaustion. She's been working all night and will probably be stuck there all day too. I feel bad for her, but I feel worse for Kasabian.

Once she catches her breath she nods at me.

"Thank you. I couldn't have held him much longer."

I look at her name tag. "Maggie." Use it. Personalize things. It always helps.

"I'm glad I could help, Maggie. Maybe you can help me. I'm looking for someone."

"You'll have to speak to someone at the desk for that information."

"But you have access to a computer, right?"

"Yeah, but I can't just tell you where someone is."

"It's my brother, Maggie. He was shot."

"I'm really sorry, but—"

And then I do my best magic trick: I get between her and the rest of the room. Pull a wad of hundreds from my pocket. Shove the bills into her hand.

"Please. He's my brother. I'm very worried."

She looks from me to the bills and back to me again. I can see the conflict in her exhausted eyes. But this is L.A., and money is the magic that anyone can do and everyone here respects. It takes her almost a full minute to work it out in her brain. Finally, she makes a fist around the bills and shoves them in her pocket.

"What is his name?"

I tell her and she points me to the farthest corner of the waiting room. I go over and lean against the wall. I was right about her. She's basically honest, so she's not going to run off with my cash. But after a thousand-hour shift, her nerves are frayed enough that she needs something to break the tension. Since sleep is out of the question, what's left? Drugs? She's not the type. A quick sweaty fuck with another intern in one of the empty rooms? Maybe. But how many empty rooms are there these days? No, she needs a release and a little rebellion. And the thousand dollars she has in her pocket will do fine for now.

"I see you."

I look around for the owner of the voice and lock eyes with another baby Shoggot with a half-scarred face. He's in a straitjacket and is being held in place by two women. One older and one much younger. Family, probably. He leans forward and gives me his biggest, wildest grin.

"I see you," he says.

I start to say something back, but the women look terrified

of both him and me in my ratty coat and the scars around my eyes. I walk to the end of the line of chairs and wait there.

"That won't help," shouts the Shoggot. "*I see you.*"

I ignore the trussed-up Cary Grant, but I want a cigarette badly.

A couple of minutes later, Maggie comes back into the waiting room. She's changed her scrubs and tied back her hair. She waves me over and quick walks me down a corridor to a row of elevators.

"Room 312," she says.

"Thanks, Maggie," I say.

"I hope your brother pulls through all right," she says before disappearing back up front into the inferno of meat and crazies.

I GO UPSTAIRS, find room 312, and look inside—keeping one hand on the na'at.

And there's Kasabian asleep on his side. He has an IV in his arm and is hooked to some kind of *Star Trek* machine. There's a slim breathing tube under his nose. Other than that, he doesn't look like he's in bad shape. Getting shot wasn't lucky, but everything else that happened was. His EMTs were legit. I wonder how many of them are left?

My first impulse is to grab him and run, but I don't know what kind of shape he's really in. After him surviving a bullet I'd rather not murder him now. I go around to the head of the bed and look him over. He's breathing all right and there isn't any blood anywhere. I wonder where he got shot. While I'm there, Kas's eyes flutter open and he looks at me like he's not sure I'm really there.

"Stark?"

"It's me. How are you feeling, Bruce Lee?"

"I'm gone, man. To the moon and waving back at everyone. Can you see me?"

"I can see you. You're a fucking hero today. You saved Candy."

"I did? Oh yeah. She's okay?"

"She's fine. The guy who shot you ran away after you went all rodeo clown on him."

Kasabian bursts out with a drunken laugh.

"Rodeo clown. You're funny, Jimbo."

"You're high. But even high, you don't get to call me Jimbo."

"Jimbo. Jumbo. Jimboree. Jiminy Cricket," he says. Then looks at me excitedly and says, "Oh my god. Is that your secret? You're a bug in a suit?"

"Where'd you get shot?"

"In the shop."

"I know that. Where on your body did you get shot?"

Kasabian sings a couple of lines from "South of the Border."

"In the ass? You saved Candy with your fat ass? Of course you did."

"Say it."

"Say what?"

"Say thank you."

"Thank you."

"Damn. You did it, Jimbo. I wasn't sure you would."

"Maybe it's time for you to go back to sleep and rest your heroic backside. I'm going to sit over there while I figure out what to do with you."

"No. Say the other part."

"What?"

"Say thank you for saving Candy because you love her."

"Okay, you're done. Go back to sleep."

"Nope," he says. "Say it. I got shot. I'm a hero. Do it."

"I can't."

"It's just us, man."

"I can't."

Kasabian frowns, like his mom told him his puppy ran away.

"Wow. So you don't love her. I didn't know."

"Of course I love her. I always have."

He smiles and points a big, stupid finger at me.

"Yes! I knew it. Don't you feel better?"

"No."

"Oh right," he says. "Janet."

"You really need to shut up before I strangle you with your tube."

I sit down in a chair near the wall at the end of the bed.

"I love her too, you know," says Kasabian. "Candy, I mean."

"I know."

"You do? And you're not mad?"

"She's a lovable person. Why should I be mad?"

"You're a good friend, Jimbo."

"Not if you keep saying that."

"You gave me back my body and now it's all fucked up."

He puts up a hand to hide his face as he cries.

I go back to his bed and say, "It's not that bad. I've been hurt way worse. You'll be back on your feet in a couple of days."

Kasabian grabs my arm.

"Don't let the crazies kill me, okay? I don't want to die like this and have people make jokes."

"You're not going to die, Kas."

"You think?"

"I know."

"Okay." He lets go of my arm, then opens and closes his eyes a couple times. "These drugs are really good. I think I need to sleep for a while."

"I'll be right over there."

"You're a real pal, Jiminy Cricket."

Lying there high, he warbles his way through the beginning of "Over the Rainbow."

I say, "Wrong song, asshole. Jiminy sang 'When You Wish Upon a Star.'"

"Sing it to me."

"Fuck you."

"Be a pal."

"I'm not serenading you."

"Always with the negative waves," he says and falls asleep.

Feeling guilty, feeling scared, feeling incredibly uncomfortable after talking about Candy, I get out my phone and call Janet. What am I doing with myself? My life? They don't deserve this adolescent bullshit.

"Hi, baby. How are you feeling?"

"A little better," they say. "I'm feeling better and eating some of your lamb chops. I hope that's okay."

"Of course it is. Whatever I have is yours. You know that, right?"

"Are you okay? You sound weird."

"I'm fine. Sorry."

"Okay. Where are you? Fuck Hollywood and I were getting worried."

"Well, it is a little weird," I say. "Right now I'm on a chair in room 312 in the L.A. County fucking hospital watching Kasabian sleep because he got shot this morning."

"What? Is he okay?"

"He will be. But I don't want to leave him alone. Hospitals aren't safe these days. But he's hooked up to all of these machines. I don't know what to do."

"Want me to come over?"

"No. Your immune system is already fucked up and this place is full of sick loons. Besides, you're safe. I want you to stay that way."

"What can I do to help?"

"Just stay by the phone for now. If I think of anything clever, I'll call you later."

"Okay. Love you."

"Love you too."

They say, "Aww. You said it right away."

"What do you mean?"

"You usually hesitate a little. I know you're shy about emotions. It's okay. Sweet, even. I just like that you said it like that."

"Well, it's true."

"I love you too."

"Stay safe. Have some more lamb."

I have to get my shit together. Candy is gone. I shouldn't have said anything to Kasabian. Now the little prick has something to hold over me. Not that he'd say anything dumb.

Probably. This is what happens when you get in too deep with real people. Monsters are so much easier. I understand them. People will probably always be a mystery to me. And that includes me. And now I think I know what I want. Who I want. But it's all such a train wreck in my head. Sometimes it feels like everything I truly love gets snatched away. Because of Mason, I lost Alice when she died. Because of Audsley Ishii, I lost Candy when I died. What's worse is that Alice's death was partly my fault. If I hadn't gone to see Mason that night, he wouldn't have sent me Downtown and Alice wouldn't have been alone.

In a way, I suppose I can say the same thing about Audsley's killing me. I'd never gotten along with the guy, and never tried. I couldn't even keep my mouth shut around him. Then I got him fired from the Augur's security team. If I hadn't gone to see Mason, I wouldn't have lost Alice. If I hadn't goaded Audsley the way I did, I wouldn't have lost Candy. So it's not some vast *Wormwood*-style conspiracy. I'm at least partly responsible for everything and everyone I've lost. Am I going to lose Janet too? Maybe I deserve to be alone.

I watch Kasabian's machines blink, spew out numbers, and draw lines describing the shape of his life at this moment. It's strangely comforting seeing someone reduced to simple readouts, like running a diagnostic on a car. We should all be so lucky to have our lives read out and tuned up every now and then. Stop by for a soul lube and a heart rotation. Free hot dogs in the parking lot and balloons for the kids.

My mind just drifts for a while. Not focused on anything. Just replaying images of King Bullet's wretched graffiti and the man himself, just before he shot me. I don't hate him. I'm not afraid of him. I don't feel anything at all. Just the weight of his presence in my city. Who the fuck is he and where did he come from?

Are these even the right questions? What does it matter where he's from? Who he is? How do I kill him—that's what I need to know. I want to rip out his spine like I'd do to a High Plains Drifter, but would that stop him? I want to know before I get that much blood and gristle on my boots.

I go back to drifting. Candy. Janet. Back to Candy again. I hate my brain. I hate my mind.

When I look up, just over an hour has passed.

Someone knocks at the door and opens it halfway. I pull the Colt and cock it. Then someone—a woman—says my name.

"Jimmy?"

"Brigitte?"

She comes in and I put the Colt away. Her surgical mask is covered with laughing skulls. She stops to touch Kasabian and look at his machines. Then she comes over and hugs me.

"Janet sent me," she says. "They thought you might like some company."

Janet looking out for me. How can you not love that?

"It's good to see you," I say as she sits on the other chair.

"How is he?" she says, looking at Kasabian.

"He'll be fine. Sore as hell for a while, but fine."

"We should all be so lucky."

"True. Janet tells me that you're still waiting for a final Immigration interview."

She nods infinitesimally.

"It's true. I just want it to be over, one way or another. But with the virus, things just drag on."

"You know that if they send you away, I can bring you back and throw a glamour on you. No one will recognize you and you can have any life you want."

Brigitte looks away like she's contemplating that solution.

"Thank you," she says. "It's something to think about."

"But not what you want."

"No."

"Me neither. None of us want it for you. Brigitte—you, just the way you are—is pretty special."

"Thank you, Jimmy. You take good care of us all."

That's not true, of course. I spend half my life getting people into trouble and the other half getting them out of it.

"Speaking of taking care of people, I've been here for over an hour and no one has come to look at Kasabian. That's weird, right?"

"A bit. But things are so chaotic right now. I'm sure they're monitoring him somewhere."

"You're probably right. Still, it would be nice to see someone check his bandages or something."

"Would you like me to see if I can find someone?"

"Yeah. Why don't you do that? I'm going to stay here and guard Snow White."

"Is that why you had your gun out when I came in?"

"Shoggots are in the hospitals. The EMTs. The cops too. I don't trust anyone I don't know."

"I didn't know it was that bad."

"It's probably going to get worse."

Someone shoves the door open. Me and Brigitte both pull our guns. The nurse in the doorway just stands there with her hands up.

"Oh my," she says. "I seem to have interrupted something. I can come back later."

"No," I say. "We were wondering where someone was. Shouldn't you be checking on the patient?"

The nurse puts her hands down and glances at Kasabian.

"Can I do it without getting shot?"

We put away our guns.

"Sorry."

Gently, Brigitte says, "We were just concerned. Given the current unusual circumstances."

"I know exactly what you mean," says the nurse. She checks Kasabian's breathing tube and IV. Looks over the readouts on his machine, then makes some adjustments.

"Is he going to be okay?"

"He's going to be fine, Mr. Stark. We don't want him. We just wanted to get your attention."

Before I can ask how the hell she knows my name, the nurse pulls down her mask to reveal heavy facial scars. The edges of her lips have been sliced and the cuts curl into spirals on her lined and burned cheeks.

Me and Brigitte both have guns out again. I move around Kasabian, backing the nurse toward the door.

I say, "What do you people want?"

She cocks her head.

"Not us people. Just King Bullet. He'd like to come by for a drink."

"Are you fucking kidding me?"

"I'm not," she says and reaches into the pocket on her scrubs.

I move fast, knocking her back against the door and not letting her take her hand from her pocket.

"Get that hand out of the way," I say. "I'll take out whatever's there."

"Whatever you'd like, you nervous goose."

She stands perfectly still as I reach into her pocket and pull out an envelope. It's streaked with grime and a couple of bloody fingerprints. I step back so Brigitte can keep her gun on the nurse while I read the note in the envelope.

It's not long. Just a few words scribbled across a dirty sheet of paper:

THE PLEASURE OF YOUR PRESENCE IS
REQUESTED TONIGHT, MONSTER. 9 P.M.

The handwriting is a childish scrawl. The letters are jagged and boxy, like it was written by someone more used to holding a knife than a pen. The note is on cheap stationery from the Hollywood Hawaiian Hotel. I look at the nurse. She smiles as much as all her scars will permit.

I hold up the paper. "Meet him here?"

"You know where it is?" she says.

"I know."

I look at Kasabian.

"I'm taking him out of here."

"If that's what you want."

"He's going to need pain meds."

She reaches into her other pocket and tosses me a bottle of Norco tablets.

"These will help," she says. "Don't worry. They're not poison and they won't magically change him into a toad or anything. Like I said, he's not the one we want."

I say, "Get out. We'll handle things from here."

The nurse opens the door.

"Then I can tell him you're coming?"

"Hell yes," I say, without thinking about it.

Before she puts her mask back on, the nurse looks from Brigitte to comatose Kasabian and does a mild snort laugh.

"The King was right. You are predictable. And soft."

When she's gone, Brigitte and I put our guns away.

"What do we do now?" she says.

"Help me get him unhooked from these machines. I'll take him back to my place."

"I'll go with you."

"Thanks."

We grab some extra bandages from a cabinet in Kasabian's room and I take both him and Brigitte through a shadow into the apartment.

JANET AND FUCK Hollywood jump from the sofa when they see us, and Brigitte and I lay Kasabian down there. Quickly sussing out the situation, Fuck Hollywood tucks him in with her blanket.

"What happened?" says Janet. "Is he going to be all right?"

"I think so. But we have to keep him still. Probably the best way is to keep him stoned for a couple days at least." I give them the bottle of Norco. "This should help."

"Should we call Allegra?"

"I was thinking that too. She should bring some clothes, because she's staying."

"It's going to get really crowded in here."

"I know. Think of it like summer camp, only there're bears and flying monkeys in the trees so the counselors are making you stay inside."

"That's a shitty summer camp," says Fuck Hollywood.

"The worst."

"All right," says Janet. "We can move some of the furniture around."

"Thanks. I need everyone to stay put while I see the King tonight."

"Why would you do that?" says Fuck Hollywood anxiously. "He'll kill you."

"I wasn't ready the first time. I will be this time."

She sits in a chair in the corner of the room.

"I don't like it. Janet. Tell him."

They say, "I don't like it either. Why is it always you who has to do these things?"

"Because he asked for me. He almost killed Kasabian to get my attention last time. What will he do if I ignore him this time?"

Janet comes over and hugs me.

"I know that all makes sense, but I still don't want you to go."

"I don't either. If Abbot had done his damn job and killed the King I wouldn't have to. But he blew it. Now it's my mess to clean up."

"I'm going with you," says Brigitte.

I shake my head.

"There's no fucking way."

"You cannot go in there alone. You need someone to watch your back."

"Why? There's going to be fifty, a hundred of them. What's going to happen except that you get hurt too?"

"There is no argument. I'm going."

"Maybe you can help her," says Fuck Hollywood. "Get her some body armor or something."

"There," says Brigitte. "You can't say no now."

"I don't have anything like that here. I'm going to have to go out and steal it."

"There's about a million boarded-up stores. It won't be hard," say Fuck Hollywood.

I look at Janet.

"What do you think?"

They have their arms around themselves.

"I'd be less scared if Brigitte went with you."

"All right. I guess I just have to find a cop supply house."

"Found one," says Fuck Hollywood. She holds up her phone so I can see the screen. "There's one at La Brea and West Third. Uniform Professional Warehouse."

"There. The matter is settled," says Brigitte.

Janet says, "When are you meeting him?"

"Nine tonight."

"That will put you out after the curfew."

"I have no intention of either of us being out in the street. We'll shadow walk both ways."

No one says anything for a minute. Then Fuck Hollywood says, "I know it's early, but can we start drinking?"

"I wouldn't mind one," says Janet.

Brigitte nods.

"Me too."

It's unanimous. I take the bottle from my coat and set it on the table.

Fuck Hollywood frowns.

"Are you wearing my coat?"

"Yeah. I lost mine. Is that okay?"

"Just don't get it burned up or anything. I like that coat."

"I'll take care of it."

"And don't get any more blood on it. It has plenty."

"Got it."

I smile at her, but she looks scared.

Janet gets some glasses from the kitchen and hands them out. We pass around the bottle. After a couple rounds, I slip out to the cop supply house and come back with enough gear to outfit a small army. We spend an hour or so dressing up Brigitte like a Transformer until we come up with a combination of gear that protects her but lets her move too. Then we pass around the bottle until it's empty.

Janet takes me back into the bedroom and we lie down together. They hold on to me tight and I pull them close. We're both a little drunk and fall asleep for a while. I wake up a few hours later and go into the bathroom to call Abbot.

"This is a terrible idea," he says when I explain what I'm going to do.

"I know it is. So give me an alternative."

There's a pause.

"I don't have one."

"Then stop talking about it and tell me about the weapon. First, why didn't you tell me about it before? It could have solved everybody's problems."

"I don't have a lot of information about the weapon beyond the fact that it exists."

"Can you get it for me?"

"I'm working on it. But the Golden Vigil is still a thorny issue with the government. There are a lot of people who want it swept under the rug, so getting some of the old equipment out of lockdown is going to be tricky."

"You're the Council. You people *are* magic. Do something. Hoodoo someone and get them to sign whatever goddamn forms they have to sign."

"I keep telling you it doesn't work that way."

"Then what use are any of you? Assuming I survive tonight, don't call me again until you have the weapon."

I hang up on him. He calls me back a second later, but I let the call go to voicemail. Fuck Hollywood and Brigitte are watching a movie in the living room while Kasabian snores away on the sofa. I make some tea and bring it in to Janet, but they're asleep. I lie down with them and wait for night to fall.

THE HOLLYWOOD HAWAIIAN Hotel is a seventies tropical oasis at the corner of Yucca Street and Grace Avenue in North Hollywood. Dozens of discreet rooms and a big pool surrounded by lots of palm trees and ferns. Chaise longues and beach umbrellas everywhere on the concrete shoreline. It's a legend among the older rock and roll crowd for its bar and debauched parties.

But the place hasn't done so well since the virus hit. It pretty much shut down early in the epidemic. I don't know when or how King Bullet took it over, but his presence is obvious from a block away.

Me and Brigitte check out the Hawaiian from across the street. She's strapped into so much body armor she looks like a miniature Gundam. Most of the hotel's lounges and umbrellas are in the pool, along with an assortment of TVs and mattresses. An early-sixties Cadillac Eldorado is nose down in the water, its tail fins pointing skyward like some chrome and plastic Stonehenge.

There are Shoggots everywhere—on this street, sitting or lying facedown by the pool, either passed out or dead. A few look our way, but none seem very interested in us. I look at Brigitte.

"You ready for this?"

"Of course not. Are you?"

"Not even a little."

We walk over to the hotel to see what kind of reception we might get. Brigitte has her gun out and I have the na'at in my hand. But we don't need them. The Shoggots couldn't care less about us. Maybe they got the word that we were coming or they're just too far gone into virus psychosis to register us as real. Still, we move slowly and carefully, trying not to make a sound.

We pass the first group of Shoggots and make it past the pool. Then, me and Brigitte look at each other.

"Where to?" she asks.

"I have no idea. He didn't say."

"Lovely. I suppose he meant to disorient you."

"He's off to a good start. Come on. Let's take a look at the front office and see if there's anything in there."

The check-in area for the Hollywood Hawaiian looks like the rest of the place—like a bunch of deranged monkeys hopped up on meth systematically dismantled the place. There's a bloody body behind the counter. It's been stripped clean of everything but the surgical mask still on its face.

We're about to head out when Brigitte spots a map of the hotel on the wall. All the rooms look pretty much the same except for three: the bar, a conference room, and the bridal suite.

The bar seems like a good choice, so we head there first.

When we get there it's full of drunk and passed-out Shoggots, but no King Bullet. Another corpse is sprawled in one of the go-go dancer cages on the side of the little stage.

The conference room is an even bigger waste of time. Just a junkyard of smashed video equipment and broken tables and chairs. That leaves only one place where the King might be.

We hear the bridal suite before we see it. It sounds like New Year's Eve on fast-forward, complete with gunshots and screams. I take off my mask before we go inside. Brigitte understands why. We have to make an impression on King Bullet and he wouldn't respect me if we came in timid and masked up. To Brigitte's credit, she slips hers off too before we go inside.

No one even notices us when we come in. There's a party going on inside, and it looks like it's been going on for days. Maybe weeks.

To the right of the door is a large hot tub full of guns and ammo. A series of long tables ring the room. One is piled high with meat and cake and booze. On another table is a mountain of cash—bundled twenties, fifties, and hundreds. Another table is covered with prescription bottles. Hundreds of them. People help themselves to whatever they want. The truly jaded Shoggots don't bother with the bottles. They grab handfuls of mystery medicine from a fish tank at the end of the table, filled to the brim with a colorful assortment of pills, tabs, and gel caps.

The screams we heard from the hall come from a far corner of the room. It's a scarification station. New Shoggots or jaded ones who aren't quite Halloween ugly enough yet get their features done by what I guess are their equivalents of tattoo artists. Only they don't work with needles. I mean they do, but they also use scalpels, branding irons, dental tools, acid, and little saws. Some of the Shoggots gobble fistfuls of pain pills. Others grin through the agony, at one with their psycho ugliness.

In another corner of the room, a small Asian man in a dirty white apron is chained to the wall.

The bridal suite's heart-shaped bed stands on end at the far side of the room. They've been using it for target practice. Knives cover the front and it's full of bullet holes.

Someone is playing Skull Valley Sheep Kill's new album at full blast so that it almost shakes the walls, and it really pisses me off they like my music.

The place reeks of sweat and vinegar.

King Bullet is sitting at a table by himself, as quiet and still as the room is loud and chaotic. He has his skull mask on, as well as what looks like the bloody shirt of the check-in clerk. Surrounding him on the table are heaps of sushi along with his kpinga and his gold narco .45s. On a TV nearby, Julie Andrews sings about how the hills are alive with the sound of music.

When we reach his table, he looks from Julie to us. I sit down. He laughs.

"There he is. Mayor McCheese himself. And he brought a friend," says King Bullet. He gives Brigitte a little wave. "Hello, dear." She ignores him, keeping an eye on the room.

A sweaty creep in a sleeveless *My Favorite Martian* T-shirt comes over. The shirt is three or four sizes too small, so his hairy gut peeks out from underneath. He looks Brigitte over.

"I know you," says the creep. "You were in *Orgy of the Murder Girls*."

I wave my arm up and down to catch his eye.

"Be nice. She's a friend of mine."

He looks to King Bullet.

"What's-her-name here does porn."

"So what?" I say. "Everybody's got to pay the bills."

He looks at her again.

"She fucks like a fucking demon."

Brigitte just stares at him. When I start to get up King Bullet says, "Go have some pills, Monkey."

A few seconds pass and the creep wobbles away to the pill table, making jerkoff gestures as he goes.

The King picks up a piece of sushi and says, "Don't mind him. This uni has more brains than Monkey."

I look at him.

"Why don't you take that mask off?"

He sets the uni down and looks over the food.

"Maybe later. When you've earned it."

"Who are you?"

He laughs again, a little giddy this time. He's playing a game and we're in his house, so we have to go by his rules. The King chuckles one last time and looks at me, all innocence.

"Who am I? Just another small-town boy trying to make it big in Hollywood."

I shake my head.

"I think you peaked too early. Just another one-hit wonder. Why don't you go home?"

"Those other people didn't have a plan."

"And you do?"

"Don't you?"

"I'm more of a mellow 'California Dreamin'' kind of guy."

King Bullet laughs at that and pushes some sushi my way.

He says, "Let's start over. Have dinner with me."

Selecting a salmon roll, he pops it in his mouth. A second later he spits it out into his hand. Roots around the mess with a finger and pulls out a shard of glass.

"Now how did that get in there?" he says.

The King takes my plate away and holds it out in the direction of the man chained to the wall. He says, "Junji. Did you do that?"

The chained man nods.

"Of course."

"Why?"

"I made it for you."

The King rubs his hand clean on the plate and sets it on the table.

He says, "I admire your honesty and ambition."

With his clean hand he picks up one of the narco guns and pumps six shots into his sushi chef. Everybody but me and Brigitte laughs. Monkey steals Junji's *hachimaki* and puts it on his own greasy head.

With a sweep of his arm, King Bullet dumps all the food onto the floor.

He says, "I guess sushi is off. Monkey, why don't you take some money and get us dim sum?"

Monkey squints.

"What's dim sum?"

"You," I say. "You're dim sum, you fucking pork bun."

The King smiles and waves a hand at the comment.

He says to me, "You need to relax and unwind a little. Want Monkey to bring you some pills?"

By the aquarium, Monkey grabs a handful of random pills and stuffs them in his mouth and chews.

I look back at the King.

"I'll pass."

He smiles to himself.

"Before this is over, I'm going to suck the marrow from your bones."

I lean on the table.

"I bet you're the kind of guy who names his cock. Big Jim or maybe Krull."

King Bullet looks where I'm leaning.

"Do you miss your special arm?" he says.

"That Kissi thing? Why would I miss that?"

"It made you special. It raised you above the ordinary drones and yet you couldn't wait to get rid of it."

"They cut off my arm and gave me that Kissi thing as a joke. Would you want to carry around that memory and look at it every time you took a shower?"

"More than anything."

I notice that the Shoggots here aren't immune to autophagia. Scattered around the room, men and women gnaw on their hands and arms. No one pays them any attention.

"Why do you have such a thing for me?" I say.

Breathing in, the King giggles a little, having a grand time.

"I don't know," he says. "Maybe you remind me of someone. Maybe I just don't like your face."

"Let's see yours, Brad Pitt."

He takes a pack of Maledictions from his pocket and sets them on the table between us. I'm shocked, but I try not to show it.

I say, "Where did you get those?"

"The same place you get them."

"You're saying you can go Downtown?"

The King ignores the question and strikes a match.

"Would you like one?" he says.

I don't want to take anything from this prick, but I have to know if it's real. I take a cigarette from the pack and he lights me up. Then he lights one for himself.

Fuck me if this isn't a real Malediction. But I'm still not buying his story that he can Lindy Hop into Hell and back. He's got another angle. I just have to figure out what it is.

"Tell me something," he says. "What are you exactly? You used to kill monsters. What are you doing with nobodies like her?"

He nods to Brigitte.

"Careful. She's a friend."

Monkey comes over and sniffs her neck. She backhands him onto the floor.

"And that ridiculous thing in your bed," the King goes on. "Not a man or a woman. A freak. Admit it."

I look around, wondering how many people I'd have to kill to get out of here if I murdered King Bullet right now.

I say, "Don't even start that shit with me."

"How can you stick your cock in something like that?"

I'm fast when I want to be. Faster than these doped-up hyenas. I slip the black blade from my coat and shove it through the King's hand and into the table. When I take the knife out, I draw it through his hand, splitting his palm in two.

The King just grins. By the time I put the blade away, his hand is almost healed.

"Nice try," he says. "But you should have taken my head."

"If that's what you want. Hold still."

He laughs and claps his hands as if he's just thought of something.

"I'll make you a deal," says the King. "I'll leave you and your friends alone. I'll even leave L.A. You just have to do something for me."

"What's that?"

Serious now, he says, "I want you to admit what you are— and to make amends for it."

"Amends. That's an awfully big word for a fuckwit in a Halloween mask."

He points to me.

"But amends are what you owe. You owe your friends. L.A. The world. Me. You have to make things right."

"What amends do I owe you? What are you talking about?"

He puts his palms on the table and leans forward.

"I want you to get down on your knees and apologize."

"For what?"

"For everything. Do you think a tenth of what's happened the last few years would have happened without you? Your whole life, you've brought doom down on yourself over and over again. The world is just your collateral damage."

"I didn't bring you here."

"Yes, you did."

"How?"

"Wrong question. The right one is *why*."

"Okay. Why?"

"You'll know that when you've earned a look at my true face."

His hands are still on the table. I grab them and pull him across to me. He doesn't resist, just laughs as I haul his ass my way. A moment later, what feels like a ten-ton octopus lands on my back. It's all grasping hands and arms that squeeze the breath from me. As bad as this shit hurts, I know I can kill King Bullet before this Shoggot octopus crushes me. But when I hear Brigitte scream, I know that they have her too, and I didn't bring her along on a suicide run. I let go of the King and he waves a hand to get everybody off us.

He stands, brushing himself off, and says, "I told you to go for my head."

Getting up off the floor, I say, "Come outside. Just you and me. I know you want to show off for the Mickey Mouse Club."

"I have a better idea."

"No more ideas."

Laughing, he says, "I'm going to give you what you love most in the world."

"Roscoe's chicken and waffles?"

"To fight a battle you can't win."

"If you mean my battle with gingivitis, I know I should floss more."

He looks at Brigitte.

"I'm going to give you ten minutes to go anywhere you want. Within L.A. of course."

"Then what?"

"My Shoggots will hunt you, kill you, and bring me *your* head."

"How about a nice game of Stratego?"

"Nine and a half minutes."

"What if I just sit right here?"

"Then you get killed here. And the Shoggots not hunting you will kill all of your friends."

"Listen—"

"Nine minutes."

"If we make it 'til dawn you call your people off."

"Deal."

Monkey is still holding on to Brigitte's arm. He sniffs her.

"I can smell your pussy."

I start out and nod to her.

"Let's go."

She shoots Monkey in the face and follows me. I pull her into a shadow.

WE COME OUT in the Beverly Center, the upscale shopping utopia at the corner of Beverly Boulevard and La Cienega. Eight floors of the kind of consumer garbage that L.A. is famous for. Need a Ferrari jacket? Sure. You're a race car driver. *Vroom vroom.* Need silk designer socks that cost more than neurosurgery? We have that too. Come on down to the Beverly Center for something bright and shiny and leave feeling poorer, puzzled, and dead inside.

Brigitte looks around.

"Why are we here?"

"It's perfect. He'll never think of looking for us here."

"I think King Bullet is smarter than that."

"Fine. If we break this place, who cares? I hate malls. Don't you?"

"I never really thought about it."

"I mean look at this shit. Louis Vuitton, Victoria's Secret, Bath and Body Works, *and* a vitamin store? It's not bad enough that they spend the national budget on looking pretty, they want to live forever too. That's just hubris."

"You worry about the strangest things, Jimmy."

"I can't help it. A pair of Simone Perele thong panties took my lunch money in high school. It scarred me for life."

Brigitte shakes her head.

"Shouldn't we find somewhere to hide?"

I look at the million stores around us.

"Take your pick."

"Macy's is large. There will be more places to hide."

"That's a good idea. If we can get into the security office we can see if any Shoggots figured out where we went."

We go through another shadow into Macy's and wait for a moment to see if any motion sensors go off. When nothing happens, we prowl the edges of the store looking for the security office. Twenty minutes of this crap and I get bored. So I kneel down in the middle of the men's suits and carve runes into the floor with the black blade, while whispering some location hoodoo. A bright gold line traces itself in the air, wavering slightly like it's caught in a gentle breeze. It runs straight, then left, right, up a floor, and stops. Brigitte and I run along the path the spell laid out in the air, and find the security office a couple minutes later.

Not surprisingly, the place is empty. Maybe they're monitoring the store from a remote location. Maybe, in the wake of the epidemic, the rent-a-cops are dead or just don't give a damn anymore. Whatever the reason, the security office is empty. I turn on the cameras and Brigitte and I settle down to watch some quality TV.

I say, "I'm sorry I dragged you into this stupid game tonight."

"Don't be silly. This is exactly what I'm here for."

"Then thanks."

"You can thank me when this night is over."

We turn back to the monitors for a while. Here's the thing, though: even when you're running for your life, a bank of monitors showing you stationary shots of tuxedo mannequins, nonstick cookware, walls of shoes, fake antique furniture, silk sheets, and faux alligator handbags is boring. So goddamn boring that you'd rather have a Terminator take an angle grinder to your skull than watch for another minute. Luckily, Brigitte is more determined than me. While I wander away to check out the room, she stays by the monitors, keeping us safe from Shoggots and any rats that have made their way into the empty mall looking for gluten-free kale smoothie mix.

It's tempting to fire up the coffee maker, but there's time for that later when we're sure the Shoggots are off looking for us in the Hollywood Forever cemetery or the Roosevelt Hotel. I pull open desk drawers and break open storage cabinets. Finally, I come up with something useful.

"Merry Christmas to me."

Brigitte looks up from the monitors.

"What did you find? Candy bars or toys to play with? Please take this seriously."

"I am taking it seriously," I say and toss her one of the two Benelli shotguns from the cabinet, along with a box of shells. "The only ammo I can find is bird shot, but it's better than nothing."

"Why does a department store have shotguns?"

"This is L.A. Everyone is always expecting Ragnarok."

She smiles and loads her gun while I come back to the monitors with my own Benelli.

"Anything?"

"Nothing at all," Brigitte says. "Maybe you were right and King Bullet doesn't suspect."

"Maybe. But we need to stay here a lot longer to make sure. Dawn at least."

"I think you're right. Is there any food?"

"I'll look around. Maybe someone left something in the fridge."

In fact, someone did leave something there. A Tupperware container of something that had transformed over the last few weeks into a white fungus, like someone was trying to grow bunnies in the security office. There's some spoiled milk and half a can of flat Coke. But in the back, I get lucky and bring the box I found over to Brigitte.

"Protein bars."

She takes the box and selects a couple bars, then hands it back to me, saying, "You can have the rest."

I look them over.

"Wait. You took all the fruit ones. All that's left are nuts and twigs."

"Just like you. Some twigs, but mostly nuts."

"You're so funny."

"I'm the one watching the monitors. That should entitle me to first choice."

"Have you seen anything?"

"Nothing."

I unwrap some kind of gluten-free nut-and-complete-bullshit bar.

"See? I told you they wouldn't look here."

"Eat your food," she says. "You're not so pretty when you're smug."

One bite of the protein bar and I flip it end over end into a trash can. I get out my phone and call Janet.

When they pick up, I say, "Hi. I just wanted to let you know that things went great and me and Brigitte are fine."

"I'm so relieved. You don't know what I was going through. What we all were going through. When are you coming back?"

"It might be a while. Probably not before morning."

"Why that long?"

"It's nothing. Just some people are looking for us and I think if we can make it tonight we'll be all right."

"But you said that things were all right. Who's looking for you?"

"Some of King Bullet's knuckleheads. But they'll never find us."

"You always sound so sure and then bad things happen."

"Trust me."

I hear them take a breath and say, "How can I help?"

"Just take care of yourself and the others."

"Do whatever you have to, but come back. Okay?"

"I'm halfway home."

When I put the phone away Brigitte says, "How are they?"

"Nervous."

"You told Janet a very nice fairy tale."

"It's not a fairy tale. We're doing fine."

"For how much longer?"

She points to a screen showing an Apple store. A small group of Shoggots mill around outside.

"Shit."

"What do you think we should do?"

"Stay put for now. There're a hundred stores in the mall. They can't search everything in one night."

"I suppose it depends on how many Shoggots there are."

"Or how many are here."

Other monitors show more Shoggots all over the place. I start loading the Benelli.

"How did they find us here?"

Brigitte says, "I told you King Bullet was smart."

"Yeah? Where would you have hidden so he couldn't find you?"

"At the hotel, of course."

I look at her.

"That's actually a really good idea. Maybe we should go back?"

The screens show the lower floors filling up fast with Shoggots.

Brigitte says, "Maybe not now. If his people find nothing the King will become suspicious."

"You're right. We have to deal with these fuckers. At least for a while."

"There are a lot of them."

"Maybe we can break them up a little. Let's see."

When I get up, Brigitte says, "Where are you going?"

"Downstairs where they can see me."

"What good will that do?"

"I'm going to hop in and out of shadows. Maximum confusion. When I have them chasing their tails, I'll come back."

"Be careful. Janet will never forgive me if I let you get hurt."

I look over her shoulder at the monitors.

"Where's a good place to start, do you think?"

Brigitte points to a Kenzo store.

"There are no Shoggots at the store, but there's a group directly below."

"Perfect. Thanks."

I slip through a shadow and come out across the mall near the top of an escalator. There's a small mob of Shoggots at the bottom. Bracing the Benelli against my shoulder, I shout, "Up here, you ugly fucks." And then empty the shotgun into the crowd before stepping into another shadow.

I come out near a bakery on the first floor and pull the same gag with a group who are all staring up at where I was. Only this time they're all facing away, so I empty the Colt into their backs before letting them see me.

On the eighth floor I pop out near a UNIQLO, reload the shotgun, and fire below. Not even aiming at anything. Just letting the sound call the King's animals to me.

After that bit of fun, I head back to Brigitte.

"How did I do?"

She scans the screens.

"You certainly have them angry and confused."

"Want me to take you out for a round? It's a lot of fun."

She thinks for a minute.

"Maybe you were right before. Perhaps staying here is foolish."

"You want to go back to the hotel?"

"No. Not yet. But if we can convince the Shoggots that we're here, we could slip out to anywhere else in the city for a few hours."

"You mean bring them into Macy's? The place is a god-damn maze. They could run around looking for us all night."

"Exactly. Shall we try it?"

"Why not? It's better than sitting here."

We leave the security office and go to the store's mall entrance, which is currently covered by a huge gate that rolls up into the ceiling. I get out the Colt and we start shouting.

It doesn't take long to get the attention of a lot of Shoggots. I mean a lot of them. They pound on the gate and try to pry it up from where it's locked to the floor. Me and Brigitte back away, still shouting, but I'm not having quite as good a time as I was before.

Reloading the Colt, I look at her.

"Seeing them all together like that, there're a lot more of them than I thought."

"And who knows how many are out looking for us other places?"

"It really is an army. The King has all the crazies left in L.A."

"And who knows how many more will be transformed when infected with the virus?"

The gate starts to crumple. Not because they've pried open

the lock, but from the sheer weight of all the lunatics massed against it. I grab Brigitte's hand and we run. We keep going for two or three minutes, until it feels like we've run to Nebraska.

"Now?" Brigitte says.

"Now."

I dodge left and pull her into a shadow.

We come out by the escalators a couple of floors below. The sounds of the Shoggots screaming and tearing the upper mall apart echo off the smooth glass walls, filling the place with grunts, crashes, and shrieks.

There aren't a lot of shadows where we are so me and Brigitte run down the escalators heading for street level.

And right into another Shoggot mob.

How many recruits does King Bullet have? Is he giving away free toasters when you sign up?

I start blasting the closest Shoggots with the Benelli I reloaded upstairs. Bird shot won't kill you from a distance but a load of it into your face from close up will 100 percent fuck up your day.

Brigitte keeps the crazies off our backs, but we don't have much ammo and have to get out of here fast. When it's empty, I throw away the Benelli and get out the Colt. I empty that too, then bark some Hellion hoodoo to blast a hole in the remaining mob. We make it to ground level and I get out the na'at, swinging it like a steel whip through the windows. Glass rains down all around us as we run outside. I shout more hoodoo and the glass swirls into the air like a glittering twister, blasting itself into the mall and cutting the nearby Shoggots into kitty litter.

With the streetlights out, I still can't find any good shadows to jump through. But Brigitte spots an abandoned Prius up the street. How humiliating. Do I really want to get rescued by a hybrid? But I have a partner with me, so I get out the black blade and open the doors so we can jump in. Then jam the blade into the ignition. We get lucky and the little car fires right up.

We pull a one-eighty and head north, trying to get into Hollywood and back to the hotel. I try turning onto Rosewood Avenue, but the street is blocked by the cops and National Guard. I pull another one-eighty and head back up the street. But every street we cross, it's the same thing. Cop cars and National Guard personnel carriers. Every one of them on the street is armed with a long gun.

Finally, after driving up and down La Cienega, I'm about to tell Brigitte that we'll dump the car and go the rest of the way on foot. There are some lights in Hollywood and that means shadows to jump through.

At Fountain Avenue a goddamn whale on wheels shoots across us and I have to jerk the car hard to the right to keep from colliding with it.

It's an L.A. city bus. But the downtown buses don't run anymore. They haven't in weeks.

Before we can even get started again, the bus turns around, as clumsy as a listing barge, and charges back at us. I try to get a look at the driver, but I don't really have to. It's a fucking Shoggot and the bastard is looking to run us down.

We play dodge up and down Hollywood side streets for a while. Brigitte takes out her pistol and fires through the rear window at the bus. She hits the windshield, but not the driver. The crazy plows through parked cars, glass-walled bus shelters, and the front of some shops in its clumsy chase until the whole front end is a mass of pounded metal. But it doesn't stop. It stays on our tail and it will be there until it kills us or I can figure out something to do.

"Any ideas?" I say to Brigitte.

"If you could stop or slow down maybe I can jump from the car, get inside, and kill the fool behind the wheel."

"You are seriously not doing that. One mistake and you're a squashed bug. There has to be something else. I just need one good shadow."

"The only lights are by the barricades."

"Then that's where we have to go."

"They'll arrest us. If they don't shoot us first."

The bus makes a burst of speed and rear-ends us, sending the little Prius into a spin. I have to fight the damn thing to keep it from rolling. But I keep the car on its wheels and he takes off again. But we're dragging. Something happened to the rear end. The bus damaged the axle or the u-joint or something. I can't get up as much speed as before and the bus keeps gaining on us.

I give Brigitte a look.

"Maybe getting shot is the best thing that can happen right now."

"Explain that to me, please?"

"Trust me."

"I have no choice."

As the Shoggot bus bears down on us, ten tons of psychotic metal, I do a screaming turn north onto Hollywood Boulevard. The Guard and cops have the way blocked with heavy armor all the way across the street. Perfect. I jam the accelerator to the floor and keep it there. The bus falls back a little but is soon catching up with us, and the Prius is running rougher and rougher. It shakes likes we're stuck in a paint mixer. But there are lights ahead. Streetlights and halogen work lights on poles around the barricade.

Brigitte braces herself against the dashboard.

"Jimmy?"

"Any second now."

The guards along the barricade aren't dumb. They see a car and a bus bearing down on them and it's obvious that neither is going to stop. I can hear someone yammering some warning or other through a bullhorn, but are we listening? Hell no.

One more time I say "Trust me" to Brigitte and grab her hand. She squeezes it like she'll never let go.

We hit the area with streetlights just as the first pop-pop-pops start from the Guard troops firing at us and the bus. A shot hits the windshield between us, spiderwebbing it. But we've reached the lighted zone. A lovely fat shadow passes over the front seats. I drag Brigitte into it.

We come out a block behind the barricade line. The little Prius has enough momentum that it's still speeding toward the National Guard. But it's so shot up there's barely anything left of it. As it slows and almost stops, the bus plows into it, still rocketing forward as the guns blast big fat holes in it.

The Guard troops hold the line until the last second. As they scatter, the bus and Prius plow into the barricade of armored vehicles at top speed. The whole grinding mass explodes into a rolling fireball that boils into the sky, turning the boulevard pumpkin orange.

When we're out of sight of the Guard troops, I say, "I'm going on alone."

"But why? You might need help."

"There's enough craziness going on that if I get to the hotel soon, I don't think he'll be expecting me. But if I'm wrong, I need someone who knows what she's doing looking after Janet and everyone."

"All right. But I don't like it."

I shadow walk her to the apartment, but don't stay to chat. I then go back through the Room and come out down the block from the Hollywood Hawaiian. Even when I get closer there doesn't seem to be anyone outside. I step into another shadow and come out behind a palm tree by the pool.

There are a couple of especially ugly Shoggots by the hotel lobby. I want to do this quietly, so I slip out of a shadow inside with the na'at in my hand, forming it into a long blade, and skewer them both through the throat before they can make a sound. Dragging their bodies into the lobby, I spot a Shoggot sitting in one of the few chaise longues not in the pool. There's one more by the entrance to the bridal suite.

I throw the black blade at the one in the chaise longue and hit him right between the eyes. He falls onto the chair like he's gone to sleep. The Shoggot by the bridal suite doesn't seem to notice, so I retrieve the blade and duck into a shadow. Come out behind him and slit his throat, lowering his body to the ground gently so he doesn't make any noise.

Jumping into one last shadow, I come out behind the table

where King Bullet had been sitting. Lucky me, he's still there watching Julie Andrews. His phone rings a moment later, distracting him. I wait for the conversation to start.

"You're still at the Center? What? How many are hurt?"

While he yammers, I get ready to take what he suggested earlier—his head.

I manifest my Gladius and he takes the phone from his face. The glow of the blade is reflected into the phone's glass. Shit.

I swing the blade down as fast as I can, but he jumps out of the way and all I kill is his table.

He runs across the room and puts up his hands to blast me with black light. I duck it, tuck and roll under the boiling black mist, and come up right in front of him. Surprised, he takes a step back. This time he's not fast enough. I swing the Gladius up and take off his right hand halfway up the forearm. He shouts for his guard, but no one answers. Falling back against the wall, he hits me with the black light from his remaining hand.

The mist sucks me in, but with King Bullet injured it's not as powerful as the first time. Still, things scramble around me, all teeth and claws. I swing the Gladius, but there are too many to stop them all. A couple dig their claws into my stomach, trying to gut me like a trout. I bring the blade down and scare them off, but not before they rip me open enough that it makes my head swim. Shouting hoodoo and swinging the Gladius, I drag myself out of the black light.

King Bullet is slumped on the floor, bleeding. His mask is askew, but still on. I want to rip it off, but he has one of his narco pistols out and starts blasting. Holding my stomach wound closed, I throw myself into a shadow and come out in the hall outside my apartment. I can't get up right away, so I sit quietly catching my breath.

Well, I didn't get King Bullet's head, but I got a piece of him and that's something. It proves he's solid and human and that means he can be hurt. And killed. I want to go back and finish him off, but I can't quite get off the floor. I'll have to pencil in his murder for another day.

My phone rings and I take it out. It's Abbot. Thumbing it on, I say, "What?"

"Stark? Is that you?"

"Who else would it be."

"You just don't sound like yourself."

"I'm just having a little lie down. What's going on?"

"Did you have anything to do with the crash on Hollywood Boulevard tonight?"

"I don't know what you're talking about."

"The mayor and governor are going insane."

"L.A. is falling apart and they weren't insane before? It's nice to know they have priorities."

"Listen, that's not all I'm calling about. I have information on the Golden Vigil's weapon. The one we think can take down King Bullet."

I'm bleeding badly and I think whatever lives in the black light rearranged some of my organs.

"That's great, but this isn't really the best time to talk."

"When is a good time?" he says, sounding exasperated.

"Three days ago."

"Do you want the information or not?"

"Sure. Give it to me."

"All of the Vigil's equipment is in a special high-security hangar at Edwards Air Force Base."

"Swell. Can you get me inside?"

"There might be a problem with that."

"Isn't there always?"

"I thought that with your unusual talents you might be able to get in on your own."

Bleeding and in a world of pain, I can't help but smile.

"You bad man. You want me to break the law."

"No, I don't. I want you to help end this. But the Vigil is still under investigation and virtually no one can get inside. You going in on your own might be the only way to retrieve the weapon."

"Where is it?"

"I don't know, but I have an inventory number."

"Give it to me."

He does and I start to fade.

"Is that all?" I say.

"Are you all right? You sound terrible."

"I'm just sad that I'm out of Cheetos."

"Goddammit. Will you go in for the weapon?"

"Sure. But not tonight. Tonight, I have to rest."

"I knew that was you in the Hollywood crash."

"Good night, Abbot."

"Get the weapon soon."

I thumb off the phone and fumble around trying to get it into my pocket. Finally, when I can get to my feet, I stumble over to the apartment door and bang on it.

Allegra throws it open and sticks the Devil's Daisy in my face again.

"Didn't we already do this?" I say. But she shoves me out of the way and shoots into the hall. A couple of King Bullet's goons vaporize behind me. They must have been staking the place out.

"Thanks," I say before falling into Allegra's arms. I don't remember what happens after that.

I WAKE UP the next morning with Janet beside me. There's a long gash in my stomach but it's stitched closed. Thank you, Allegra. Janet stirs awake as I sit up. They kiss me on the cheek.

"How do you feel?"

I rub my stomach.

"All right. But I could use a cigarette and a drink."

"You can have coffee and a donut."

"Where did you get donuts?"

"There are other donut shops in L.A."

"That must have hurt."

"It did. But just a little. Everything is so crazy right now, I don't know what to expect next. At least you're safe."

I put an arm around them and we lie back down.

"What time is it?" I say.

"Just after one. Why? Do you have to be somewhere?"

"Not have to, but I want to. I had an idea while I was asleep."

"Unconscious. You were unconscious."

"I feel a lot better now."

They sit up, leaning on an elbow.

"I was so scared when you came in."

"I've been hurt a lot worse."

"I'm glad I wasn't around when that happened."

"Me too."

"Come and have some coffee."

I follow them into the crowded living room. Before I can even say hello, Brigitte wants to know what happened after she left. I tell everyone, but Brigitte is the only one who gets excited.

"You took his hand? You should have kept it as a souvenir."

"I wish I'd thought of it."

"Good for you," says Kasabian. "That asshole won't be bothering anyone for a while."

I scratch my ear.

"I wouldn't count on that. He heals fast too. And he's really going to be out for my blood after this. We hurt a lot of Shoggots last night, but we don't know how many he has left."

"What are you going to do?" says Allegra.

I don't answer right away because I don't want to have to tell them, but there's no way around it.

"I'm going to see someone who might be able to help."

"That's great news," says Janet. "I want to come with you. You need looking after."

I shake my head.

"You can't. None of you can."

"Why not?"

"I'm going to see the Dark Eternal."

"Who's that?"

"Vampires," says Brigitte, and I'm a bit surprised she doesn't spit on my floor.

"They can't hurt me, but the rest of you are lunch snacks to them."

"Are you sure they can't hurt you?" says Janet.

"My blood is toxic to vampires. And they know it. They won't lay a hand on me."

Janet gets up and goes back into the bedroom. I follow them in and find them lying down again.

I sit on the edge of the bed and they say, "I know you have to go see those people. The vampires. But this kind of thing is still new to me, you know. It's hard to deal with sometimes."

"I'm sorry. I know my life is a train wreck. I want to forget all of this kind of thing. Vampires. King Bullet. I want to be quiet. Be boring."

Janet sits up.

"Is that what I am to you? Somewhere boring you can play house?"

Goddamn my mouth. This is what happens when I try to be a person.

"That's not what I meant. I meant ordinary. Someone who isn't afraid to be ordinary or go into a grocery store."

Janet takes a breath and looks away.

"Being called ordinary isn't much better than being boring, but I'll take it for now."

"Look, I'm terrible at talking about these things. I've been a killer most of my life. Everything that isn't that is new and strange and hard."

Janet puts a hand on my arm.

"I know. It's new and hard for me too."

I lie down with them.

"Let's just stay here for a while. I can go out later."

They lay an arm across me, careful to avoid the stitches.

"I thought vampires were asleep during the day," Janet says.

"They're up all hours. They just can't go outside in daylight."

"I suppose garlic and crosses don't work either."

"Don't ever show a vampire a cross. They'll laugh in your face. And then tear open your throat."

"There's a lot to learn about your nonboring world."

"There's nothing boring about yours," I say.

We lie there together for a while, not talking. Half-dozing. My mind flashes to Candy for a moment. Another killer, I never had to explain anything to her. That was the ordinary world. Not this one I'm trying to learn to navigate. But I have to learn to love it or Janet will be gone the way Candy is. Then I really will be alone, and I'm not good at that. Even Kasabian doesn't need me anymore. Maybe I should just give up and get a goldfish. They don't need a lot of upkeep and they'd always be happy to see me when I show up with dinner. Maybe that's the quiet life I've really been looking for. Just me and a shiny dimwit in a little bowl watching movies until we each go belly-up. *Requiescat in pace.*

That's so depressing I almost want to laugh. Instead I get my PTSD pills.

Later, when I'm feeling more functional, I get out of bed and put on fresh clothes. Janet is asleep or just doesn't want to deal with me, so I leave them under the covers and go out through a bedroom shadow because I can't handle talking to anyone right now.

THE DARK ETERNAL used to be based out of a club in West Hollywood, but since the epidemic they took over a boutique movie theater and bar complex closer in on Sunset. They still have the same club atmosphere in the bar, but the theater lets them show old movies 24/7 to bored shroud eaters who can't go outside during daylight hours. Rumor is that they franchised the idea to other vampire clans in virus hot spots in the Valley and Glendale.

The front doors are blacked out and locked. I don't bother putting my mask on. Just go in through a shadow and stroll by a concession stand that looks more like a butcher shop than a place to get overpriced M&M's.

It takes the bouncers all of two seconds to realize I'm not one of them before I'm surrounded by heavy security. I put up my hands and open my coat to show them that I left my weapons back at the apartment.

"What do you want here?" says one, a huge beef cutlet with a Nick Fury eyepatch.

"I'm here to see Cole."

"Forget it. He's watching the movie."

"What are you showing?"

"Neill Blomkamp's *Alien 5*."

I frown.

"You can get that only at Max Overdrive. Does he have a membership?"

"Him and Kasabian have and understanding."

"So, it's like protection money."

The cutlet shrugs. "Call it what you want. Cole is tied up."

"Damn. I'd like to see that on a big screen. Do you think—?"

"I think you can leave before there's trouble."

I show meat mountain my throat.

"Why don't you go ahead and take a bite, big boy? Or don't you want to turn into minestrone soup?"

"No one's going to bite you, but that won't stop us from breaking every bone in your body."

There is that. "What if I told you I have Max Overdrive's only copy of *Danger: Diabolik* with Alain Delon as Diabolik? Would that get me a meeting with him?"

The beef cutlet looks at another mound of bloodsucker muscle. Cutlet number two nods. Nick Fury says, "Don't move," and goes into the theater, leaving me surrounded by a deli platter of seven-foot-tall luncheon meat.

I look at one and raise my arm to make a muscle.

"You lift, bro? I used to until I blew out my patty melt."

He squints at me. "A patty melt's a sandwich."

"I know. It shot right out of me while I was working my core. Hit another bro in the eye. The pickles blinded him. I still feel bad about it. And to this day, I haven't touched another patty melt."

"Why don't we make the lobby into a library and not talk for a while?"

"Why don't we."

"Everything about you is aggravating."

"Okay. But don't ever do dead lifts after eating chicken vindaloo. That stuff will go right through concrete."

"What did I *just* say?"

I hold up an imaginary key in front of my mouth and turn it, locking my lips shut.

A minute or so later, who comes out of the theater but Cole Sumner himself? He's only five foot six or so, but is supposed to be a major danger in a fight and smart as Mr. Peabody.

"Hello, Stark. I understand you have a movie I might want."

"I do," I say. "But more than that, I'm willing to make you an offer."

"What's that?"

"Partner with me to take down King Bullet."

Cole raises his eyebrows and the meat smorgasbord around us laughs.

"And why would we do that?" Cole says. "We already have an understanding with the King. He leaves us alone and we stay clear of him."

"Yeah, but think about it. The city has to be slim pickings right now with everyone locked in their apartments and no one on the streets but heavily armed cops and crazies. You partner with me and we take down the King, you'll have his entire Shoggot army to feed on."

Cole checks his watch.

"They've paused the movie for me, so I'm going to make this quick. I'm a man of my word. When I make a deal, I stick with it. And for your information, Shoggots aren't exactly prime meals for us. The virus in their blood ruins most of the nutrients we need, so why should we want more of them? And last, you're crazier than the King and I don't partner with crazies. So the answer is no."

This is exactly what I was afraid of. They think they have no stake in this fight. That King Bullet isn't going to come after them once he's done with the mortal population of the city. But I can tell that it's pointless to argue.

"I get it," I say. "You cut a sweet deal for you and your people. But you can't like that fucker. Is there anything you can tell me about him? Where's he from? What's his ultimate goal? Some kind of weakness?"

Cole is already walking away when he says, "There's no deal here for you, Stark. We're set up. Maybe you should check with the Dreamers. Those freaks will talk to anyone. But you better scoot. I hear the virus got a lot of them too. Happy hunting."

"Okay, but you're really missing out not seeing this *Danger: Diabolik*. There's a flying car."

He stops and looks at me.

"Diabolik has a flying car?"

"No. But wouldn't it be great if he did?"

"Give him some popcorn and throw him out, boys. I don't want to see you again, Stark, movie or not."

Samuel Jackson cutlet shoves a jumbo popcorn carton into my hands. He and the meat patrol frog walk me to the door and toss me out. The popcorn flies everywhere, but I manage to stay on my feet, leaving me with half a carton. So my life continues to suck but, hey, free popcorn. I'm already coming out ahead. In between bites I dial Abbot, but he's not there. I start making calls, trying to track down the remaining Dreamers. It takes a while, but I finally get an address. When I finish the popcorn, I steal a Mercedes and head down south to Compton.

THE DREAMERS USED to work out of a secret site in Hollywood—the power spot for most of the country's collective unconscious—but a year or so ago they moved to a new facility after their Hollywood home was destroyed by a quake that none of them even saw coming.

The Dreamers are reality stabilizers. Their thoughts and visualizations hold the fabric of our existence together. Without them, humanity's seething fears and desires could rip apart what we think of as the waking world. If Cole is right and the Dreamers are dying off, King Bullet might not be the only thing we have to worry about.

When I get near the Dreamers' new digs on Alondra Boulevard I dump the Mercedes in a mini-mall parking lot and go the rest of the way on foot. The building has an intercom system at the front door, but none of the buttons are labeled. I decide to push all of them, but before I can raise my hand the intercom crackles.

"You can't come in."

It's a female voice. Young. Very young. Like trick-or-treat young.

I look around and find a camera looking down at me from over the door.

"This is important. I'm James Stark. I helped you people once."

"I know who you are, but you still can't come in."

"Why not?"

"You're not wearing a mask."

I fumble around in my pocket and slip on She-Ra as fast as I can. Then I look up so the camera can get a good look at me. A moment later the door buzzes and unlocks. I go inside.

And find myself at the bottom of a long staircase. At the top is a girl. Maybe twelve years old. She's grown a lot since I last saw her, but I'd know her anywhere. Keitu Brown. The leader and most powerful member of the Dreamers.

"Hi, Keitu. Look how you've grown," I say, which is stupid because it's the last thing kids want to hear. I take a couple steps up the stairs, but Keitu holds up her hand.

"I'm sorry, Mr. Stark. No one but Dreamers gets inside anymore."

"So the virus really did get to your people?"

She nods.

"Badly. Most died. Some became—unstable. We can't afford to take any chances."

I'm down here looking up at a little girl with the weight of existence on her shoulders. Twelve years old going on forty.

"How many of you are left?" I say.

"I can't tell you. Things are unstable enough."

"It's that bad, is it?"

She nervously plays with a strand of her long brown hair and for a moment she looks her age. When she realizes what she's doing, she turns all business again.

"Things we might have prevented before—earthquakes and lightning strikes that lead to million-acre wildfires—get by us now. Understand, we're not helpless, but we're not what we once were."

"What about the virus? Did you let that in too?"

"I suppose you could say that, but not the way you mean."

"Then how?"

Keitu looks at her shoes.

"If you think King Bullet holds any ill will toward us you're wrong."

"That's not what I asked." But it's what I was thinking.

"I say that because he doesn't consider us a threat. We're too weak for him to bother with."

I look at her.

"What you mean is that like the quakes, you didn't see him or you couldn't stop him from coming."

She touches her hair again.

"I know what you want, Mr. Stark. You want us to fight him for you."

"Not for me. With me."

Shaking her head, she says, "That's not possible. We're too busy holding what's left of the city together. But I can give you information that might help."

"I'll take anything you have."

"King Bullet isn't a rogue angel. He isn't a demon or an escaped Hellion. We don't know exactly what he is. When we look where he should be, all we see is a void."

"Where did he come from?"

"We don't know."

"Did he cause the virus?"

"No. But he's the cause of it. It's not a spell or something he did. It's who he is. A pestilence. He came to Los Angeles, so the plague came with him."

"What would happen if he went away?"

"So would the virus."

For the first time in days, I don't feel helpless.

"Great. So all I have to do is get him to leave town."

When Keitu frowns it's not the face of a twelve-year-old girl. It's haggard and worn.

"He's unlikely to do that," she says. "He's here through a desperate desire. A deep hunger. Until he's fed, he won't ever leave."

"Then I'll either get him what he wants or I'll kill him."

"You'd be better off trying your first idea. We don't think killing him is an option."

I give Keitu a look.

"Kid, I've gotten rid of old gods. I can get rid of this creep."

"Good luck. I mean that sincerely. But I have to go now."

She starts to walk away, but I yell up to her. I hold up my hands to indicate the world outside the door.

"What happens to all of *that* when you're gone?"

"Then reality is on its own. Take care, Mr. Stark."

"Thanks."

I start out of the building.

"And, Mr. Stark?"

I look back up at her.

"Yeah?"

She smiles.

"I really like your mask."

"Yeah. She's a lot cooler than He-Man."

"Totally."

MY GUT STILL hurts enough that I'm not ready to take on the entire United States Air Force while looking for the Golden Vigil's superweapon. Instead, I detour back from Compton to Max Overdrive to fill in Candy and Alessa about Kasabian.

Too, I wouldn't mind seeing them. Well, one more than the other.

I come out of a shadow in the alley beside the shop, and all of a sudden, it's like when I first got back to the world in Hollywood Forever—the world is smoke and heat and I feel like I'm on fire.

I duck my head and run out of the alley and fall down on the sidewalk, my lungs full of smoke. When I look back where I was, I freeze for a moment. My brain can't accept what I'm seeing.

Max Overdrive is on fire.

Hell, it's more fire than shop now. All that's left is the front facade and part of the apartment where Candy and I used to live.

That's when I really panic. I run back as close to the building as I can and scream, "Candy!"

I'm trying to think of what fire protection hoodoo I know so I can go inside and look for her when someone yells my name. I look around and see Candy and Alessa crouched by the curb a few houses down. I run over and hug them both. Their faces are streaked with soot and Alessa's left hand is blackened and badly burned. I whisper one of the only pieces of healing hoodoo I can think of while my brain is screaming at me. A moment later, Alessa is able to move her fingers.

"Thank you," she says.

"Allegra can fix the rest," I tell her.

She nods and I realize I'm still holding on to Candy's arm. I let go, feeling ridiculous and awkward, but neither of them seems to notice because we're all looking back as Max Overdrive drifts away as smoke into the afternoon sky.

I say, "What happened?" pretty sure I know the answer already.

"I don't know exactly," says Alessa.

"We were upstairs when we heard a window break," Candy says. "When we went down, the whole first floor was burning. We jumped out of an upstairs window into the dumpster."

"I didn't think we were going to make it."

They hug and Alessa starts to cry. It's a strange thing to see. I always saw her as so solid and even hard at times, but here she is bawling away while Candy holds her.

I want to tell them that I know who did this and who will pay for it. I want to say the name King Bullet and tell them this is payback for taking his hand last night, but I can't. Everything they'd built over the last couple of years, including their home, is gone. I simply don't have the courage to tell them that this might be partly my fault. So, I keep my mouth shut about that and, instead, tell them that Kasabian is all right and at my place.

Candy looks at me.

"Kasabian isn't going to handle this well."

"He's flat on his back on my sofa. There's no reason he needs to know for a while."

I hear sirens in the distance heading this way. If it's the fire department, there's nothing left for them to save. And if it's the cops, fuck them. I'll just disappear. But it's neither of those.

A couple of ambulances round the corner and scream to a stop in front of Max Overdrive. I've had about enough of crazy ambulances at this point, so I reach in my belt for the

Colt—and remember that I left it back at the apartment when I went to see the Dark Eternal. I don't have the na'at or black blade either. By then it's too late.

Eight Shoggots pile out of the ambulances, running straight at us. Candy looks at me and gets what's happening. She shoves Alessa behind her and goes Jade. Between her and me, we might be able to handle all of these Shoggots long enough to get away.

But things are never that simple in L.A.

A low rider pulls up behind us, full of more Shoggot crazies. King Bullet is going for heavy payback and he's trying to make it very personal. And it looks like he's going to get his way, because even with Candy gone Jade and me with my Gladius, I don't know if we can hold off the sheer number of lunatics.

Then I remember something. Something I didn't need, but still have. I feel around in my pocket until I find Samael's pyx. Pull out the Host and bite it in half. As I manifest my Gladius, he appears across the street, behind the ambulance of Shoggots. Candy lets out a Jade howl and leaps at the closest crazies. I follow her right in. Across the street, Samael manifests his two Gladii and begins ripping his way into the mass of Shoggots.

They come at us with knives, axes, and guns. We take out the shooters first. Me and Samael aim for their arms and heads, while Candy goes for their throats. A tall Shoggot with a glass eye all askew comes down at my head with an ax. I split him in two with the Gladius and shove the ax into another Shoggot's head. Candy, all teeth and claws, disembowels a Shoggot who tried to get to Alessa. Samael . . .

the fucker must have massacred ten Shoggots by himself, all without breaking a sweat.

Between the three of us, we take down all the Shoggots just in time for the fire department. That usually means cops aren't far behind, so I grab everybody and drag them into a shadow.

We come out into the apartment, which is starting to get a little crowded. Still, everybody is safe and accounted for. Everybody except one. I call Carlos from the kitchen, but it takes him a while to answer.

When he finally picks up, I say, "Are you all right? Get away from the bar."

"I'm at the bar, man," he says. "Some crazy motherfucker in a truck tried to throw a Molotov cocktail through the window."

"Are you okay?"

"I'm fine. I shot his donkey ass and he took off out of here. What the fuck is going on?"

"I hurt King Bullet bad last night and now he's taking it out on everybody I know. He's already burned Max Overdrive."

"What? No."

"He might make another play for your place. You and Ray should come to the apartment. You'll be safe here."

"I don't know, man. I think I'd rather be here in case those pricks come back."

"If they come back, it's not going to be a guy in a truck. It's going to be an army with pitchforks and torches. Please. Get out of there."

"If you're so sure."

"You'll come to the apartment?"

"I hate hiding out. I'm not helpless. I know you have a plan. Let me help."

"You don't want to."

"Tell me what it is and I'll tell you if I want to."

"Me and Samael are going to break into Edwards Air Force Base."

"Yeah, I don't want to help with that. I'll get Ray and come over."

"Make it fast."

"Do you have any food in that dungeon of yours?"

"We have about ninety pizzas."

"That's what I thought. I'll bring some people food too."

"Thanks."

I go into the living room, where every piece of furniture is full, and Brigitte and Fuck Hollywood are sitting on the floor. They look a little like kids at the saddest birthday party in history. Samael leans against the wall and Allegra comes over to examine Alessa's hand. Candy sits down by Brigitte.

"Oh good. More people," says Kasabian. "Are you going to move in bunk beds or are we supposed to sleep hanging from the ceiling like bats?"

I go over to where he's sitting on the sofa.

"It's nice the way you have your arm propped on that pillow. You know, you're taking up enough room for two people."

He shifts in his seat, looking uncomfortable.

"I have an affliction."

"If it's too cozy here for you, I can take you to the Beverly Wilshire. I bet they have a lot of vacancies these days."

"Okay. Okay. You made your point," he says. "But seriously, are we supposed to camp out here like rats in the wall until the virus is gone?"

"No. Just until I get rid of King Bullet."

"How long is that going to take?"

"With Samael's help, it'll be a lot faster than before."

Samael raises his eyebrows slightly. "Oh good. Someone noticed I'm here. I feel so warm and welcome."

"Calm down," I say. "You're going to love what I have planned for you and me."

"What's that?"

"The stupidest thing I've ever done. We're going to break into a high-security military base and steal a weapon I know nothing about and hope we live long enough to use it on King Bullet."

He smiles and says, "I love everything about this. It really is a very stupid idea. When are we hatching this master plan of yours?"

"We'll go tonight. I can shadow walk us onto the base and into the bunker. Then we just have to find the right crate, hope it weighs less than a Camaro, and get out before the alarms go off and we have the entire base shooting at us."

"That would be nice. This is a new suit."

"You always have a new suit. I don't think I've ever seen you in the same suit twice."

"Of course you have. A couple of years ago. When I was in town working on a movie and you were my valet."

"*You* were a valet?" says Janet.

"No. I was his bodyguard."

"Still," says Samael. "I remember you fetching me clothes."

"I also stabbed you and left you for dead. Remember that?"

"Well, I didn't say you were a good valet."

"Stark?" says Fuck Hollywood. "Who's your hot and kind of scary friend? He doesn't exactly look like the kind of people you usually hang out with."

Samael crosses the room in two strides and holds out his hand to her. "Hello, my dear. I'm Samael."

"Hi. I'm—"

"Don't tell him your name," says Kasabian. "He's the Devil."

"He's what?"

I give Kasabian a look and tell Fuck Hollywood, "That's an exaggeration. He isn't the Devil."

"Not for years," says Samael. "In fact, our boy Stark here was old Nick more recently than I was."

She looks at me. "Stark?"

I pull Samael away from her, saying, "It's a long, dumb story. I wasn't Lucifer for very long at all."

Alessa looks up from where Allegra is bandaging her hand.

"Stark's the Devil?" she says. "That explains a lot of things." She frowns at Candy and says, "And you didn't think to tell me?"

I shout, "I'm not the Devil. I was—briefly—but only on a technicality."

"He's telling the truth," says Samael. "Hell was much more of a franchise operation in those days."

Alessa says, "I don't know if I'm comfortable here anymore."

Candy takes her good hand and says, "It's okay. Really. It's even a little funny. Right, Stark?"

I think back on the hundred days I was Lucifer and lie. "Yeah. Some of it. Sure."

"Tell us all about it," says Fuck Hollywood.

"It's a long story."

She looks out the window.

"It's the afternoon. You're not going anywhere until tonight."

"She has you there," says Janet.

"You're supposed to be on my side."

"I am. But it's crowded in here and we're all tired. I think we could do with a good yarn."

I can tell I'm cornered.

"Fine. I'll tell you."

Samael chuckles quietly to himself as Fuck Hollywood shouts, "Wait."

She opens a pizza box, takes out a cold slice, and looks at me.

"Begin."

AROUND TEN IN the evening, I steal a panel van and me and Samael take a bumpy ride ninety minutes north to Edwards Air Force Base. We leave the van about a mile away from the base and Samael does some location hoodoo to find the right hangar. It's not that he's better at that kind of thing than I am, but he's always more convincing about it, which is a little annoying. He comes up with an isolated hangar in the northeast part of the base. We put on glamours we hope make us look enough like air force personnel and I shadow walk us in as close to the hangar as I can without ever having seen the layout of the base.

I bring us out in the middle of a group of parked trucks so we can look around without being seen. It doesn't take long to spot the hangar. It doesn't look like much from the outside. No guards, but it's surrounded by a high fence topped with razor wire, along with a lot of warning signs. A *lot* of signs. Angry-looking signs. It's a good thing we're ignoring them or I'd be intimidated. But something occurs to me.

"I didn't think of it before, but aren't they going to have all kinds of alarms inside? Like thermal sensors or motion detectors?" I say. "I don't think I can hide us from that."

"Oh, I can do that," says Samael. "There's nothing to it."

"Really? How?"

"This isn't really the right time for thaumaturgy lessons, don't you think?"

"You're right. But you have to show me sometime."

"Certainly."

We sit there for a minute.

I say, "When are you going to do it?"

"It's already done. Stop dawdling and get us inside."

I take Samael's arm and shadow walk us into the hangar.

It's DARK INSIDE. Blacker-than-black dark. I get the feeling no one has been inside here for a long time. I whisper some hoodoo and a pool of pale light forms around us.

Samael looks around and says, "A lovely glow. And you didn't even blow anything up."

"I can do the subtle stuff. Sometimes."

"True, but why don't you leave that to me for the rest of the evening? I don't fancy ending up on fire when you mess it up."

"Fine. Be like that."

"I will and I am."

The hangar is monstrously large. Nearby are groups of armored vehicles, some with weapons mounted on them and some without. We're standing in long rows of enormous crates that could hold anything from smaller vehicles to a sleeping brontosaurus. In the distance are dozens of shelving units piled to the ceiling with smaller boxes.

We head out and I start checking serial numbers on the nearby crates. Right away it's bad news.

"Shit."

"What?"

"I was hoping everything would be in some kind of alpha-numeric order. But it looks like they just piled boxes wherever they would fit and stuck bar codes on them. There's probably some kind of manifest that shows how they're grouped, but we don't have it and this place is full of crap. We could look for a week and not find the right box."

"All right. Settle down," Samael says. "Let's use our heads, shall we? We're looking for a weapon, right?"

"Right."

"And presumably the Golden Vigil wouldn't send someone into one-on-one combat with a tank."

"That makes sense."

"So, what we're looking for is probably small enough to be carried by a single person."

"Keep going."

"With luck, what we're looking for is anything from the size of a pistol to a bazooka, which means it wouldn't be on the floor with all of these vehicles and large crates. It would be on those shelves with the smaller items."

I look around at the hundreds of gigantic crates around us and decide that Samael is right simply because the alternative is too damn depressing.

"I have no idea if your logic is military logic, but we can't stay in here until New Year's. Let's do it your way."

We head to the shelves. Unfortunately, the numbering system here is just as random as it was on the floor. This whole thing is starting to give me a headache and I want a cigarette, but I'm sure that would set off some kind of asshole alarm, so I just grind my teeth.

"Fuck me."

Samael says, "Calm down. Let's think this through."

I look over the shelves for a minute and say, "You're right. I know the crate number. Maybe I can just do location hoo-doo on that."

"No. I'll do it. We just discussed this. You stand looking dapper and I'll handle the real spellcasting. Now, what's the crate number?"

I tell him and he draws a circle in the dust on the floor with his finger. He fills it with a triangle and a square inside that. Around the edges, he draws numbers, runes, and a series of arcane symbols, some of which I don't recognize. I hate to admit that Samael knows this stuff better than me, but he really does.

A moment later a mote of light appears in the air. It hovers there silently at eye level before moving off down the rows of shelves. We follow it as it floats through the dark, a firefly I hope is going to save me from having to go hand-to-hand with King Bullet ever again.

We wander the rows for ten minutes or more. Long enough

that I start to wonder if Samael's Tinkerbell knows anything more than we do or if he's just putting on a show to impress me. But finally, after a few more minutes of wandering, it stops and rises into the air to a point two shelves above our heads. When it reaches that point, it simply hovers there like a dog who did a trick and expects a treat.

I grab a nearby ladder and drag it to where the mote is hanging in the air. Sure as hell, the little fucker found the crate. And it's no bigger than a rifle case, though it feels a lot heavier when I try to move it. The moment I touch the crate, the little mote winks out and I feel bad for ever doubting the little bastard. If I had its address I'd send it a fruit bouquet.

I'm feeling really good right now and even Samael is smiling. It's a little smug. Like he's pleased with himself for showing me how much better he is at the subtle stuff than me. But right now, I'm in no position or mood to argue the point. I haven't felt this relieved in a long time.

Naturally, that's when everything goes to shit.

All I can figure is that while Samael's hoodoo kept us hidden from the hangar's alarm system, it didn't extend to anything we touched. Maybe we pushed a secret button or broke an infrared beam, but it didn't occur to either of us that the individual crates themselves might be hooked to the alarm system. Whatever we did wrong, the response is immediate— and I see the smugness fade from his face.

An alarm that screeches like a freight train giving birth to a banshee echoes off the walls as every light in the hangar comes on. A second later, the front of the building opens and armed soldiers pour in, heading in our direction. Me and Samael grab the crate and run toward the hangar's far wall. I look around as we go. Each light overhead seems as bright as the noon sun, and the illumination intersects so that there aren't any dark areas, which means no shadows for us to jump through. I already know what Samael is thinking. He's a rebel and a warrior and he'd be just as happy turning around and fighting our way out of here. I, on the other hand, am tired of getting shot. And the grunts rushing in our direction are just some slobs doing their jobs. I'd feel bad about killing them. So we keep running while there isn't a damn shadow in sight.

Finally, we reach the back wall.

"Now might be a good time to get us out of here," Samael says.

"The shadows are no good. I need something darker. Maybe if we knock over one of these big shelving units."

"Or just move some damn crates. We don't need a shadow the size of the Colosseum. I'll hold off the guards."

"No killing!" I yell.

"You have one minute before I manifest a Gladius."

While Samael runs at the soldiers, I try to muscle some crates over to create a dark patch. The problem is that everything this far back in the hangar is the size of an Escalade or bigger. I can barely move any of them and I'm sure as hell not going to be ready for Samael's sixty-second warning. Instead of knocking over the crates, I manifest my Gladius and cut them into big sections, which fall onto the floor at all kinds of crazy angles. When there are six or eight big pieces of machinery piled up around me, I've created enough darkness that we can get out. It turns out that Samael had a similar idea. He used his Gladius to cut through the supports on several shelving units, toppling them like redwoods in the path of the soldiers. When I call his name, it only takes him a second to run back to me.

But a group of guards is right behind him and they open fire when they see the abstract art I've made out of their crates. As the shots tear into the walls and crates around us, Samael turns toward the guards and does the biggest show-boat move I've ever seen any angel or devil make.

He turns into a fucking dragon.

It's twenty or thirty feet tall. I mean, he doesn't really turn into an actual dragon, but he shifts his glamour to look like something out of a Sam Peckinpah version of an R-rated King Arthur movie. The shooting stops when the dragon appears, and the guards scatter in all directions when Samael belches a tsunami of white-hot fire at them. Before the guards start shooting again, I grab him and pull him into the shadow and back outside to the panel van. Wiping sweat off my forehead, I give him a look.

"Really? A dragon?"

"You didn't want anyone getting hurt. I was thinking outside the box."

"But a fucking dragon?"

He picks some lint off one of his lapels.

"Yes. Let them put *that* in their official reports."

"I guess we didn't kill anyone."

"Didn't even muss their hair."

I kick the crate at our feet.

"Let's get this home and see what this is."

"If we got the wrong box, I'm going back and burning the place down for real."

"I'll go with you."

I'm hot, I almost got shot, and I'm not looking forward to another ninety-minute drive in a van with shocks like concrete. So we ditch the van where it is and go home through a shadow. In a few minutes I'll know if Abbot gave me the right crate number or if I'm going to have to kick his ass to Neptune.

EVERYONE CROWDS AROUND us when we get back. Even Kasabian hauls himself up from the sofa to have a look. Janet puts the pizza boxes on the floor so I can set the crate on the coffee table. We don't have a crowbar and I don't want to chance using hoodoo to open the weapon, so I use the black blade to pry up the edges and tear the top off with my hands. Imagine everyone's surprise when what we find nestled in custom-shaped high-impact foam is what looks like plumbing supplies.

There're four sections. Two hollow pipes, each the length of my forearm. A metal cap that goes over something. And a smaller hollow pipe about the size of my hand.

"The plan is that you're going to fix King Bullet's toilet?" says Kasabian. "I feel safer already."

I look at Samael.

He shrugs and says, "It is a bit of a letdown, as far as doomsday weapons go. Don't you think?"

I pick up the long pipes and see notches at the ends where they probably fit together. Beyond that, none of what's in the crate makes any sense.

Allegra hands me a couple sheets of paper.

"Look at these. They fell out when you opened it."

The papers are covered in numbers and diagrams—assembly instructions for the doomsday plumbing. At the bottom of the crate I find a strap I missed earlier. Following the diagrams, we put the thing together quickly. Once it's done it looks sort of like a robot arm in a big-budget fifties science fiction movie. It would look perfect in *Forbidden Planet* or *This Island Earth*, just like most Vigil tech. I just have to hope that it works better than some I've seen in the past.

"How does it work?" says Janet.

I turn the instructions over. The last page is covered in long streams of numbers and letters.

"Great. It's in some kind of code."

"At least try it on," says Samael. "Get the feel of it. Maybe that will tell you something."

I slip the idiotic thing on. The smaller piece fits well over my hand, while the two longer pieces enclose most of my right arm. The rounded piece is an end cap that fits snug over my shoulder. The strap I missed earlier goes over my shoulder, securing everything in place.

When I stand up Fuck Hollywood sniggers.

"You look like Inspector Gadget."

I look around the room. "What do you think I should do from here?"

Kasabian points to a small ring attached to the hand that seems designed to slip over one finger.

"Try that maybe?"

I put my middle finger into the ring and a sudden jolt of static electricity shoots right through me. Hidden lights and strobing sensors hidden along the length of the doomsday plumbing come on and I can feel the damn thing vibrating with power. The ring stiffens against my hand.

"It's the trigger, I think."

"Turn it off," shouts Allegra.

Janet adds, "Yes, please."

I slip my finger out of the ring and the whole arm goes quiet. I'm quickly surrounded by half-smiles and nervous laughter.

"Go-go gadget, what the hell?" says Fuck Hollywood.

Samael claps a hand on my shoulder.

"Well done, old son. You didn't cock things up after all. I'm proud of you. A little nervous with that blunderbuss so close, but proud too."

I look at him.

"Want to take it out for a test drive? Kill some Shoggots?"

"That sounds delightful."

Janet comes over.

"Wait. You just got back. Do you have to go out again already?"

"King Bullet isn't taking the night off," I say. "The sooner we get him, the sooner this will be over."

"I understand that, but still—"

I steal a glance at Candy. She looks nervous too.

"Listen, I'll have Samael with me for backup. We've done this kind of thing before."

Janet doesn't seem convinced.

"Please just be careful and come back in one piece."

"I promise."

She nods, pressing her balled-up hands to her mouth.

I throw my coat over my shoulder to hide the pipes and look at Samael.

"Let's go fuck up some monsters."

"Let's."

WE GO THROUGH a shadow and come out across the street from the Hollywood Hawaiian Hotel, ready to bum-rush the place and kill everyone. But we're too late. The place has collapsed into ruins, engulfed in a huge fire. The whole neighborhood is burning. To the north, wildfires cover the foothills and the HOLLYWOOD sign has just burst into flames.

This is a big-boy tantrum. This is lashing out. This is someone not wanting to eat his vegetables and go to bed. This is someone cutting off his favorite hand so he's taking his ball and going home. The sheer petulance would make me laugh if Samael didn't point out that a huge section of Hollywood Boulevard is also on fire.

We shadow walk and come out on North La Brea Avenue. Everything from the Roosevelt Hotel to the Chinese Theatre to the Hollywood Wax Museum and the Egyptian Theatre blazes away. And the fires are moving east as a rolling riot of torch-wielding Shoggots runs wild on the street, setting ablaze everything in sight. At the front of the mob is King Bullet. He holds his kpinga in the air, where it sprouts flames like some kind of holy relic. What's worse is that he's holding it in his right hand. The hand I cut off. Either he got himself a nice, fast prosthetic or the fucker is a starfish and can grow back limbs. One more goddamn thing to worry about.

I don't know where the National Guard, the sheriffs, or the cops are, but it's sure as hell nowhere near here. King Bullet is going to murder all of Hollywood—*my home*—because he lost a brawl. I need to kill him right now. Maybe that will at least slow his Shoggots, and the Guard and whoever is left can take them down.

Me and Samael go through a shadow into the recessed doorway of a vape shop near the Musso & Frank Grill. I wish this doomsday plumbing was a sniper rifle. I don't like being on street level with the crazies, but I don't know the range of the weapon, so I'm going to have to get as close as possible to the King. As the mob reaches us, me and Samael put on glamours and join them.

There's no time to fuck around. We shove our way to the middle of the pack and start moving forward, closer and closer to the King. The crazies' screams are deafening and the stink of the burning buildings and cars gets caught in my throat so that I have to cough. It feels like the wildest parts of Downtown have finally come north to the streets of L.A. Welcome to my world, kids. The tension I felt when I realized what the King was doing fades as the procession begins to feel familiar. A Hellion fever dream. The instincts that got me through a thousand bouts in the arena kick in and I can't wait for the killing to start. I move up through the crowd, elbowing Shoggots this way and that. I don't even know where Samael is anymore. I don't care. My entire focus is on one man, one freak of nature, that I'm going to skin alive in front of his followers.

Then the slightest flicker of doubt pops into my head and I look at the weapon, hoping to hell it works.

Time to find out.

Finally, King Bullet is just ahead of me. He's put Junji's bullet-ridden chef's apron on over the hotel clerk's uniform. I'm so close now that I can almost touch him.

I shout, "Next time I'll take both hands."

He whirls around, slashing the burning kpinga down in a defensive arc. But I'm out of range. The King recognizes me through the glamour and the part of his face not covered by the mask twists in anger. He's about to call on his Shoggots to kill me, but he never gets the chance.

Samael utters some Hellion hoodoo and I feel a concussion all around me as he explodes the center of the mob, sending Shoggots, cars, and everything else nearby flying back onto the street. Then it's just me and King Bullet.

He puts out his hand to use his black light, but I get my finger through the weapon's trigger. Electricity bristles through me as it heats up and a ragged yellow light explodes from the weapon's handpiece straight into King Bullet's chest. It knocks him onto the ground and pushes him back several feet. I move with him to pour on the force. It takes only a second to turn the King into a flailing pyre. He rolls and crawls on the street, trying to get away from the light emitting from the weapon. His clothes burn away, leaving only his body and that goddamn bone mask. Soon, his skin begins to bubble and slowly roll off him like candle wax. In just a few seconds, he's utterly unrecognizable.

Still, the bastard is strong.

A burning, bony scarecrow now, he manages to get to his knees and raise his hands to hit me with the black light. Only Samael is already there and rips off King Bullet's bone mask. Then, to my surprise, he does something really stupid.

He just stands there for a few seconds and says, "Stark. Look!"

I don't know what I'm supposed to see other than burned

bacon with an attitude, but the moment of hesitation gives the King just enough time to shove the kpinga into Samael's side. As he falls, King Bullet opens up with the black light at Samael at point-blank range.

I try to grab him before the light hits, but he disappears in the boiling darkness. I expect him to fight his way out the way he did in a hundred battles during the war in Heaven, but he doesn't. There's just the light and Samael is gone. I pull the trigger on the Vigil weapon again and blast the King.

Finally, the light goes out and there's Samael in the street, covered in blood and the kpinga still in his side. I yank it out and toss it at King Bullet. But he's facedown, burning and not moving a muscle. I blast him one more time, but nothing changes.

Fuck it. He's done and not getting up. But I can't say the same thing for his Shoggots. They're coming around again, closing the circle around the three of us. I can't take them all on, especially with an injured Samael to protect. I take one more look at King Bullet—unmoving and sizzling away like a pork chop on the griddle. Then I pull Samael into a shadow and away from the crazies.

We come out in the Room of Thirteen Doors. The air is clear and cool and I take a deep breath before setting Samael down on the stone floor.

I've never seen him like this before. Burned and scarred. It looks like whatever lives in the black light went at him like a wood chipper, ripping his skin and breaking his bones. I roll him onto his back and he sputters a couple of times before trying to sit up. And failing.

"Where are we?" he says.

"The Room. Relax. You're safe here."

"Are you sure? I know you think it is yours alone, but what if you're wrong?"

"What are you talking about?"

"Is King Bullet dead?"

"Yes."

"Are you sure?"

"He was a goddamn charcoal briquette. Yeah, I'm sure."

Samael looks up at me.

"Yes, but did you take his head or his heart? I don't want to rain on your victory party, but until you see him in pieces you can't trust that you've done anything but piss him off further."

"I didn't exactly have time to give him a pat down. We were dying."

"Go back," says Samael. "Right now, while he's weak. Go back and take his head. His heart. His limbs. Obliterate him."

"I can't leave you."

"Do it. Do it now or all this will have been for nothing."

I look at him, his blood pooling behind him on the floor.

"You're sure about this?"

"Hurry."

I go back out to Hollywood Boulevard. And right back into the riot, only this time the National Guard is there, fighting Shoggots in the street. The air is full of tear gas and rubber bullets. Then the rifles open up and real bullets start whizzing by. I stay low, trying to be small and nonthreatening to both sides, until I can get back to where I left King Bullet's body.

Samael was right. There's nothing there but a scorch mark in the street. The vague outline of a body. A ragged line moves away from them. Maybe from the Shoggots dragging him away. Or maybe from the fucker crawling away on his own? Whatever happened, King Bullet's corpse isn't here now, but a shitload of trigger-happy cops and crazies are. I go back to the Room.

Samael is sitting with his back against the wall when I get there. I can tell he's in a lot of pain, but his ego wouldn't let him be seen on his back more than once. I've seen him hurt before, but never in such bad shape. He smiles when he sees me.

"He wasn't there, was he?" Samael says.

"No. He wasn't. But it's not like he just walked away. Some Shoggots took his body so the Guard or the cops wouldn't get it."

"You keep telling yourself that if it helps you sleep at night, but we both know it isn't true."

"You're giving this guy way too much credit. You should be his publicist."

Samael tries to stand, but his legs won't hold him.

"I can't help you now, Jimmy. You're on your own from here. I'm sorry."

"I'll take you to Allegra. She can help."

"It's all right," Samael says. "Just take me home."

I pick him up and go through the closest door, coming out in Mr. Muninn's palace in Heaven. Going by feel, I take Samael to what I remember is his room, and lay him on the bed. There's a phone on a bedside table. I grab it and dial 0. There's no response. I dial 911. Still nothing. I start pushing buttons at random, hoping for something. At least a damn dial tone. Finally, I hear laughter. It's Samael.

"If you'd beaten King Bullet the way you're beating that phone, this would all be over with by now."

"Who should I call? Give me a phone number or a room to go to."

"It's all right. Father knows I'm here."

"I'll wait with you."

"I'd prefer you didn't. It's likely to be a father-and-son moment."

I get up.

"Tell him—tell him I'm sorry."

"I'll tell him you're going to kill King Bullet and not cock it up this time."

"You're going to be all right?"

"Yes, but there was something I wanted to tell you. Something important. But I—"

I reach for him just as a frowning Mr. Muninn bursts into the room. He walks with a cane and when he sees me he doesn't say a word. Just holds up a hand.

And I come out on the floor of the Room of Thirteen Doors like someone kicked me off a moving train.

I stand there for a minute, as alone as I've ever felt in my life. Did I just watch Samael die? Did I just see the place where I lost King Bullet? Am I that much of a fuckup that right when I could have ended all this madness I didn't? At least I hurt the bastard, right? At least Samael is back with Mr. Muninn and the other angels. Those fuckers built the universe. They can fix a few scrapes and broken bones, right? Of course they can. Samael is home and safe and I have a job to do. I have to make sure King Bullet is 100 percent dead and if he isn't, to rip him apart with my bare hands.

This isn't a fight anymore. It's revenge, pure and simple.

I take off the Vigil weapon and when I drop it on the floor some of Samael's blood splashes onto my boots. There's a funny sound coming from somewhere. A soft electric tone echoes gently off the walls. I check my phone. Nothing. Then I look at the Vigil weapon. It begins to glow faintly.

Shit.

I dive out of the room and into the apartment just as the explosion hits.

EVERYBODY RUSHES ME at once with hugs and questions and I have to back away and shout "Stop!"

I sit down on a kitchen chair.

"Are you all right?" says Candy.

"Did you kill King Bullet?" says Kasabian.

I feel around in my pockets for a Malediction and say, "Can someone bring me a drink?"

Fuck Hollywood is there a moment later with a tumbler full almost to the top with bourbon. I take a sip and set it down. Light the cigarette. Think.

That's it then. I'm not just paranoid. The weapon was booby-trapped. I use it and solve the Council's problem with the King. Then it solves their problem with me. I wonder if Abbot knew. Fuck it. Of course he knew. He's the goddamn Augur. He had to know. And he gave me everything I needed to get the thing.

After seeing Samael go down, I feel double gut-punched. I mean, I was suspicious of the Council's games, but I didn't see Abbot pulling something like this. We're going to need to have a discussion soon. A little moment over this. Oh, yes, we are. But before that, there's a room full of my friends who want an adventure story.

What the hell am I supposed to tell them first? I'm sure not going to mention what happened with the weapon. Maybe something about how I might have possibly maybe killed King Bullet or how I most probably got Samael murdered. Allegra saves me the trouble of deciding.

"Stark," she says. "Where's Janet?"

"I don't know. Check the bedroom."

"They're not in the bedroom. You called and told them to meet you somewhere. Where? And why are you here?"

I get up and push through everybody, going to the bedroom, then pounding on the bathroom door before going in.

I go back to Allegra.

"How long ago did I call?"

She looks at me.

"It wasn't you, was it?"

"How long ago?"

"Just a little while. Four or five minutes ago."

I stand there like I did in the Room, feeling vacant and very alone. Janet could be four or five minutes dead now and I'm here helpless because I didn't finish things when I had the chance.

Candy says, "Stark. What's going on?"

I sit down on the sofa. My phone rings. It says it's Janet, but I know it's not.

"Where are you?"

"Nearby," says King Bullet.

"Is Janet alive?"

"Is that friend of yours I skewered?"

"Please don't hurt them."

He laughs.

"Them? They? Who are you talking about? I see only one dumb bitch. Is that who you're referring to?"

"Let me speak to Janet."

"I will if you say it for me."

"Say what?"

"That she's one dumb bitch."

"Never mind. Just tell me where you are and I'll come without weapons."

"Nope. I want to hear you say it first."

"I can't."

He sniggers.

"Then you can listen to me splatter the bitch's brains on the wall."

"Fine," I say. "She's one dumb bitch."

He laughs so loud I have to take the phone from my ear. Everybody in the room looks at me.

"There. I said it. Now where are they? Where's Janet?"

The laughter goes on and on. Finally, when it dies down a little I hear "Griffith Observatory. And don't bring that pop-gun of yours. It hurt."

I don't even wait for him to hang up. I jump through a shadow and come out in the park. Everything around me, every tree and bush in sight, is on fire. I go to the observatory's doors and push my way inside.

The atrium of the observatory has a circular railing around a pit in which swings a large eternally moving gold pendulum that lets you follow the movement of the Earth. Seeing it still working in the midst of all this madness isn't so much comforting as it is bizarre. Nothing here is normal. The world isn't revolving or circling the sun. It's unmoored and adrift in space. Who's in charge? No one. Don't look for any saviors around here. No pilots or train conductors. Most of all don't waste your breath on prayers. God's away on business and he's not returning calls at this time, but if you'd like to leave your number . . .

King Bullet is on the far side of the circular pit with a knife to Janet's throat. He's dressed in the scorched remains of the uniform he was wearing when I zapped him with the Vigil weapon.

His skin isn't burned so much as melted. Like a Ken doll after a kid tortured it in the garage with a hair-spray-can flamethrower. He smells worse than ever. His usual unwashed vinegar reek is there, but now it's perfumed with overheated flesh. Janet, with the blade to their throat, is wide-eyed with fear. Why did I ever agree to start seeing them? This isn't their life. The funny thing is that we got together because I saved their life a couple of years ago. Now it might all end because if I don't play this right, I'm going to get them killed.

I start around the room toward them, when King Bullet pulls Janet tight against him, pressing the knife harder against their throat. Even burned beyond recognition he seems to be having a good time. He laughs.

"That's close enough, lover boy."

I hold my hands out to show him that I'm not holding any weapons.

"You got me here. You don't need Janet anymore. Let them go."

He ducks his head behind Janet's, not because he's scared of me but because he's having a good time. Playing hide-and-seek.

"No. The bitch stays here. We have a lot to talk about, you and me. Some of it will interest her too. She should know who she's fucking."

I say, "Janet knows who I am. I haven't held anything back."

"Except that you're still in love with the other bitch. Candy is her name?"

"Is that what I'm here for? Junior high note passing? Do you like me? Check yes or no."

He giggles.

"You should be so lucky, Romeo. The problem is the bitch doesn't know who she's fucking because you don't even know yourself. You're pathetic and ignorant and you've wounded everyone around you so many times over. And you don't even know why. Worst of all—and this is the part that brought me here—you're lucky."

I don't say anything for a minute because I'm waiting for the punch line. When there isn't one I say, "Lucky? Me? You're holding the person I love hostage. How is that lucky?"

"Lies. You love the other one."

I ignore him and move slowly around the edge of the pendulum pit. He moves back with Janet at the same pace.

"Look at me," I say. "I'm fucking *ugly*. There isn't one inch of my body that isn't scarred. And I still dream about all the fights and wounds. Every night. I take fucking pills for it.

I've been dead and dragged across Hell and brought back to this world only to find it's gone on and it's better without me. How the fuck does any of that make me lucky?"

"Because it happened. Because of all of it," says King Bullet, only now he isn't grinning. "You move. You live and die and come back. You have lovers and enemies. You have a life. You have *something*, unlike others who have nothing."

"I have no idea what you're talking about."

"You will."

"Let Janet go."

"Say that again and I'll start tossing you pieces."

Janet is rigid. Tears run down their face, but they don't scream or fight back. Good. With luck, I'll get them out with just a case of PTSD as bad as mine. For me, it's time to fight back.

I take a step forward. Then another. I don't look at Janet, but keep my eyes on the creep with the knife.

I say, "King Bullet. Did you make that up? It looks good tagged on a restroom wall, but I bet the bank won't put it on your checks. Just who the fuck are you really?"

He ducks his head behind Janet's, then out again. He pushes them away from him, leaving his body open, then pulling them back, just daring me to attack. But I don't. It's too early for that. The fire outside won't hurt the observatory. We're safe in here and have all the time in the world.

"Well? Who are you?" I say again.

He laughs to himself and with his free hand takes off his mask. The face he reveals is handsome in an unremarkable way, but it bothers me because it looks vaguely familiar. When he speaks, he does it slowly.

"I am the lost. I am the seething. I am the filth God banished to the cesspool of creation. I am pestilence and revenge and the end of everything. And I will drag you to Armageddon with me because quick deaths are mercy and I have none in me."

I shrug.

"Nice words, but they don't answer the question."

With the tip of the blade, he digs into the skin around his neck, working something out of the soft, warped flesh. It's a thin, barbed silver necklace. Like someone took a length of razor wire and tried to turn it into a teen girl's prom-night present.

He says, "This belonged to my mother. My father gave it to her. He put it around her throat, and more lengths around her torso, arms, and legs. He bound her to a cross and placed her in the dark, so far away that no one would ever find her—in the farthest reaches of the chaos at the edge of the universe. And no one did find her for millions of years because she'd been shunned and no one was looking. Except for me. And when I found her, dead, desiccated, barely there at all, I took this burden from her and for the first time knew what I had been born to do."

"And what's that?"

He drops the necklace back against his skin.

"Kill you. But not before I make you suffer first. Not until I take away everything you love."

I stare at him, taking in everything he said. Trying to make sense of it. And I can't. There's nothing to do now but keep going.

"Look, I'm sorry about your mommy and daddy issues, but what do they have to do with me?"

He looks at me, then Janet. He gives them a quick kiss on the cheek and laughs.

"What was your father's name?" he says.

"What's that got to do with anything?"

"Tell me about your daddy."

"He was Garrison Stark. A salesman and an asshole."

"No," shouts King Bullet. He presses the knife into Janet hard enough to draw blood. "Your *real* father," he says.

I look at him. What does this fucker know about this?

"Fine," I say. "Uriel. An archangel. One of the guardians of the Earth."

King Bullet says, "And he fell in love with a pretty mortal girl and lay with her. Then nine months later, you slithered out of her belly with a little piece of Daddy's power."

"That's no secret. Lots of people know it. I'm a Nephilim."

"The only one. Alone in the whole lonely universe."

"Yeah."

"Wrong!" he shouts, and the sound bounces off the marble walls. "Behold another wretched Abomination. Doesn't it feel good to know you're not alone?"

This time there are tears in King Bullet's eyes too. I don't want to believe him, but I'm getting a very bad feeling he isn't lying. Maybe, if I'm lucky, he's just crazy. But his power. I can't ignore that. He has both hands again.

I say, "What the fuck are you talking about? Explain it all to me now or I'm going to take Janet away from you and rip you apart."

The King looks at me, calm again.

"Did it ever occur to you that if Daddy could fall in love once that he could fall in love a second time?"

I was afraid he was heading this way. But it doesn't make any sense.

"No. If there was another one of me here, I would know it. I would have met him or her long before you creeped into town."

"Not here, you idiot." He's shouting again. "My mother was loved and abandoned millions of years ago. Not on this stupid mortal rock, but in an infinitely older realm. The realm of the Kissi."

I look at him hard.

"You're saying my father fucked a Kissi and had a darling little baby and left them there?"

"No. He left *me*. But he imprisoned my mother. Because of his shame. These barbs I wear around my neck held her. But our father pricked his finger on them and left a drop of his blood there. That's why I'm stronger than you. That's why I can regrow a limb. That's why you can hurt me, but never kill me."

I was wrong earlier. This guy is nuts. He has a good story with a lot of cute little details, but it's complete bullshit.

I say, "That arm could be a prosthetic for all I know. If you're so powerful, why don't you regrow your face? You look like someone melted a candle on a baboon's ass."

"Look closer, you idiot. My mother was Kissi and so am I. But I'm part Uriel too."

My mind goes blank for a second. I can almost see something familiar under all the ugliness. But no. It isn't possible. It's just a clever con. It goes right to the soft spots of my family memories. My mortal father wanting me dead. Then almost knowing Uriel, only for him to get murdered by Mason Faim before that could truly happen. But what's the angle? What does this guy really want?

Something else occurs to me then. His smell. Kissi always reeked of vinegar. That's a weird detail to know about, even for a good con man. It's not like there are a lot of books on the Kissi in the library. They're practically unknown outside the celestial realms. But this still doesn't make sense. It can't be right.

King Bullet says, "I know what you're thinking."

"You don't know anything about me."

"You're thinking that what he says can't be true because there are no more Kissi. I killed them all."

"That's right. I did. I finished the last one Downtown and that was the end of it."

"But you didn't kill me. I wasn't there during your great betrayal with the Hellions. I was in the Kissi realm looking for my mother. And I found her at the bottom of the farthest westerly hills. Where there are no stars to light the way, and so she was hidden in darkness from all eyes. Including God's. I found her and here I am. Truly, the last Kissi."

My guts feel like someone has been working them over with a baseball bat. I don't want to believe a word of this, but just enough of it maybe makes sense that it's possible King Bullet isn't entirely full of shit.

I breathe another lungful of the vinegar. It's there and real.

Damn you, Mr. Muninn, for your half-baked universe. You made weak and stupid angels and they brought nothing but misery to humanity and maybe even the monsters who lived in the chaos at the ass end of the universe.

But I can't show that to the King. He wouldn't like me being weak.

"Okay, Norman Bates. You've had your fun with making me miserable. I mean mission fucking accomplished. What else do you want? You want me dead? I say fine. You and me. Right here and right now. You're stronger because you have our daddy's blood on the necklace? Prove it. I took your hand and I took your skin. Now I'll finally take your head."

King Bullet laughs and presses his face to Janet's cheek.

"Who do you bet on, sweetheart? Which of us was Daddy's favorite? Me?" He takes the knife from their throat and points to me. "Or that piece of shit?"

Janet doesn't wait. The moment he moves the knife away, they lean forward and dig their teeth into his wrist until they draw blood. King Bullet bares his teeth and stifles a grunt.

I sprint at him with the black blade in my hand.

The King elbows Janet back hard enough that they almost fall into the pendulum pit. He slashes at me with his knife when I'm close enough. He wants to fight, but I've won already because I don't. I'm just going to run away.

I angle around so that Janet is to my back. Thrusting forward with my knife hand, I grab Janet with my left and pull them to a shadow.

We almost make it.

I'm halfway into the shadow when King Bullet jumps on us. We both have hold of Janet and when he swings his knife I'm sure he's going to stab her. Instead he brings it down hard on my hand, which is holding Janet's arm. There's a second of blinding pain before I look down and see my left hand lying on the floor. Blood splatters onto my boots. Janet screams and rakes their nails down King Bullet's face. He still has hold of them, but it blinds him long enough for Janet to grab his barbed necklace and snap it off his neck. They throw it to me and push me the rest of the way into the shadow.

I come out in the observatory parking lot. The park burns around me. The smoke fills my lungs and I'm bleeding badly. My left arm is pressed against my body while I hold the black blade and broken chain in my right. I'm done, but I can't leave Janet. I take a few steps to a nearby shadow, cough, and fall on my face.

When I come to, the most beautiful woman I've ever seen is lowering me into the passenger seat of a silver Corvette convertible. My head swims and I can't focus on anything but her evening gown. She takes off a long silk scarf and wraps it around my wrist.

"You are the biggest mess, Stark. There. That should take care of that nasty arm of yours. But you got blood all over my nice leather seats."

I blink twice.

"Mustang Sally?"

"I was on my way out of town when who comes stumbling out of the dark right in front of me, but you. It must be kismet. Want to get out of here?"

"I can't. I have to go back for Janet."

I try to climb out of the car, but Sally—strong as any goddess of the road—shoves me back down.

"Not with that arm you're not. Now let's get out of here before you choke to death on smoke."

Sally revs the Corvette, does a donut in the parking lot, and rockets us down the hill.

There's a shot behind us. One. Then two more. Sally jerks forward, blood erupting from the side of her head.

The Corvette skids off the road and plunges down through the burning park. Flaming branches and hot stones pelt my face and arms. When the car hits the street below, Sally throws herself on top of me. We flip once, twice, and the Corvette comes to a stop resting on its twisted wheels. I have my good arm over my face.

"Sally?"

She isn't there. I crawl out onto the road and look around and under the car.

"Sally!"

She's gone. There's blood on the steering wheel, but all that's left of her is the silk scarf on my mangled hand.

"I'm sorry, Sally. I'm so sorry."

I hear shots coming from somewhere above. Bullets slam into the ground all around me. I don't have a choice but to dive into a shadow, a mangled fool leaving Janet and Sally behind.

STUMBLING. PANTING. BANGING off walls in the Room. I crack my head. I try to push off with the hand that isn't there and smash it into the stone wall. I want to throw up. I want to scream. I fall on the floor, dreaming or hallucinating. I don't know which.

King Bullet laughing. Janet crying. Flying down an endless hill of flame. A bloody Samael in bed. The burning hill seems endless. But I hit the ground, flipping over and over. Candy's face covered in soot outside Max Overdrive. Mustang Sally. There one minute. Gone the next. Glass-filled sushi. Then the burning hill again. Turning over and over. Rolling for a million years into a starless canyon surrounded by towering mountains. Then nothing.

I come to on the floor, cradling my mangled arm swaddled in a dead woman's scarf. The silk, or whatever crazy magic stuff it is, has stopped the bleeding. The funny thing is that I can still feel my hand. A phantom limb, I think they call it. The addled nerve endings twitch, sure they're moving fingers that aren't there. I felt this once before. When I lost my arm in a gladiator battle Downtown. I look at my right hand. There's King Bullet's necklace. The barbs have cut deeply into my palm, but I still have it. The necklace grew back the King's hand. I wonder if it will do the same for me? I put it in my pocket and hope for the best.

Janet and Sally. I lost them both in the span of, what, three or four minutes? But can you really kill Sally forever? A goddess of the road. *The* goddess, if you ask me. No, you can kill an incarnation, but you can't kill her. I think. I hope. I've never seen a goddess die. Not one I cared about. I don't have the rule book. Please don't be gone forever, Sally. I can't carry that kind of weight on my back.

But Janet is alive. That much I know. King Bullet wouldn't kill them yet. They're too useful a way to get to me, and that's what he wants. They're okay. As okay as you can be in the hands of a Kissi lunatic.

Kissi.

So, do I believe him now? He's not just another fruit bat, but the real, living, last Kissi and, like me, an Abomination? Nephilims don't grow on trees. I need to know for sure. Just as soon as I can walk. Can I walk? Am I walking now? No. I'm sure of that, at least. Maybe I'll just lie here for another thousand years until my hand grows back or I sprout horns. Whatever it is the necklace wants to do to me.

Stop it. Stop. I can't be like this. Janet is alive, but they're still in danger and I need answers. I can't pull myself up with one hand, so I brace my back against the wall and push myself upright using my legs.

There. One job accomplished. Now what?

Once I can stand upright and walk in a straight line, I go to the far side of the Room of Thirteen Doors. There, I lean against the last door. The Door to Nothing. I boarded it up after the last Kissi died, but now I need it again. With my good hand, I start ripping away the boards. It's hard work. Points to me for doing such bang-up carpentry.

After working for several minutes, I'm sweating and shaking. My phantom hand aches and the pain is getting distracting. I have to work faster than this. Taking a few steps back, I growl some Hellion hoodoo and the Door to Nothing explodes, showering the Room in splinters and shards of wood. A cold wind blows into the Room. It carries the faintest hint of vinegar—the last remnants of a dead race.

There's a deep darkness beyond the door. I take a breath and step inside.

THE KISSI REALM is cold as a deep freeze. I can see my breath as I walk. All around me are the insectlike husks of the few Kissi who escaped Hell and came back to die on their home turf. I'll give them credit. They were tough fuckers. Was I wrong to wipe them out? They'd tormented mortals for centuries, causing wars, pogroms, and plagues. They fed on mortal terror. No. They would have never let up. Never given humanity a moment's peace. In the end, I wasn't wrong to stop them. But that still doesn't mean I can't feel a little sympathy for what they were. God's first big mistake. Imperfect angels, banished to chaos forever. And then he and all the other angels pretended it never happened. That the Kissi never existed. That would put anyone in a bad mood.

I start walking west to a line of distant mountains. The riot of stars above me is a mess. A wild jumble of pinpoints, then vast dead holes of empty space between them. I'm light-headed, but I keep going. I have to know for sure.

King Bullet is a killer and a monster. But that doesn't necessarily make him a liar. What if what he said about me is true? Then I haven't just ruined my friends' lives, but maybe wounded the world too.

It all comes down to hubris. My ego. I was a stuck-up little shit when I was in the magic circle with Mason. The two of us were locked in a kind of Cain and Abel game of who was the best magician. Only Mason was the smart one and got rid of me in the best way possible, by sending me straight to Hell. The one place in the universe there was no coming back from. That one night changed everything. And it didn't have to happen. Alice, my old great love, told me not to go. But my ego wouldn't let me stay home. I knew that Mason had something special planned and I had to see it, just to prove that I could do something better later. Alice begged me, but I went anyway. And went to Hell. And then Alice died. Sure, she killed herself to keep Mason from killing her—her small fuck-you to him— but she didn't have to die at all. I caused that. I murdered her. Maybe like King Bullet said, I have to make amends.

The ground in the Kissi realm is cracked and littered with rocks and boulders. I trip frequently as I go. Each step and misstep jars my mangled wrist. The pain is starting to get to me. I whisper a little healing hoodoo. It doesn't actually fix anything, but it will keep the pain at bay for a while. I take the plastic bottle out of my pocket and have to hold it between my knees so that I can twist off the cap with my good hand and get out some PTSD pills—I don't bother to count. I dry swallow them, put the bottle away, and start walking again.

The only reason I'm Sandman Slim is that I went to see Mason that night. If I hadn't done that, I might have just spent the rest of my life with Alice. I would have been a drinker and a bit of a showoff who could do slick hoodoo with no effort whatsoever.

Would that have been such a bad life?

Instead, I went to see the circle. Then I went to Hell. If I hadn't fought in the arena, I wouldn't have become the monster who kills monsters. Eleven years later I wouldn't have escaped and gone looking for revenge. I wouldn't have fought Lucifer or become Lucifer. I wouldn't have fought the Angra Om Ya. I wouldn't have died and come back. And I wouldn't have killed an angel named Zadkiel and she wouldn't have released King Bullet.

The fucker is right. I have amends to make. A lot of Hallmark cards to send out.

To Whom It May Concern,
Sorry for everything. None of this was necessary. Please accept this Starbucks gift card as my way of making up for ruining the world.

Yours sincerely,
Sandman Slim

But it isn't just my fuckups that I have to make amends for. There's what Uriel and Mr. Muninn did. I had a life and King Bullet had nothing but torment.

Uriel, you asshole. In the end, you were no better than my mortal father. And now I have to clean up your mess.

And Mr. Muninn. Granddad. You're the worst of all. You made angels weak and then tried to hide the worst of them where no one would ever find your mistake. If you hated the Kissi so much, why didn't you just wipe them out? You caused floods and burned cities. Why didn't you clean up your biggest mess? Because you're weak too. A weak God—a caretaker, a janitor—making weak angels who made weak and stupid mortals. Why didn't you kill me? You had plenty of chances. Me being gone would have improved the lives of a lot of people. Maybe yours too. But I guess you needed me just enough to clean up some of the mess you made, so you let your Abomination off the hook. Thanks a bunch for that.

Finally, the stars go out and the sky is black. I manifest my Gladius and hold it up like a torch so I can keep going. How long have I been walking? How long was I unconscious? How many hours or days have passed back home? It doesn't matter now. I'm in too deep. I have to know.

Eventually, I come to a wall of mountains. There's nowhere farther to go. I'm as far west as I can get, staring at a sheer rock wall with no openings and no markings. I hold the Gladius up high and look around. The light is bright, but it doesn't extend far enough into the dead dark that surrounds me. I bark some Hellion and a fiery ring appears above me, like a twenty-foot halo. I expand it farther and start down into a deep valley at the base of the mountains. If I was going to hide a body, this is where I'd do it.

At the bottom of the canyon, something glitters. Tiny sparks in this black world. I run down toward it, tripping over stones and slamming my knees into rocks. I can't help myself.

And there it is. A cross made of the same smooth stone as the whole Kissi realm. I move closer to it until I can clearly make out the lengths of barbed silver chain used to secure *something* to the high cross bars. I can't say for sure if it's King Bullet's mom or not. The body is too far gone. But it's where he said it would be. And it looks the way he described. Like I said, he might be a monster, but it doesn't necessarily make him a liar.

I sit down on a boulder for a moment to catch my breath.

So, King Bullet was telling the truth. We're both Abominations and maybe I'm the worst of us. I almost feel sorry for the bastard. I definitely feel sorry for his mother. Betrayed by Uriel and abandoned by the other Kissi for taking an angel for a lover. It must have been a cold and lonely death. And it couldn't have been fast. I'm sorry, Ms. Bullet. If I'd been around and known what my father was up to, I would have tried to stop him. But here's the thing. I can't let your kid—my half brother—get away with what he's doing any more than I could have let Uriel off the hook. I feel sorry for your son. Hell, I feel sorry for all of us. But I'm still going to kill him. Because, like the rest of you Kissi, he isn't going to stop. Even if he kills me that isn't going to stop him. It isn't the hubris talking this time. It's the understanding of a simple reality: that I'm the only one who can do it. It's absolutely my job. Maybe more than that. Maybe it's me making amends.

I whisper some hoodoo and a few ragged roses sprout from some nearby rocks. I pull them up and lay them at the base of Ms. Bullet's cross.

I let the flaming halo that lit my way in the valley go out as I head back the way I came. I know what I need to do, but I have a few questions. And there's only one person I trust to give me the answers.

I GO BACK through the room and come out again by the Devil's Door Drive-In. I don't know how long I was in the Kissi realm, but it's night in L.A. Normally, there would be a line of cars bumper to bumper waiting to get in for the night's double feature. But those days are over, at least for now. The Devil's Door is as locked down and dark as any tomb in the graveyard. Still, that doesn't mean there's no one home.

But before I can go inside, my phone rings. I'm so clumsy one-handed that it takes me a minute to answer the damn thing. But I finally manage it. Again, the caller says Janet, but King Bullet's voice comes out of the speaker.

"I've been calling. Where were you?"

"Paying a call on Mom dearest. She sends her best, but says you never visit. I think you ought to go see her and consider staying."

"If you've seen my mother then you know I was telling the truth."

"So what? You think that changes anything? I'm sorry you had a shitty childhood. Mine wasn't *Leave It to Beaver* either. But I don't go around shitting on the world. You want to feel better? Get yourself some pills and a shrink. Now let me speak to Janet."

"You might want to modulate your tone while I have a gun to her head."

He's right. I'm letting my anger get the better of me.

"Okay. I'm calm. See? Don't take this out on Janet. But if you want to make a deal or something, I have to know they're still alive."

"Sure. Sure," he says. "But I want you to apologize first for being rude."

The anger burns in my throat like bile, but I keep my voice calm.

"I'm so sorry. Please forgive my earlier rudeness."

"That sounded pretty sarcastic. Try again."

I have to take a few breaths and really get ahold of myself. Finally, I say, "I'm sorry."

"What was that? A big, strapping lad like you shouldn't sound so much like a mouse. Now apologize like you mean it or I'm going to hurt the bitch."

"I'm sorry," I shout. "Please don't hurt them. I'm sorry."

There's a long pause.

I say, "Hello? Are you still there?"

"I'm here," he says. "I'm just savoring the moment. How's the hand, by the way? I have it if you want it back. Well, I don't. Your little bunny has it. She doesn't like holding it, but I told her that if she drops it, I'll hurt her. That's fair, don't you think?"

Another breath before I speak. Because King Bullet isn't the only one with an angle.

"I still have your mom's charm bracelet and I know why you called. You want to make a trade."

"Of course I do. But it's not that simple."

"What else do you want?"

"I told you earlier. I want you to make amends."

"How?"

"I want you to come to the trade not as Sandman Slim, with your big balls and your Downtown magic. I want you to come to me as a penitent."

I try to figure out what that means.

"I don't get it. What is it you want?"

"Figure it out. You have twelve hours."

"Not until I speak to Janet."

I hear some noise on the other end of the line. Then breathing. Then Janet says, "Stark? Are you okay?"

"Don't worry about me. Did he hurt you?"

"Not yet."

"Hang on, baby. I'm on my way."

But it's King Bullet who answers.

"You cheap liar. You're not on your way anywhere. You have work to do. Amends to make and twelve hours to do it in."

"I still don't understand what you want."

But it's no use. The line goes dead.

I stand by the side of the road as a line of armored vehicles speeds past, on their way to—or from—a skirmish or maybe it's just lunchtime. Maybe they'll even stand a chance tonight with King Bullet out of the picture. Good luck putting down whatever gaggle of Shoggots are still out there stealing candy from babies. I find a nice shadow and go into the Devil's Door and then an office behind the concession stand. I knock on the door and Flicker opens it. She's wearing a surgical mask and has a .38 in her hand. She relaxes when she sees it's me.

"Fuck me, Stark. I thought you were one of the nutjobs running up and down Sunset. What are you doing here?" Then she looks at me closer. "Oh shit. What happened to your hand?"

"Can I come inside? I've been walking for hours and I'm a little worn out."

She steps from the door and I go inside. She sets the gun down on her desk while I drop onto her battered sofa. Flicker looks sympathetic, but she gets a surgical mask from her desk and tosses it to me.

"Nothing personal, but put that on."

I hold up my mangled hand.

"I can't."

She says, "Don't breathe," and comes over to loop the sides of the mask over my ears. "Okay. You can breathe again. Why don't you start off by telling me what happened to your hand? I mean, I have some herbs and potions that can help if it hurts, but that's about it."

Flicker is a powerful magician. A geomancer. Her power is in the Earth. She can manipulate it and speak to it. She answers to the King Below, a powerful earth spirit who saved my ass in Little Cairo a few months ago.

"I'm okay," I tell her. "I just need to rest a little."

"At least tell me how you lost it and why you have a ladies' scarf around the stump."

"The scarf belongs to a friend. How I lost it is to the lunatic who's been behind all the chaos in the city these past few weeks. He's even responsible for the virus. And he has Janet. I have to stop him. I have to kill him."

"How can I help?"

I get the necklace and toss it to her.

"What can you tell me about this?"

Flicker holds it up to the light and smiles at it.

"Wow," she says. "It isn't from this world."

"I knew that much. What else can you tell me?"

She balls it up in her fist.

"It's practically screaming with power. There's a lot of potential magic in this baby."

"Good hoodoo or bad?"

"It's pure power. It'll go wherever you want to take it."

I think for a minute.

"King Bullet says there's angel on it. He says it makes him more powerful than me."

"So that's what it is. I knew there was something special beyond the metal itself."

I lean forward hopefully.

"It healed him when I took his hand. It grew back in a night."

She looks at me and shakes her head.

"If that's what you're hoping for, don't waste your time. This wasn't made for mortals."

"I'm not mortal."

"This wasn't made for anything you are. I'm sorry."

I drop back against the sofa.

"Fuck."

Flicker turns the necklace over in her hands. Sniffs it. Listens to it, smiling often. But when she looks at me, her smile is gone.

"You are one *tulled* son of a bitch, Stark."

"What the hell does that mean?"

"You're caught between two worlds and you're not at home in either."

Now I smile.

"I'm just another black lane walker."

"Yeah. But a good one. You're not exactly lost. You just lack direction."

I sit up again.

"Not anymore. King Bullet has Janet."

Flicker frowns.

"I'm sorry, but if you think this is going to get them back for you, you're wrong."

"That's okay," I say, thinking things through. "He said it made him stronger than me and that I couldn't kill him as long as he had it. Well, I have it now and that makes us equal."

Flicker hands the necklace back and I put it in my pocket.

"Then what's the problem? Why don't you go out and *bam*?"

She holds up her fists like a boxer and throws a right cross.

"The problem is he wants something else, and I don't know what it is. I should know. He wouldn't have told me to do it if I couldn't. But, for the life of me, I can't figure it out and I only have twelve hours to do what he wants."

"What did he say?"

"He wants me to make amends. He wants me to come to him as a penitent."

She thinks for a minute and shakes her head.

"Yeah. That is a puzzler. But I have something that might help."

From a filing cabinet she takes out a pint bottle of something with a cork on top sealed in wax. She brings it back to me.

"Try this. It's a wine I brew from honeysuckle flowers growing on a killer's grave. It's potent stuff. It brings you visions. It can help answer your deepest questions."

I take it from her and put it in my pocket.

"Can I drink it here?"

"Oh no. You have to go to your power spot to do it. And it probably wouldn't hurt to have the King Below on your side anyway. He misses you."

I hold up my good hand.

"I don't have any offerings."

Flicker opens a bag on her desk and takes out an avocado sandwich and a cup of tea.

"It's a small offering, but I don't think you have time to scrounge up anything better."

She gives me the bag.

"Now take this to your power spot. Do you know where that is?"

I laugh a little.

"Yeah. There's only one place in L.A. that qualifies for that."

"Then go there fast. The wine can take some time to work. Hurry."

Flicker takes my head in her hands and kisses me on the forehead.

"Good luck, Stark."

"What was the kiss for?"

"I don't know if we're going to see each other again."

"What do you mean? Are you going somewhere?"

She opens her office door.

"Go to your power spot. Drink the wine. And good luck."

I head out and she closes the door behind me.

I don't know if we're going to see each other again.

I don't like the sound of that. If Flicker is in trouble too, I'll come back to help her right after I rescue Janet.

I step through a shadow to my power spot. The one place in the world that's called me back time and time again.

Hollywood Forever cemetery.

AT THIS HOUR, the place is deserted. I sit by the lake, put Flicker's bag and bottle on the ground beside me, and take out a Malediction. I spark it up and just sit there for a minute wondering where I might go that I won't see Flicker again. But I can't figure it out. But why should I? I can't figure anything out these days. That's why I'm here. I take a few more deadly puffs of the Malediction before flicking it end over end into the lake.

Another moment and I start digging with my good hand. I pull up grass and clods of earth until I get down a good six inches into the graveyard dirt. Then I put in the avocado sandwich. Bread and vegetables. Products of the earth. I pour in the tea, more earth produce. After that, I shovel the dirt back over the hole and pack it down, feeling slightly foolish.

"Hi, King Below. You helped me once. If you can still hear me, I could use a little help again. I'm fighting another king and I don't know what to do. I'm lost. If you're there, help me see the way."

I lean back against a marble grave marker—a tall angel holding a sword to the sky. A moment later, the ground rumbles. An earthquake. But a mild one. Still, it's enough to unsettle the grave I'm leaning on. The angel topples and shatters. The sword flips once in the air and buries itself in the ground beside me.

I guess someone heard me. The sword didn't skewer my leg or cut off my head, so I'm taking it as a sign that King Below approved of the offering and is maybe on my side. I'm glad someone is.

There's only one thing left to do now. I get the wine bottle and rip the cork out with my teeth. Down the whole bottle in a few gulps. Then I lie down on the warm grass to see what's going to happen.

The wine hits me like a freight train. Quickly, I'm dizzy enough to be glad I'm already on the ground. There's no way I could stand with this brew in my belly. I fight the feeling of losing control for a few seconds, then let go. This is what I'm here for. Let the flower from a killer's grave show me what I'm meant to see.

I close my eyes and just drift.

What I'm ready for is a psychedelic acid trip, but I get the opposite. Instead of expanding out in a million directions, the wine anchors me to the ground, digs deep into the soil, and holds me there. My consciousness doesn't expand. It narrows to a single point of flickering light, a fire of greens and blues. I feel the grass roots around me. Hear the insects in the grass and under the soil and moving around me. I might as well be a goddamn tree. A hippie earth child worshipping at the altar of the ancient thing I've become. Hundreds of years old, I've seen generations come and go. My wisdom is slow, but it's deep. Humans come and go like mayflies around me. Over time I've come to understand the desires and fears of the lost souls flitting around me. And my vison becomes even tighter until I'm a pinpoint. Maybe an atom. A mote of light. But something bright and focused.

My stomach convulses and I roll over, vomiting up the honeysuckle flower wine into the grass. When I'm done, I wipe my mouth with my hand and splash lake water onto my face. I'm back. Not in the earth, but on it. When I look up, I can see stars above the half-lit city.

I grab the stone sword and pull myself onto my feet.

Thanks, King Below. Thanks, whatever nameless killer whose grave the flowers came from. I'm back. Not a mote of light, but me again. And I know exactly what I have to do.

First, I take out my phone and dial Abbot. It rings a few times before he picks it up.

"Hello?" he says, like maybe he's talking to a ghost. "Stark?"

"You missed, motherfucker. I'm still alive. And I'm coming to see you."

"Stark. No. You don't understand. I didn't know—"

I thumb the phone off. Let him call the Council. Let him call the troops. There's nothing he can do to me now. I know who he is. But that reckoning is for later.

EVERYONE IS ASLEEP when I get back to the apartment. They're sacked out on chairs and squeezed together on the sofa. Fuck Hollywood is curled up like a small animal on the floor. I shrug off the coat I borrowed and cover her with it, returning it to its rightful owner.

Allegra is in a chair by the bedroom. I put my hand over her mouth. When she startles awake, I put a finger to my lips and she nods in understanding.

I lean in close and whisper, "I need you to come with me to your clinic."

"Are you hurt?"

"We can talk about it there."

She gets her medical bag and we go out through a shadow. The last things I see as we leave are Fuck Hollywood's wide, bright eyes watching us from the floor. I give her a small wave and she waves back.

Allegra turns on all the clinic lights and we go into the exam room. I've kept my mangled arm behind my back up until now, but let it drop to my side. She takes a step back when she sees it.

"Goddammit, Stark. Why didn't you tell me? Get on the exam table."

"It's fine. The hand isn't why we're here."

She pushes me back to the table.

"I don't care why you're here. I'm here for this, so shut up and lie down."

I do what Allegra says, and she carefully unwraps Mustang Sally's scarf. When she starts to throw it away, I say, "No. I want that."

Allegra frowns as I take it from her, but then her attention goes right back to examining my left arm.

"What happened here?" she says.

"King Bullet took it."

"How long ago?"

"I don't know. A few hours."

Allegra stands back and shakes her head.

"It's healed. The wrist is completely healed. The skin is perfect. No signs of infection at all."

Thank you, Sally. You always were too good to me.

"Great. Now that we have that out of the way, can we talk about why I brought you here?"

"Of course," she says lightly, but she crosses her arms, suspicious of why I wanted to talk here of all places.

I sit up on the table.

"King Bullet has Janet."

"Oh shit. That's why we're here? How can I help?"

I want to blurt it out, but I don't. I understand Allegra enough to know I need to bring her with me on this. Slow, but wise.

"I'm sorry that I'm always asking you for help and favors. But I promise. This is the last one ever."

"Don't be silly. We're friends. It's what we do. Now tell me. What do you need?"

"King Bullet is going to call back in a few hours and I have to be ready for him."

"Ready how?"

"I want Janet from him, but he wants something from me. I didn't know what until a little while ago. But now I do and I need your help getting ready."

"Do you have any other wounds you want me to look at?"

"No. It's nothing like that. You're not going to like the favor I want."

"Let me be the judge of that."

"If there was any other way, I wouldn't have come to you."

"Stark," Allegra shouts. "Just tell me."

I look at her, hating myself for what I'm going to say.

"I want you to make me into a Shoggot."

Allegra tightens her arms across her chest. She looks away. Frowns. When she turns back to me, she says, "You can't ask me to do something like that. It's disgusting. I won't."

I get up from the table.

"I understand. I thought you might say that. And it's all right. But it still has to be done."

She takes a couple of steps back and leans on a counter.

"Why?" she says.

"He wants me to humble myself. Come as a penitent for my sins, my father's, and even my grandfather's."

"Stark. No."

"It's the only way to get Janet."

She looks around the room.

"I've seen your magic," she says. "I've seen you work miracles. You came back from the dead. There has to be something else you can do."

"There isn't."

"What about a glamour? You're always making yourself handsome. Make yourself ugly."

I gently move her away from the counter and start taking her surgical tools from a drawer.

"He can see right through my glamours. If I'm going to save Janet, I'm going to have to do this for real."

She watches as I pile the bright metal blades on the counter.

"Do you even know what half of those are for?"

"They're sharp. That's all I need."

She shoves me away.

"And you're going to perform this transformation with one hand?"

"If I have to."

"Stop it," she says.

"I can't."

She shoves me hard and I stumble back into the exam table. There are tears in her eyes.

Allegra says, "Just park your ass there for a minute. I need to think."

"Okay."

After a while I'm sorry I gave Fuck Hollywood her coat back. I left the Maledictions in the pocket. Not that Allegra would let me smoke in here. Still, it would be comforting to hold and smell one.

From the corner of the room Allegra says, "What do you want me to do?"

I look at her. She seems shaky, but I can't wait around forever.

"First, take off my ears."

She puts a hand to her face and for a second, I think she's going to start crying again. Finally, she takes the hand away and says, "Listen. You heal quickly, but if I take your ears off, I don't think they're going to just grow back."

"I know. It's all right."

She tilts her head slightly and looks at me hard.

"You're not planning on coming back, are you?"

"I don't know."

"Yes, you do. You want me to do this and you're just going to leave me here without even Vidocq to cry to. You're going to leave us all."

I get up and go to her.

"I promise you. If I can come back, I will."

Now she does start to cry.

"I can't do this."

"King Bullet is going to kill Janet. Then he's going to destroy everything else connected to me. Including you."

She shakes her head.

"There has to be another way."

I'm seeing and thinking clearer than I have in a long time. "There isn't another way."

Tears stream down Allegra's face.

"I can't."

I push her into a nearby chair.

I say, "It's okay. Just show me where there's some Novocain or something to dull the pain and I'll do it myself."

She sits there, just crying and looking at me. In a minute she gets up and pushes me away from her tools.

"Stop it," she says. "You're going to fuck it all up."

"Then you'll help me?"

"Sit down on the table. And hush."

A few minutes later she comes to me with a syringe. She injects something into the skin around each ear.

"Let me know when it's numb."

No one talks while she arranges her tools.

A couple of minutes later I say, "I'm ready."

She comes to me without hesitation. There's a bowl with

scalpels and shears. She sets towels on each side of me and pulls on nitrile gloves.

"Are you ready?" Allegra says.

"Yes."

And she begins the work.

I can't see anything, but I can hear every slice into the skin. Every snip of the shears where she cuts away the cartilage at the base of my lobes. I feel blood running down the sides of my face and onto my neck. Allegra wipes me clean with the towels. A lot of towels. I didn't think ears would bleed this much.

Finally, after what feels like an hour she says, "It's done."

I touch the sides of my head. They're smooth except for some tiny ridges of cartilage around my ear canals.

Allegra sets the bowl on the counter and draws a long breath.

"Now what?" she says.

"My cheeks and forehead. I need scars."

"You have scars."

"You know what I mean. Something nasty. Something ritualistic. What do you have that will burn me?"

She stares into space.

"I have a few potions that might do it. Not that you're supposed to use them that way."

"Get them. Then we're going to work on my lips and teeth."

"What about your teeth?"

"You have drills, don't you? Dental drills?"

"Sure."

"You're going to drill off the edges of my teeth. Make them sharp like shark teeth."

She sits back down in the chair.

"Cut you. Burn you. Drill you. What will you want after that?"

"Remember this is for Janet. You want them back too, don't you?"

"Of course."

"Then please keep going."

Allegra drags herself out of the chair and goes through her cabinets.

"I'm going to need some things. And you're going to need a lot more painkillers."

"Yes, please."

IF I WAS a real Shoggot, my transformation would be a lot more brutal and take maybe an hour. But what Allegra does, with all her care and knowledge, takes most of the rest of the night.

When her sink is full of tools and towels and my blood she says, "I'm done. I can't do any more."

She sinks back down into the chair, her head in her hands.

I go to a large chrome paper-towel dispenser and look at myself.

"Look at me. Hello, Dr. Phibes."

Allegra says, "Is it everything you hoped for?"

"And more. Thank you. Ow."

I bite my tongue with my new pointy front teeth.

Allegra shrugs and looks at her watch.

"I'm numb," she says. "I may never feel anything again."

"You'll be okay. Do you have any bandages to wrap up in? I don't want to scare any kids or dogs."

She gets some from a cabinet and mummifies my head.

I say, "Thanks. Let me help you clean up the place."

She holds up a hand.

"Leave it. I'll clean it up tomorrow."

"Let me take you back to the apartment. You'll be safe there."

Nodding a little, Allegra says, "Sure. I could use a drink."

"Then let's get you liquored up."

She looks at me.

"What the hell am I going to tell people?"

"Nothing. Not a word."

"Not even Candy?"

"Especially her. You've helped me enough. Let me deal with the rest."

She gently puts her hand on my mutilated cheek and bursts into laughter. I can't help it. I laugh with her.

"Oh my god," she says. "Look at us. What a couple of absolute loons."

"The Three Stooges. Well, two. We can put out an ad for number three."

She laughs until there are tears in her eyes.

"I knew someday you'd ask me to do some crazy-ass shit. I just didn't know it would be this. Or today."

"Admit it. I'm your favorite patient. You get to do all your fanciest work on me."

She pulls me to her and says, "I love you, you complete asshole."

"I love you too."

"Now take me out of here and go save Janet."

I lead her out through a shadow.

I LEAVE ALLEGRA in the kitchen and go straight to the bedroom. If things go the way I think they will, this is the last time I'll probably see the place. So many good and bad memories. I'll miss it here.

I put the Colt down on the bed and the na'at and black blade next to it. There's a few hundred dollars in my pocket, so I toss that down too. My shirt is soaked in sweat and streaked with blood. I drag it off me and go to the closet for another. However, it's still dark and I'm clumsy with one hand. I knock half the goddamn clothes off the hangers and onto the floor. A moment later someone knocks on the bedroom door. They open it a crack.

"Stark?"

It's Candy. When she sees me, she comes inside, gently closing the door behind her.

"The others are still asleep. Where did you and Allegra sneak off to?"

I stay in the dark of the closet.

"Her clinic. I just needed a few stitches."

"Funny," Candy whispers. "That's the kind of thing she could have done here."

"I didn't want to wake everyone."

She stands there frowning at me.

"This is me, remember? I know you're lying. What are you hiding? Come out here where I can see you."

"No."

Her frown melts from annoyance to concern.

"Stark. What's going on? Come out or I'll drag your ass out."

"Okay. But don't make a sound. I don't want to wake the others."

I step out into the vague light filtering in through the windows.

Candy rushes to me when she sees my bandages.

"What happened? Who did this?"

"Be quiet. I'm okay. This was all necessary. King Bullet won't meet me otherwise."

She feels my face through the bandages.

"What's wrong? Let me see you."

I push her hand away with my one good one.

"Fuck. Your hand."

"It's all right. Allegra says it healed perfectly."

But Candy isn't listening. Instead, she's tearing at the bandages around my head. She's a Jade. She's good at ripping things, so it doesn't take long. Afterward, she takes a step back, but doesn't say anything.

"I'm sorry," I say.

"What have you done to yourself?"

"King Bullet wouldn't let Janet go if I didn't do it. And, I guess, I'm paying off some heavy debts."

She shakes her head.

"You can't possibly owe that much."

"I owe so much more than this to everyone," I say. "You know, my life has been one big shitshow and most of it has been my fault. I thought if I hadn't gone to see Mason that night so many bad things wouldn't have happened. But then

I thought, if I hadn't spent all those years in Hell, I never would have met you. So, all things considered, I figure it was worth it."

I hold out the shirt in my hand and she helps me put it on. She looks at my things laid out on the bed and says, "Where are you going?"

"Far away."

"When will you be back?"

I don't know what to tell her so I stand there like an idiot not saying anything, which is worse than telling her the truth.

"Oh," she says. "No."

Candy puts her hands on my cheeks and pulls me to her. Kisses me hard.

"Whatever else has happened between us, you're my monster. And I'm yours. Take me with you."

I want to tell her no, but I can't.

I say, "Are you sure? Look at my face. There's no coming back for me. But if you come with me now, there's no going back to your old life."

"I don't care."

"You might die."

"I don't care."

I have so much to pay for. Amends and apologies to make. But I can't just walk away now.

I say, "You might—"

She grabs me and kisses me again.

"Shut up," she says. "Let's go."

FIRST, I SHADOW walk us into the hall and dial Janet's number. King Bullet picks up.

"How's the hand?"

"I did what you wanted."

He giggles.

"Did you? Let me see."

I hold the phone at arm's length and take a shot of myself. Hit Send.

I know he's received it by the big laughs that come out of the speaker.

"Spectacular. Your outside finally matches your inside, daddy's boy. Oh, and I shared the photo with your paramour. She's delighted by your new look."

"I'm ready to make the trade."

"Smart boy. Meet me—"

"No. You meet me. In Enoch Valley."

King Bullet doesn't say anything for a few seconds, then, "Where the hell is that?"

"In the desert. Buy a fucking map."

"No. We're doing this my way."

"Not anymore. Not if you want Mommy's necklace back."

"Yeah. What if I kill the bitch right now while you listen?"

"You won't. If you hurt or kill Janet, then you lose the moral high ground. It will only prove that Uriel was right and the Kissi are the kind of scum who deserve exile and punishment."

"Okay, Prince Charming. But now I want something else too."

"What?"

"You wanted my head. I want yours."

"Like you weren't already going to try to kill me."

He laughs lightly.

"But now I don't want to have to fight about it. You have to give yourself to me willingly."

"Done."

"Oh my. Not even a snappy comeback."

"I've been dead before. It's no big deal."

"It's not the dead part that hurts. It's how you get there. And I've been planning your death for a long time."

"High noon then. Enoch Valley."

"If you try any tricks or don't show up, I'll burn the bitch alive."

I hang up on him.

Candy says, "Is everything all right?"

"Fine. The exchange is all set up."

"I don't like you saying things like death being no big deal."

With my good hand, I squeeze her shoulder.

"You can still back out of this."

"Not a chance."

"Then we have one more stop to make before we go to the desert."

"Where's that?"

"An audience with God."

"What?"

"Here we go."

"Oh shit."

WE COME OUT in a hallway in the lobby of Mr. Muninn's palace. Candy holds on to my arm like a kid who's afraid she's going to get lost at the circus and eaten by a lion. She looks all around.

"This isn't what I was expecting at all. I thought it was going to be a lot Gothier, you know?"

"Like Frankenstein's castle or Notre-Dame."

"Yeah."

"And instead it's just like a nice hotel. Not a great one, but above average."

"Weird."

I take her to the elevators and push the button for the penthouse.

"Is he going to let us in just like that?"

"He knows we're here."

"I mean, he's God, right? I mean, isn't he busy?"

"He was injured in the war and has been taking some time off. I'm sure he'll have a couple of minutes for us."

"I don't even know why we're here."

"You knew Doc Kinski. Uriel. My dad. Now you get to meet Grandpa."

She gets a little pale as we ride up.

"I don't think I'm ready for this. I'm not even human. What if he smites me or something?"

I smile at her.

"He's not going to smite you. But he might smite me. We've got business to discuss."

Candy squeezes my arm harder.

"I won't let him hurt you."

I kiss her cheek.

"I know you won't."

It takes a couple of minutes to reach the penthouse. When we do, the doors open right up.

I say, "See?" and stand aside so Candy can step out first.

She shakes her head no, so I go out into the opulent living room and she follows. Tall windows wrap around the place, giving a view over half of Heaven. I can tell Candy wants to look, but she's too afraid to leave my side.

A voice comes from a room or two away.

"I'll be right out, children. Make yourself at home."

Candy mouths "Was that him?"

I nod and take her to a turquoise tufted sofa.

A minute later, Mr. Muninn comes in, wearing a silk robe and carrying a silver tray with a teapot on top.

"Here we go," he says. As he leans over to set things down, he glances at us and drops the tray the final couple of inches. Tea splashes on the coffee table and sugar cubes go everywhere.

"Oh, Stark. What have you done to your face?"

Candy reaches over and takes some napkins to wipe up the spilled tea.

"This is my friend Candy," I say.

"Hello, my dear," he says, then looks back at me. "Let me fix that awful face for you."

"Looking like this wasn't my first choice. But I have to stay ugly for a meeting."

He looks me over and sees my missing left hand.

"What about that? Must you remain hobbled for your meeting too?"

I glance at the stump.

"I guess not. Yeah. You can fix that."

"It's already done. Tea?"

I look down and my hand is back. I flex my fingers, grateful to see them again.

"Thanks," I say. "But there isn't time for tea."

Mr. Muninn sits down across from us and fills three cups.

He says, "I invented time, and I say there's always time for tea."

He hands the cups all around.

I take mine and set it on the coffee table. He lifts up the cup and slips a coaster under it. Candy holds hers in her lap.

I say, "How's Samael?"

Mr. Muninn's forehead creases.

"I'd rather not discuss family business."

"But he's alive. Right?"

He looks at me hard.

"What did I just say? Now, explain to me exactly what you did to your face."

"You know how you say I look bad? Well, isn't this how you always really saw me? The Abomination? The dog-faced boy?"

Muninn puts two sugar cubes into his tea.

"Don't be absurd," he says.

"I'm not sure I believe you, but okay. Anyway, I had to cut myself up to fix Uriel's mess. He was a bastard. I hate to say it, but it's the truth."

Muninn breathes in and out.

"He was a foolish and ill-considered boy. Not unlike some people in this room."

"Sure, I'm a bastard too. But the difference is that he was part of your crew. You made an army of weak angels. And the universe is still paying for it."

Muninn clasps his hands together.

"It's true. I've made so many mistakes."

"So have I," I say. "We both have a lot to make up for. So you have to help me and don't give me any of that you-don't-want-to-get-involved bullshit."

Muninn looks like he's about to turn me into a pillar of salt.

"Stark, I know you're upset, but if you came here for a favor, remember who you're talking to."

"Uriel was my father, which makes you my grandfather. I know exactly who I'm talking to."

He shakes his head and turns to Candy.

"He was never any good at respecting his elders."

She says, "I love Stark. Please listen to him."

"I can tell you care deeply. You're a Jade, aren't you?"

"Yes. Please don't kill me."

Muninn laughs.

"I don't kill my children. And you are my child as much as that troublesome one next to you. Now, tell me about this favor."

"It's not really a favor. It's more like a deal."

"Go on."

"I want you to take the Key from me and give it to Candy."

Candy looks at me in shock.

I squeeze her hand and say, "Hear me out."

Muninn sips his tea and says, "If you don't want it anymore why not just leave it with me?"

"No. Candy needs it more than you do. If you're worried she'll use it to rob banks or something, forget it. She's not built that way."

Mr. Muninn leans back and crosses his legs.

"I'm curious why she needs it."

"I don't want it," Candy says. "I don't want the Room of Thirteen Doors. I don't want any of it."

"There, you see?" says Muninn.

I get close to Candy.

"Listen to me. You might not want the Key, but you need it. But only once. After that, you can give it to Mr. Muninn." I look at him. "Does that sound fair?"

He looks at Candy.

"Will you give it up willingly?"

"If Stark says so."

He picks up his tea again.

"Then we have a bargain."

I turn my cup on the coaster, not looking at him.

"That's not the whole deal. You get the Key back, but I need you to trust me on something big. And I need you to do something that you said can't be done."

Mr. Muninn looks from Candy to me.

"Do you have any idea what he's talking about?"

She shakes her head.

"I want you to give me the first fire. The Mithras."

He looks at me and chuckles.

"You're serious. I can't do that. If it gets loose, you'll burn down all of existence."

I point at him.

"Not if you do your part. Look. This is a deal based on trust. You trusted me with the Mithras once. I'm asking you to do it one more time. And when all this is over with, you get the Key *and* the Room of Thirteen Doors. I know you've always wanted it."

"Don't misunderstand," Mr. Muninn says. "I do trust

your good intentions. It's just your methods I worry about. I'll need to know more before I can hand you the Mithras."

"First do the Key exchange. Then I'll tell you everything."

"All right."

Candy tries to set down her teacup and almost drops it.

"I'm afraid," she says.

I put an arm around her.

"It's okay. Mr. Muninn won't let anything happen to you. Right?"

He leans forward, looking as beneficent as any kid's Bible drawing.

He says, "You'll be all right, my child. But the Key goes into your heart. It might hurt a bit at first."

She looks from me to Mr. Muninn and back to me again.

"Do it."

"Excellent," he says. "Both of you lie down where you are. There's plenty of room. Open your shirts and try to relax."

We lie down head to head on the long sofa. Our arms dangle off the side and we hold hands.

Mr. Muninn stands over us and says, "Here we go."

I close my eyes as I feel his hand slip into my chest. It's warm and when his fingers enter my heart, it still hurts. I can feel it as his fingers wrap around the Key. When he tries to pull it out it resists. Becomes heavier. Digs into me. It burns and I can't help groaning. Candy squeezes my hand.

Mr. Muninn never lets go of the Key, but pulls it slowly, insistently, out of my heart, up through my breastbone, and out of my chest. It glows a bright gold. Like the rising sun.

Then he moves to Candy and very gently slips the Key into her chest. She cries out at one point. When it goes into her heart. I remember the feeling. I sit up and hold her hand with both of mine. Her teeth are bared as Mr. Muninn gently removes his hand from her chest.

"It's done," he says.

Candy's face and body relax. Her breath becomes regular.

"She'll sleep for a while," says Mr. Muninn. "She's strong, but she doesn't have your constitution."

He goes back to his side of the coffee table and wipes his hand on a napkin.

"Now we have a chance to talk one-on-one. Tell me what you want with the Mithras."

I need something to drink, but tea is all that's on the table. I run my hand along my forehead. The new scars ache.

"Do you have anything stronger than Earl Grey?"

Mr. Muninn leaves and returns with a bottle of bourbon and two glasses.

I say, "You don't happen to have any Aqua Regia, do you?"

He gives me a look.

"Sorry. Bourbon is fine."

He pours us both good portions from the bottle. We clink glasses.

"There," he says. "You have your drink. Now tell me, finally, what do you intend to do with the Mithras?"

I smile at him.

"It's not what *I'm* going to do with it. It's what *you're* going to do."

We get to Enoch Valley well before noon, so we rest in the shadow of one of the mountains that ring the place. Even in the shade it's still pushing 110 degrees. Mr. Muninn gave us a couple of bottles of water to take with us. Me and Candy sit back on the smooth rock wall, shoulders touching, and pass one of the bottles back and forth.

"How's your chest feeling?" I say.

She squirms a little.

"It tickles."

"It'll do that for a while. You'll get used to it."

"I don't want this thing in me long enough to get used to it."

"Not even to take it out for a test drive? Go some places you've never been? Did you ever want to go to Paris or Rome or see the Northern Lights? You can do that through the Room. No twelve-hour flights or Customs assholes to hassle you at the airport."

"Did you want to see those places?"

"Maybe. Someday. With the right person."

Candy wiggles in closer to me.

She says, "I always thought you'd shrivel up like a prune if you ever left L.A."

"I should have gone to those places years ago. Time just sometimes disappears, you know?"

"When you spend all your time fighting monsters."

I sip some water.

"Still. We had some good times at the Chateau Marmont. Didn't we?"

"Oh man. The room service in that place."

"And the beds."

"And then Kasabian managed to weasel his way in there."

Candy laughs.

"It was a nice thing you did for Kas, giving him his body back."

"He's been through enough. We'd both been through enough."

"I'm going to say something now."

"What?"

"You're a romantic dork. A sweet, secret romantic."

I hold up the water bottle to the desolate valley.

"And I take you to all the nicest places."

Candy sits up, takes the bottle, and drinks. Wiping her mouth on the back of her hand, she says, "You haven't told me why we're here. Why this particular spot?"

"Do you know anything about Enoch Valley?"

She thinks for a minute.

"I've heard people joking about it. It was supposed to be some kind of huge land development thing a long time ago. But everything went wrong."

Spread out in the near distance is a dead landscape of ruins to rival Pompeii. A hundred or more abandoned mansions bleach and crumble to dust in the dry air. In the center of the site is a salt-choked lake surrounded by the desiccated bodies of millions of dead fish.

There are two low points in the valley wall. One east and one west. I point to the west.

"In the seventies, the railroad was supposed to come through here from L.A. Enoch Valley was going to be the Palm Springs of the north. An exclusive enclave for the super super rich to live, go boating, fish, and generally do rich people stuff away from the prying eyes of the little people. There was even a shopping center with Versace, a Lamborghini dealership, Prada. All kinds of luxury shit."

"What happened to it?"

"State funding ran out and they never built the railroad. The real estate company went bankrupt and the site sat here for years. In the eighties, some of the investors tried to make their money back by letting companies dump toxic waste in the lake, but the state shut that down and now the valley is one big biohazard site."

"And not another person in a million miles."

"That's the idea."

Candy picks up a rock and throws it at a weathered NO TRESPASSING sign.

She says, "Who needs the Northern Lights when you have toxic sludge to spoon to?"

The shadow we're sitting in is getting smaller by the minute. I check the time on my phone. It's eleven twenty.

Candy says, "How does it feel to have the Key out of your heart?"

"Weird. Lighter. It's strange to know that if I tried to jump into one of these shadows I'd just crack my head."

"It was freaky for me to bring us here."

"You'll get used to it."

"No, I won't."

Candy checks the time too. Now we both know that things are going to wrap up one way or another very soon.

I look at Candy, so beautiful sitting on her rock, and say, "I'm sorry."

She looks at me.

"For what?"

"Everything. Losing you. Letting Audsley Ishii murder me. Being dead for a year so that you had to move on with your life. I'm sorry I did that to you."

"You didn't know that Audsley was going to kill you."

"Yeah, I did. In a way. I always knew he was unstable. But my ego wouldn't allow me to let up on the guy. I cost him his job and that pushed him over the edge. Like so many things I did back then, I hurt everyone around me."

Candy looks out over the dead city.

"It was hard seeing you die. It was hard trying to get over you."

"I'm glad Alessa was there."

"Me too."

"You think she'll forgive you for coming with me?"

Candy shakes her head.

"You mean for kissing you. For never getting over you. I don't know. Maybe not. I don't want to talk about that now."

I say, "I wish I had a cigarette." But before I can say anything else Candy is on top of me, tearing at my clothes. She rolls off long enough for us both to get undressed, then climbs back on top and slowly lowers herself onto my cock. We move together slowly. This isn't crazy breaking-furniture sex. It's something else. Two people—two monsters—trying as hard as possible to absorb the other into their skin and bones so that whatever happens next, they'll carry this moment and the essence of the other person with them forever.

We're still lying in the last of the shade, just holding each other, when a plume of dust appears at the valley's eastern entrance. Me and Candy scramble into our clothes and walk hand in hand down to the fetid lake at the center of Enoch Valley.

The plume of smoke grows as a gleaming black Chevy pickup speeds across the empty house lots in our direction.

Candy pulls me around to look her in the eye.

"I love you, James Stark."

"I love you, Candy."

"I don't want to leave you here with him."

"You have to. That's the whole plan."

"You're sure? There's no other way?"

"There isn't. I've been over this a million times."

"Okay then."

"Okay."

The Chevy comes to a long, sliding stop about fifty feet from us. It disappears for a moment as the plume of smoke becomes a dust cloud around the truck. A few seconds later, King Bullet and Janet emerge from the cloud. Janet looks like hell. There are marks around their throat from when he held the knife to it. Their face is streaked with the tracks of dried tears. The King, on the other hand, couldn't look jollier. As soon as he sees me he lets go of Janet and heads in my direction, laughing. He has what looks like a god-damn Viking battle ax in his hand. But he doesn't come at me with it. He wants to savor the moment. He swings the ax in an arc and buries the head a few inches in the packed valley floor.

King Bullet walks all around me, taking in the view.

He says, "You know, for a few minutes yesterday I thought you were fucking with me. That the photo you sent was a Photoshop phony. But here you are. Wow. You are one beautiful hunka-hunka burning ugly."

He turns to Janet.

"Come closer, princess. Join the party and get a good look at your main man."

Janet is crying again and when they don't come forward, King Bullet grabs them by the wrist and drags them to me.

"Look at him," he shouts.

Janet is trying to be strong, I can see it, but the last twenty-four hours have been too much for them.

"Are you okay?"

Janet half-smiles.

"I'm holding up."

I say, "You don't have to listen to him. Close your eyes. Look away. This face, it isn't for you. It's for his amusement."

They shake their head.

"No. It is for me. You did that to yourself for me. I'm—I'm sorry."

I take a step toward them, but King Bullet gets between us.

"Look, but don't touch," he says.

I stay where I am.

"Don't be sorry. This was my decision. I had to get you away from him."

King Bullet laughs and says, "You hear that, princess? He did all that to himself for you. Really, in a way, you did it to him."

When Janet looks away again and the King grabs their wrist, they wheel around and slap him. He looks genuinely shocked. But then laughs and slaps them back.

I'm on him in a second and plant a fist to the side of his head. He goes down hard. But before I can stomp his brains all over the valley floor he comes up with a little 9mm pistol aimed not at me, but at Janet. He goes to them and puts the pistol to the back of their head.

He says, "Let's not do that again, shall we?" Then looks at Candy. "What's the extra bitch for? I told you, no tricks."

"No tricks," I say. "Candy is just here to take Janet away so you and me can get down to business."

King Bullet looks around.

"I don't see a car."

"They won't need a car. It's all been taken care of."

"Huh," he says. Still a little suspicious, he looks at the sky like he's expecting an *Apocalypse Now* helicopter raid, complete with Ride of the Valkyries. Eventually, he looks back at me.

"Where's my necklace?"

I take it out of my pocket and hold it up so it glitters in the desert sun.

He holds out a hand to me.

"Throw it here."

I stamp the toe of my boot into the ground, raising a little dust. Then I put the necklace back in my pocket.

"No. You let Janet go first."

"Fuck you."

"The moment Janet is with Candy, you and me can finish things. You said you wanted my head."

"Sweet baby Jesus yes."

"You let Janet and Candy go. I kneel down all penitent like you wanted. You use the ax. And that's all there is to it. Get the necklace from my pocket and you've won."

He laughs, but his eyes are hard.

"You know if you try to trick me I'm going to find your bitches again and kill them. Kill them bad."

I shake my head.

"You keep saying shit like that when you could be killing me. Look. If you've changed your mind it's fine with me. But let's do something besides standing around. It's hot and your threats are boring."

"Get on your knees," he says.

I do what he said.

"Hands behind your back."

I do that too.

He throws a length of rawhide to Candy.

"You. Tie his hands tight."

Candy looks at me and I nod. She gets behind me and knots the rawhide around my wrists.

King Bullet says, "How's it feel being completely helpless?"

Now I laugh.

"Are you kidding? This isn't the first time Candy's tied me up."

When she's done, Candy stands up.

"Get away from him," says King Bullet.

Candy takes a few steps back. King Bullet comes around behind me and checks the ties on my wrists with his boot. He moves in front of me again and says, "Good." Then he looks at Janet and says, "You and the other bitch, get out of here. The menfolk have things to do."

He lets Janet go and they run to me. Throw their arms around me.

"You don't have to do this," they say.

"Yeah. I do. This has been a long time coming. Payback for all the mess of my life."

Janet kisses my ravaged lips. They look at Candy.

"Stark used to warn me that he attracts trouble. That this wasn't the life for me. I know he never loved me the way he loved you. And that's okay. Because he was right. This isn't the life for me, as much as I tried to pretend it was. I'm glad for the time Stark and I got to spend together. But, in the end, I'm glad he has you."

Candy doesn't say anything, but holds out her hand to Janet. They give me one more soft kiss and go to Candy.

"Boo. Fucking. Hoo." King Bullet still has the gun out. "Go on," he says, gesturing with it. "Shoo."

As Candy walks Janet back into a shadow to safety I manage to smile one last time at both of them.

And then they're gone.

"Finally," says King Bullet. "Alone at last. I didn't think you'd do it, you know. With your history, I thought you'd do something stupid and make me kill them both."

I say, "Dad was a bastard, but you're an idiot. You have so much power, but you wasted it on this shit. You're not the king of anything except the playground, you fucking child. We could have done amazing things together. But you decided a tantrum was enough."

"You would have trusted a Kissi enough to call him brother?"

"With some time."

"Well, I never wanted to party with you, so if this is a plea for forgiveness it's not going to work."

"It's not a plea for anything other than to shut your yap. Like I said before, you're boring. Now, let's get going. Mason Faim could have sent me to Hell a dozen times by now."

King Bullet puts the gun away and jerks the ax from the ground.

"Do you want a moment to pray to Dad or Granddad?"

"I'll pass. They know what I think of them."

"Cool. Get up on your knees and bow your head to me."

I do what he says. But instead of chopping me, King Bullet has one more look around, like he's expecting some angelic cavalry to rush to my rescue.

I say, "You're safe. No one's coming."

He scans the horizon one more time and says, "It looks that way. Ready?"

I tilt my head up toward him.

"Still bored," I say.

King Bullet swings the ax.

And Enoch Valley disappears in a mushroom cloud of pure fire.

So here I am. Wherever that is. Everywhere and nowhere at all. Just drifting. Like a trash bag in the wind, blown this way and that. I'm pretty sure I'm not alive. I guess this is— what? Not death. I've been there before. This is weirder. Maybe something in between. Maybe after the explosion there wasn't enough of me left to go on. So I just drift. It doesn't hurt, and I can see a lot. I mean fucking everything. Across time and stars and goddamn galaxies. But I turn away from the light show and focus back on the stupid little rock I just came from.

How long have I been drifting? Weeks maybe. The first thing I see when I look again is Max Overdrive. The rubble is gone and the ground is clear. Candy, Kas, and Alessa are there. They're rebuilding the place. They look happy. I wish I were there with them, but unlike the last time I died, this time it's good to see them moving on. I plant one ghost kiss on Candy's cheek and the wind blows me away across the city.

Hollywood is full of people again. The virus must be gone

and there isn't a Shoggot in sight. It's all cars and buses, and people going to work and partying. Good for you, assholes. Have some tamales for me.

There's a gust and I tumble through the streets. Finally, I bump my way into Bamboo House of Dolls. Carlos is giving out a free round to the unmasked crowd as Brigitte shows her new green card to everyone who'll hold still. Allegra and Fuck Hollywood stand with Janet between them. Nice. They're part of the family now. I reach out to touch Janet's hand, but another gust grabs me.

I'm tossed end over end across the city. Past the Devil's Door Drive-In, where a long line of cars winds itself inside for a triple bill of the first three *Frankenstein* movies. Flicker always had good taste.

Before I get sucked up into the sky, I grab one of the signs marking the exits along the Hollywood Freeway. Cars flash by below. But my eyes fall on a small figure hitchhiking on the shoulder of the freeway with a sign that says EVERYWHERE. She looks younger and a little smaller than I remember her. She's not dressed as well as usual—and clearly not quite back to her full power—but I'd know Mustang Sally anywhere. You can't kill the road queen forever. Not in L.A. She needs a car to get back to herself again, but if I know Sally, she'll have her pick of a dozen before dawn.

I think I've figured out this drifting thing enough to drag my skyward ass across town one more time, all the way to Abbot's mansion.

Yeah, the fucker is in there. Barricaded in a room blazing with light in every direction, so there are no shadows a certain Abomination can slip through. He's not Augur anymore.

I don't know how I know, but I do. I guess when he didn't kill me, the Council cut the cord. He's all on his own now, waiting for the hammer to fall. Quake in your boots, Richie Rich. You got off easy this time. But we're not done yet.

I can feel myself fading. Sheering apart to nothing. But I'm not quite ready to go. I hold myself together just long enough to go back to the apartment one last time.

It's empty, but I can feel all the life collected there. It's warm and reassuring. People are safe here. People will be safe. I see my old coat nailed to the wall by the TV. Fuck Hollywood must have done it. How do I know? Because she put the damn She-Ra mask on a shelf right above it with a little Godzilla figurine looming over it like a guardian angel.

And that's all I get. Whatever's left of me comes apart. I blow to pieces in the emptiness of space. Just some motes of cosmic dust drifting through nothingness forever.

I wake up in bed in a hotel room. I can tell it's a hotel by the pointless art and the fancy but generic fixtures. Every inch of me hurts. Groaning, I sit up.

Samael is sitting on a sofa, sipping tea and reading a book. He notices I'm awake and raises his eyebrows when he sees me.

I say, "How long have I been out?"

"It's been a while. Father told me to look after you."

"Yeah? How did that go?"

"You talk in your sleep."

"What did I say?"

"Nothing I can repeat in polite company."

"I'm glad to see you're in one piece."

He slaps his chest.

"Fit as a fiddle." He holds up his cup. "Some tea?"

"Why are you people always trying to get me to drink tea?"

"It's good for you. You have some healing to do."

I touch my face.

"Don't worry. Father fixed it. He couldn't stand to look at you the other way."

Looking around the opulent room, I say, "Where am I, by the way?"

"Where do you think?"

"It reminds me of the Beverly Wilshire hotel."

"Classier than you're used to?"

"Classier than I deserve."

"That's certainly true."

I try to get out of bed, but my back and shoulder are stiff and sore.

Samael waves a hand at me.

"Later, Superman. There's plenty of time for that."

I forget getting out of bed and settle for leaning against the headboard.

"Where exactly am I?"

Samael chuckles.

"You blew yourself to teeny tiny atoms. Where do you think you are?"

"Hell again?"

"You're getting closer."

I look at him.

"Heaven? No no no. I never signed up for this."

He says, "It gets worse."

"How could it possibly?"

He takes a hand mirror from the dresser and hands it to me. I look at him before looking at myself.

Oh shit.

I shout, "Where are my scars?"

Samael leans back on the sofa, delighted by my suffering.

"When Father fixes things, he fixes them all the way."

"But my scars. They were—mine."

"It's your fault. You made yourself so ugly that he couldn't stand it, so he gave you a tune-up."

I drop the mirror on the bed.

"This is a fucking nightmare. Please tell me I'm still asleep."

"Nope."

I sit there for a moment just staring at the ceiling before I remember something.

"I know what you were trying to tell me when the King stabbed you."

"Of course. He was the spitting image of Uriel."

"Maybe not quite that close, but I saw him in the King's face. Hell. I wish I'd known earlier."

"What difference would it have made? Would he have pulled you into a warm embrace and called you brother?"

"I don't know. I just know what it's like to be fucked over. Maybe I could have done *something*."

"Yes. I'm sure some hot cocoa and a teddy bear would have fixed things right up."

Before I can tell him to fuck off, he says, "Father told me about the trick you pulled with the Mithras. Very clever."

"He was so scared of it. The gag only worked because I talked him into chipping off a tiny piece and putting it inside me."

Samael looks concerned.

"If he failed it could have been fatal for all of us."

"But he didn't. He came through when he had to."

"That he did. And so did you."

He gives me a conspiratorial wink.

"Wait. Is that why I'm in Heaven? I'm some kind of fucking *hero*?"

Samael shrugs.

"Father just assumed you'd like to stay this time."

"Well, I don't."

He makes a face at me.

"Stop whining. People have waited millennia to get in here. And don't even think about leaving. Father wants you here and that's that."

"He has angels watching me?"

"One or two."

"You?"

Samael gets up, goes to the closet, and tosses me some clothes.

"Time to get dressed. Your fans are waiting to meet you."

I sit up straighter.

"What fans?"

"Every human who's ever lived since the beginning of time," he says. "Remember that little trick where you opened Heaven's gates?"

"Everyone really made it?"

"Come outside and see."

"How many are we talking about?"

"A hundred billion or so. Give or take."

My stomach knots.

"Shit. I don't have to say anything, do I?"

"Please don't."

"In that case I guess it's okay."

"I'll tell Father you're up. And, Jimmy?"

"Yeah?"

"I know you're already plotting an escape, but forget it. Remember: you don't have a body anymore. There's nothing for you to escape into. No Wormwood to resurrect you. You're part of the family now."

I haul my ass out of bed.

"Go away and let me put my damn pants on."

Samael leaves laughing and I fall back onto the blanket. So, this is what it feels like not to have a body. I hope they have aspirin in Heaven.

GETTING CLOTHES ONTO my stiff body takes a while. Worse, there's a button-up shirt and tie with my clothes. I haven't tied a tie in a million years. It takes me a half hour and fifty tries to get the damn thing an approximation of right.

Finally, I limp out into the hall. There are a couple of big guys out there, also in suits. Soldiers, probably, from the loyal angelic army.

I say, "What are you? My bodyguards?"

The taller of the two says, "We're just here to make sure you don't get lost."

"And it takes two for that?"

The short one points to the tall one.

"He makes sure I don't get lost too."

The tall angel nods to the shorter one.

"And he makes sure I don't get lost. See? It's all a beautiful system."

"You're hilarious. You're the ones who make sure I don't jackrabbit out of here."

"There's that too."

I go over to them.

"Let's get this over with."

The short one starts out and the tall one waits for me, so I'm pincered in from both sides. It's diabolical.

We go down to the third floor. They lead me to a conference room with a balcony that normally overlooks a garden. Only the garden is gone, replaced by a mob of people. A big mob. Like from the hotel to the horizon and, for all I know, beyond. Mr. Muninn and Samael are on the balcony too. I look down into the crowd and front row center are Alice, Vidocq, and Father Traven.

Samael walks behind me and as he does, he whispers, "Wave to them, you idiot."

I raise my hand and do what he said. And a hundred billion people whoop and scream my name. It's just a little overwhelming. I don't know what to do, so I keep waving until Samael comes back and gently pushes my hand to my side.

"I think they saw you," he says.

The shouting continues.

I say, "What happens now?"

"Father says a few words, then dinner."

"Can we just skip to dinner?"

"Father did you one favor. Don't expect another so soon."

"I'm not cut out for this hero stuff."

"We're going to have to do something about that whining if you're going to be around for eternity. *And you are.*"

"Whatever you say, man. But I'm not saying grace."

WE HAVE DINNER in the biggest room I've ever seen. It's like someone took all of California and put it under one roof with chandeliers and gold filigree along the edges of the ceiling. Mr. Muninn puts me at the head of the center table and sits to my right. Thankfully, Alice, Vidocq, and Father Traven are around me too. There's good food and wine and everybody is happy and chatty. Strangers come over to shake my hand or kiss me on the cheek. It's all so goddamn heartwarming that I want to die all over again.

After a couple of hours of people thanking me, I'm about all out of graciousness and charm.

Thankfully, Samael pulls me aside, through a red velvet curtain, and out onto a small balcony. He slaps a pack of Maledictions and a lighter into my hand and says, "Enjoy. But don't be too long. Father will have the hotel guards out looking for you."

"Thanks, man." It's the first time I've genuinely felt that emotion since I woke up.

He goes back inside and leaves me alone, looking out over Heaven's absolutely perfect lawns and clean streets. It's pretty awful.

My mind goes back to the desert. Saying goodbye to Candy and Janet. My breath catches in my chest for a second reliving the moment. But I relax again thinking of Candy kissing me in the bedroom. Of making love in the desert by a dead lake with a million dead fish watching us.

I think of all my friends at the apartment. Candy trying to explain to them what I'd done. Man, I hate the idea of her having to do it, but it was her idea to tell them, and I know she'll do a good job. While we were in Heaven together, I told her that Fuck Hollywood had nowhere else to go so, if she wanted it, she could keep the place. Candy, Alessa, and Kasabian were welcome to stay too while they rebuilt Max Overdrive. I know they and the others would be all right, but I missed them all so much already.

I smoke two Maledictions and head back into the party, thoroughly sick of this hero business.

AFTER THE DINNER breaks up, I get a better look at my room in the palace. It's actually pretty nice. A soft bed, big shower, and an entire wall that's a TV with every movie ever made on call anytime I want. It's paradise in a way. For someone. For me, it's going to take some getting used to.

Maybe I'll see you again sometime. Not as Stark or Sandman Slim. Maybe just as a flicker in the corner of your eye. A quick blur in Bamboo House of Dolls. A breeze on your shoulder at the movies. Maybe just hanging out, keeping an eye on my friends.

Not right away, of course. I still hurt all over. And I have some old friends in Heaven to catch up with. Besides, Samael and his Mouseketeers will be watching me 24/7. Still—

Someone once asked Warren Zevon what he'd been up to

and he said, "Just surfing and shoplifting." I wouldn't mind giving something like that a try.

Never forget: Hell couldn't hold me. This cosmic retirement home doesn't stand a chance.

You think I'm done?

I'm just getting started.

Richard Kadrey is the *New York Times* bestselling author of the Sandman Slim supernatural noir books. *Sandman Slim* was included in Amazon's "100 Sci-Fi & Fantasy Books to Read in a Lifetime," and is in development as a feature film. Kadrey's other books include *Hollywood Dead*, *The Everything Box*, *Metrophage*, and *Butcher Bird*, and he also writes comics and screenplays. He lives in Austin, Texas.